To Leslie —

Girls In Ice Houses

Good knowing you all these years. Enjoy!

Linda Morganstein

Linda Morganstein

Regal Crest Books
by Regal Crest

Texas

ISBN 978-1-61929-222-2

First Printing 2015

9 8 7 6 5 4 3 2 1

Cover design by AcornGraphics

Published by:

Regal Crest Enterprises, LLC
229 Sheridan Loop
Belton, Texas 76513

Find us on the World Wide Web at
http://www.regalcrest.biz

Published in the United States of America

Acknowledgment

I would like to thank my dedicated readers, Mary Jaeb, Meg Petersen, Mary Ann Kavanaugh, Honey Zelle, Joan Wilson, Nancie Swanberg and Kate Ledger. To Kate Ledger, also, a thanks for her astute literary advice. I would also like to thank Nancie Swanberg for her help with art and photography questions, as well as her aesthetic wisdom and friendship. Thanks to Diane Ferreira for patiently answering legal questions. A huge thanks to Don and Rhoda Mains for their generous support, including many insights into the shoe business. Thanks to Gordon "Bart" Scott, a friend and generous dispenser of legal information. For insider information about paparazzi, thanks to Giles Harrison of London Entertainment Group. A former sports agent, John Wolf, provided his experiences. As always, thanks to my publisher, Regal Crest, and my editor, Judy Kerr.

Dedication

For Melanie, who helps me to see the big picture

Part One

Chapter One

Summer 2013

MAXIE WOLFE LAY sprawled across a plush hotel mattress with her eyes shut tight, indulging in a mortifyingly generic porn fantasy. A stripper in a Zorro mask gliding down a golden pole on a smoky raised platform in the middle of a tawdry circular bar. The fantasy was tacky performance art that would have illuminated Maxie's unorthodox psychological roots, if she were inclined to illuminate roots, which she was not. Maxie gasped, her back arched.

She opened her eyes to find her lawyer, Helen Dubois, staring at her. Helen was a top-notch attorney, but she looked like a beach blond bikini warrior. In fact, Helen had almost made Team USA in beach volleyball before she went to Harvard Law School. Helen was a super-achiever. Maxie was very attracted to super-achievers. To top it off, Helen was married to the director of a star-studded addiction rehab clinic, which enhanced the ironic thrill of the escapade.

"Can I ask you something?" Helen asked.

Maxie squirmed. "I don't know. I guess so."

"Why can't we look at each other when we're making love? I know you're a badass for your work, but you don't hide your vulnerabilities as well as you think you do."

Maxie rolled to the edge of the bed. Seductive light from a wall of windows lit the hotel suite with a cinematic glow. Beyond the balcony, Santa Monica sand culminated in ocean waves streaked with red from the rising sun. The affair with Helen had started after a champagne celebration in this very hotel two weeks ago. A sociopathic minor celebrity had made damaging claims against Maxie. Helen had gotten the (mostly) false charges dismissed without breaking a sweat.

Maxie knew the laws for journalists as well as anyone, but a key part of getting the job done for paparazzi was getting away with what you could. Anyway, Helen was a genius at getting her off if she did get into trouble. It probably wasn't a good idea to have seduced Helen, but misgivings didn't help Maxie with impulse control.

Maxie glanced over at her bedmate, whose face was distorted like she was going to weep, causing a small throb of guilt in Maxie's heart. The ring of her cell phone saved her from any more threats to her protective sheath. She glanced down at the number and another jolt shook her. It was the long-term care facility up north in Sonoma County. "Gotta take this," she said.

Maxie threw on a plush hotel robe and went into the hallway for privacy only to find the corridor occupied by a surprising number of

Ancient Grecian deities delivering newspapers and room service to early birds. She slipped into a fake marble vending room and took the call. The ice machine rumbled like Mt. Vesuvius, making it difficult to hear the distant voice, but Maxie knew who was calling.

"What's up?" she asked warily.

"I've taken care of your mother for seventeen years," Susan said. "Advance warning. She's getting difficult."

Maxie's tight shoulders relaxed with relief. "She's always been difficult. What else is new?" Maxie watched a huge shiny ebony cockroach scuttle across the faux granite counter, from under a microwave to under a hot chocolate dispenser. The roach was a luxury model befitting a luxury hotel. One, two, three, four, five, six, Maxie counted. Six swift legs scurrying for safety.

"She's been tormenting one of the new orderlies, making false accusations, lashing out physically. It was bad last night. I'm worried it's going to escalate. If so, we may have to take restraint measures. You're her legal guardian. You'll need to approve them."

"Whatever," Maxie said, then realized her remark sounded callous. "Okay," she said in a more conciliatory tone. "I trust you, Susan." It was true. Maxie wasn't big in the trust department, but her mother's long-time nurse was someone who qualified. Susan was in the Mother Teresa category of compassionate caregivers.

Maxie stepped into the hallway to find the Grecian deities replaced by a brigade of starched multi-ethnic chambermaids rolling an arsenal of well-fortified cleaning carts. Maxie smiled with genuine affection. Chambermaids were some of her best snitches. Maxie wasn't a snob. Her informants appreciated her egalitarian nature.

When she slipped back into her room, she wasn't shocked to find it deserted. Maybe the affair with Helen was over. If not, it would be soon. On the gilded dresser, she found sixty dollars in crisp twenties and a note.

Can't drive you home. Here's cab money. H.

Maxie retrieved her underwear draped on a vase of roses and the rest of her clothes scattered in a trail to the bed. She dressed slowly and picked up the money from the dresser.

THE CAB PICKED her up from beneath the protected column-lined entrance portals of the Acropolis inspired hotel. It wasn't until she climbed out in a gated private cul-de-sac off Carmelita Way in Beverly Hills that Maxie felt the full force of the Santa Ana winds. The blasts took her breath away.

She could take the heat. If she ever went to hell, it wouldn't be the flames that broke her. More likely running a gauntlet of ex-lovers cursing her immaturity. Heat always kindled the worst in humanity.

Nothing to cry about, not that she ever cried about anything.

She punched in the security code to the locked gate, head down, fighting the searing heat and moisture-sucking air, fought her way past the Tudor mansion looming ahead, and went around back to her sanctuary. A middle-aged Iranian couple with shaky finances and libertarian values owned the estate. Maxie was surprised to see Zari, the wife, emerging from the converted pool house.

"Something wrong?" Maxie asked.

"I was just passing by," Zari said. "I saw flashing lights. I let myself in. Your lava lamp was erupting! Maxie, we don't care what you do with your life. But you can't endanger our property. This is the fourth time you've left something dangerous on. We want you to think about moving."

"I'm sorry. It won't happen again."

This wasn't good. Maxie's home was one of her few comforts against chaos. The pool house came equipped with IKEA furniture, neglected cookware and insipid designer artwork, but the banality comforted her. What the place lacked was personal mementos. No photos, no trophies, no framed diplomas, nothing revelatory on display, from the life of Maxie Wolfe.

Without showering or brushing her teeth, she flopped into her bed and fell asleep. A call from Bruce Fein of *People Weekly* woke her. Bruce called everyone whenever he felt like it and expected people to pick up immediately.

"Danny King's scrounging for the lead in *A Winter's Tale* on Broadway. Shakespeare, for god's sake. He's screwing the girl playing his daughter, maybe. Get me some pictures of him. I have someone in New York tracking down the supposed daughter."

"Already screwing the unknown daughter in a play he hasn't gotten the part for?"

"Maxie sweetheart, since when did you discover logic? You're a paparazzo."

"Bruce, for the millionth time, I don't cover Danny King."

"It's counterproductive, babe. Besides, Danny's a pussycat with nine lives."

"I don't care if he has nine hundred lives."

Screw Bruce Fein. Screw all the editors who nagged her about Danny King. She was thirty-two and on track to becoming the greatest female paparazzo of all time. Doubt and misgivings lived in the same Pandora's box with crying, lid shut tight. Already today she'd come close to feeling extreme doubt and she didn't like it one bit.

Maxie rolled out of bed, did a series of modified Navy Seal calisthenics, then made an espresso with the fussy Italian machine she'd inherited from her dubious mentor, Marcello. As the pressure built in the gadget's water tank, an ominous hiss threatened to blow up the cottage. She'd promised Marcello she'd have the prima donna repaired before she used it, but had never gotten around to it. Admittedly, she had a serious procrastination issue involving getting things fixed.

In addition to super-achievers, repair specialists turned Maxie on. She adored therapists, surgeons, masseuses, acupuncturists, Reiki instructors and car mechanics, to name a few. Maybe it was time to seduce an espresso machine repairperson.

She choked down a stale doughnut while she prepared her equipment. She ran her fingers lovingly over her Nikon DSLR. The camera was the only thing she maintained with obsessive love. It was more like a body part than a device. She attached her 28-300 mm lens for close and midrange shots. She loaded her 70-400 mm telephoto lens along with the rest of her necessities into a large floppy bag that hid her intents until she went into action.

As soon as she opened the door, the Santa Ana winds rocked her again like a detonation. Maxie struggled to her 1984 Porsche 214, tilting sideways with the force of the gusts. The air-conditioning in her beloved chariot was on the blink. Another poorly timed repair situation, she had to admit.

For hours, she cruised in the sweltering heat, hitting some of her favorite spots, including the kid-friendly Brentwood Country Mart and Bristol Farms. Shots with kids were moneymakers, but most people, including celebrities, would be crazy to be out in weather like this with their little darlings. A good blast could blow one of the littler ones into the ozone. What a great story that would be.

Maxie had some of the best contacts in the business, but not this hellfire day. No hotel maids calling, no busboys or airline employees, not even vengeful ex-husbands or professional autograph hounds. Even the police radio scans remained uninspiring. To make matters worse, wannabe paparazzi scoured Los Angeles thinking their incompetent efforts were going to make them rich.

Maxie sighed. A few years ago, paparazzi kept to a code of sorts. Like the Mafia, maybe a little fractured, but the players felt a kinship and followed a set of commandments. Nowadays, jerks with cameras and cell phones haunted the streets doing whatever they felt like. Their pictures sold fast and cheap. A good shot got half or less than what it used to. A day of zero pictures was going to be difficult on the pocketbook.

Just when it seemed things couldn't get any worse, her cell phone rang. She noted the number, shivered and let the call sink into voice mail purgatory from which it would be deleted unheard. She was about to flee back to her cottage with a pepperoni pizza and a Lily Tomlin video, when her cell rang again. She read the caller ID and took the call.

"Marcello, please make my day. It's miserable out here."

"You know me, *bella*. I share all my best tips with you."

Maxie listened, disconnected, raced to Hollywood and parked south of Sunset in the driveway of a weed-infested foreclosure on a block where the cops rarely patrolled. She jogged three blocks north to the bustling boulevard as sweat trickled down her armpits. The atmosphere was still sweltering, although it was nearly eight o'clock. At least the wind had died down.

OUTSIDE THE BAD Mama Supper Club, minor personalities trolled the sidewalks. Fans called out listlessly, rehearsing their screams for when the famous arrived. Bad Mama was the current hottest restaurant in town, meaning a gaggle of tourists, autograph hounds, groupies and media lurking around for almost guaranteed celebrity sightings. It was too soon for the real moneymakers, but Marcello had promised the early arrival of the most notorious lesbian couple in town.

"Outside the Bad Mama/ the atmosphere burned hot/ the conceit burned hotter/ celebrities crowded the sidewalks/ sending sparks of narcissism bursting into the smoggy summer sky," Maxie whispered.

She shivered. That's the kind of day it was. She was making up bad poetry, an impulse that hit her at odd times and that she never revealed to anyone.

Marcello leaned on a lamppost, smoking an unfiltered Camel. He wagged his cigarette at her, like a handsome dissolute actor in a Fellini movie. She felt a spark of affection for the pseudo-journalist.

"*Buone notizie, bella.* Petra and Tiffany are due early. *Nu?* Am I a *mensch* for notifying you or what?" Marcello had picked up Yiddish from a former girlfriend, which he incorporated joyfully into his multi-lingual commentary. His language fluctuated from erudite to Ellis Island pidgin. He was, hands down, the oddest paparazzo in town.

"I hopes this pans out," Maxie said. "I'm feeling edgy today."

"As you know, I pay *molto* to someone who doesn't bullshit about these things. They'll be here *pronto.*"

"Bitch number one and bitch number two."

"You're a harsh critic."

"You created me. Kidnapped me from Piper Trueblood, Professor Higgins, and took me under your wing. I emulate you for better or worse."

"I plucked you from your ennui, *bella.* Do I dare to eat a peach? You were ripe as a peach."

"T.S. Eliot. What do you know about T.S. Eliot? Did one of your former girlfriends summarize him for you?"

Marcello squashed his cigarette into the butt-filled sand of an outdoor ashtray, looking offended.

Maxie almost apologized but Marcello frowned on verbal regrets. "Petra Lindstrom is a sports product placement and Tiffany El is insane. Worse, they're pretentious snots."

Marcello shrugged. "If I coached you about anything, I coached you to be one with those you pursue. See past bitch to oneness of humanity."

"I don't mind self-defense. But shoving a fan so hard that the kid trips over a curb?"

"People in ice houses, *shaine maidela.*"

Maxie laughed. "It's people in glass houses."

Marcello gave her one of his enigmatic looks. "No, *bella,* I meant ice houses."

"Okay, okay. Since we're mixing metaphors, we're David and Goliath, remember? Puny paparazzi versus egos on legs."

"All God's children suffer from their sins, even egos on legs."

"Father Marcello, don't go Catholic angst on me." Maxie raised her camera. "Screw sin and redemption too, for that matter."

"I've a created a harpy who mocks faith."

Maxie raised her fist. "Power to the harpies."

Marcello pointed to Maxie's camera. "You love your camera, yet you take stock pictures to fit in with the guys. You still do the best work. Who are you, Maxie?"

"*Vaffanculo!*" Maxie said. "Did I pronounce that little screw-you reference correctly?"

Marcello grinned. "*Perfetto.*"

They were interrupted by a cry from the crowd. "I'll be damned," Maxie said. "They are early."

As part of her training, Professor Marcello had taught Maxie "Marcello's Paparazzi Way," his method of non-intrusive intrusion. Maxie took a breath from her belly. She felt her focus sharpen. She didn't just have a camera. She was a camera. She pushed through the jostling media. The screaming and frantic pushing became a dance. She worked her way to the front of the crowd to gain a clear view of the street in front of the club.

Fisher Jacobs, one the few female sports agents, a legend among her kind, popped from the limo parked at the curb. Fisher was a known girl-magnet among the chic L.A. lesbian crowd. She had a compelling look, dark-haired, slim, athletic, an All-American Jewish Princess. At the moment, she radiated confidence shielding her client and client's girlfriend from the swarming paparazzi.

Petra Lindstrom, winner of four LPGA majors, gripped a Callaway seven-iron, which she used as a walking stick and a lucrative product endorsement opportunity. Tiffany El, certified diva, was doing her Celine Dion interpretation. Maxie fought to the front of the pack. Males, even frantic paparazzi, still had qualms about belting women. Maxie used this to her advantage, weaving through the chaos while using Marcello's teachings to remain calm and focused.

Her feverish cohorts shouted. "Smile, girls! How about a nice kiss?"

"Heard you broke up!"

"Heard you're getting married! What gives?"

No one expected the women to answer.

Maxie had only to get around Fisher Jacobs and she'd be able to snap some priceless shots. She made her usual vow to contribute part of her profits to a local women's shelter. Maxie attempted to slip into the gap separating Fisher and the couple. Maxie bumped hard into Fisher. Fisher flinched and grabbed Maxie to prevent a fall.

"Let go," Maxie said, coming out of her zone.

Fisher had a reputation for being super-charismatic. Today, however, a wild, demented look marred her face.

"Parasite," Fisher said.

"Who's a parasite? Sports agent blood-sucker."

"Back off." Fisher stuck a palm over Maxie's camera lens.

"Leave the camera alone!" She kicked Fisher's shin, not hard, but enough to make a point.

"Ow!" Fisher grabbed Maxie's camera tighter, nearly twisting the lens from the body.

Maxie pushed into Fisher's chest, sending her sailing. Fisher clung to the camera, bringing Maxie into the tumble. As Maxie tried to recover, the camera flew from her hands and skittered into the road, where it was promptly run over by a Corvette convertible.

Maxie felt like an arm had been severed. She raised a fist at Fisher. Fisher put up her dukes, like she was in a bar brawl.

"Girl fight!" A teenage boy called from the crowd. The masses crashed in, like high surf waves. People pushed and shoved, while a bodyguard tried to escort Tiffany El and Petra into the restaurant.

Tiffany El shoved the bodyguard away and pointed an accusing finger at Maxie. "She's a menace. Someone call the cops! She's assaulting our agent." She snatched her girlfriend's seven-iron and waved it at Maxie. When Petra tried to calm her, Tiffany El shoved Petra and swatted at the bodyguard again. Fisher Jacobs, most likely trying to avoid more bad publicity for El, tried to snatch the club, resulting in a tugging match.

At that moment, a pair of squad cars appeared, lights flashing.

Everyone on the scene was either shouting, batting at each other or recording the mess. Maxie recognized one of the approaching cops as a woman she'd run into trouble with several times in the past. The stocky blond officer headed straight for her, along with a beefy male partner.

"Hands behind your back," the blond officer said.

"I'm not the one with the weapon," Maxie said.

"Am I going to have to restrain you?"

There'd been a lot of tasering going on lately. Maxie put her hands behind her back. Click. As she was being led away handcuffed, Maxie could see that the ruckus was far from over. Fisher Jacobs argued with one of the officers. Maxie had shut up after a single line. Fisher was not letting up. Before she was guided into the back seat of the patrol car, Maxie observed Fisher committing one last stupid move, spitting on the ground near an officer's shoe. In short order, Fisher was cuffed and being led to another squad car.

In her peripheral vision, Maxie noticed Marcello and the rest of the paps snapping away at the altercation. Television crews filmed the situation. Fans were probably sending tweets all over the world.

Chapter Two

The Slammer

FOR THE FIRST time in her life, Maxie Wolfe spent the night in jail. It was after midnight by the time she'd been booked by a bored female officer. An hour later, another officer discussed bail with her. Maxie reflected on the people she could call to get her out. She imagined the lectures and hopeless sighs. The worst would be calling Helen, considering their last hotel room encounter only yesterday. Maxie refused bail. Her possessions were taken from her and she was issued baggy orange jail garb.

Like a bad remake of *Dinner with Andre*, Maxie was locked in a cell with an elegant middle-aged escort named Franny Glass. Their toilet had a blown gasket and wasted vast amounts of precious drought-land water with an endless gurgle. The dank, tiny room reeked of urine. Maxie tried to ignore the repair issue, which seemed ironically punishing.

Franny Glass explained to Maxie that she'd made the unfortunate mistake of refusing to perform a rather disgusting act on a prominent local politician, resulting in her eventual arrest while she was innocently enjoying an expensive cocktail in a five-star hotel bar.

"It's amazing how so many law-abiding people get apprehended in conspiracies," Maxie said.

"Whoa, girl," Franny said. "This is going to be a long night. Where are your social skills?"

"I didn't know they applied in jail," Maxie said.

Franny laughed. "Even more here. I'm going to ignore your rudeness. I believe in making the best of a situation."

Franny Glass had a deck of cards. She proceeded to beat Maxie at a variant of poker called Follow the Queen. She told her entire life story and insulted Maxie endlessly, which at least made the time pass.

"My mother worshipped J.D. Salinger," Franny said. "Hence my name. I don't suppose you know what I mean."

"I read all the Franny and Zooey stuff. Don't make assumptions because I'm a paparazzo. I hate Salinger. He's morbid and depressing."

"Honey, being locked up in a piss-smelling dungeon is morbid and depressing. Great literature is liberating."

"You've got a point," Maxie admitted.

"Who do I look like?" Franny asked in the early hours of the morning.

"I don't know who you look like."

"Come, come, darling, you're supposed to be the hot shit celebrity photographer."

"Really, I don't know."

Franny groaned. "Jane Fonda."

"Do all call girls aspire to be Jane Fonda in *Klute*?"

"Don't ever get convicted to prison time, Maxie. With that attitude, you'll be messed with bad." Franny pointed to Maxie. "Audrey Hepburn."

"What?"

"Audrey Hepburn was tall like you, a lot of people don't know that. You remind me of her, kind of androgynous. Cute bad girl with a heart of gold."

"I don't know about the heart of gold," Maxie said. "I forget how the queen works in this game."

"Let me see your hand. I'm not going to help you anymore after this."

"What do you care? I already owe you fifty pretend cigarettes."

"Try and concentrate on your hand now," Franny said. "Wise mouth and you suck at cards. I really hope you don't get jail time."

Succumbing to Franny's persistent grilling, Maxie eventually related every detail of what had landed her in the pokey. She never got better at the card game.

"MAXINE WOLFE," a guard called out. With zero hours of sleep under her belt, Maxie stumbled towards the opened gate the next morning. "See you around," she said to Franny.

"Here." Franny handed her the Queen of Hearts from her deck of cards. "Your new lucky charm. You're gonna need it, honey. Down the rabbit hole and back up again, that's where you're headed."

Still wearing her ugly prison jump suit, Maxie signed a promise to appear and got back her things. "Where's my camera?"

"Seized for evidence," the officer said.

"Evidence for what?"

"None of your business."

"Did they arrest Fisher Jacobs? Does that mean I can get restitution?"

"Didn't you hear me, lady? Now, why don't you just toddle off like a good girl?"

Maxie hailed a cab outside the station. Once she was in the backseat, she called her lawyer. She was relieved to be shunted into voice mail. Time enough to smooth things over with Helen before her court date. The cab dropped her off in front of the driveway where she'd parked her car in Hollywood. By some miracle it hadn't been stripped or towed, but there was a ticket on the windshield for a healthy sum of money to add to the indignities of the last few days.

MAXIE ATTEMPTED TO go about business as usual in the thirty days before her court date, but she was not herself. She even stooped so low as to chase third-rate wannabes from tacky reality shows at the airport. All her snoops were either on vacation or shunning her. She was using her back-up camera, which felt like a less favored child.

Three weeks after her release, however, Marcello broke her ennui. It was 9 a.m. on a sunny day, typical California paradise weather.

"*Bella*, I'm out of town. Take this tip. Be discreet. Don't risk another arrest."

"No lectures, Professor."

"You're correct. I shouldn't pre-judge your actions." Marcello gave her the scoop.

Maxie whistled softly. "I owe you."

"You owe me nothing. Unconditional love."

"I don't believe in it."

AT ELEVEN A.M., she was nestled behind a dumpster outside a ratty bodega on the fringe of the Silver Lake district. A Cadillac sat in the filthy parking lot with litter stuck to its tires.

Superstar macho-man Boyd Gruber and a tall, well-built male companion in drag staggered out of the bodega. They clutched each other and juggled paper bags. Boyd was on a verifiable meltdown as of late. He'd recently tainted his nice-guy married man image with a drunk-driving arrest during which he'd hurled anti-Semitic and racial epithets at the arresting officers. Now he and his companion swigged from bottles in a crummy parking lot. They didn't bother to get back into the Cadillac, instead they stood drinking and leaning into each other.

Maxie shot a series of tawdry shots of the sodden duo hugging and shoving one another in a bipolar display of affection and aggression. A few blocks away, she e-mailed the photos to Bruce Fein. The story broke a few hours later on *People Weekly's* Web site, including speculation about Boyd's companion being a male prostitute. She would get top dollar for the pictures, enough to pay the rent and more, thanks to Marcello and his tip. She felt a little sorry for Gruber. He had seven kids and a nice wife. He was digging his own grave, however. She was only the messenger.

Once she returned home she was distracted enough to burn a frozen bean and pork burrito in the toaster oven, nearly setting the pool house ablaze. Fortunately, the battery was dead on the fire alarm and she was able to put out the flames without alerting her landlords.

A WEEK LATER, Maxie faced her day in court. She took three wrong turns on the way to the courthouse. Maxie would possibly have admitted — if anyone probed — that she was expressing her increasing inner agitation by going adrift. No one asked, which is how she liked it.

Note to self: Don't arrive late to your arraignment.

Her heart sank as she caught sight of the presiding judge. A few months ago, the Honorable Kate Sullivan-O'Leary's teenage son had been arrested for selling Ecstasy. The paparazzi devoured the poor kid. Sullivan-O'Leary was as notorious as a Deep South magistrate for barbaric drug sentencing. The press, including Maxie, had had a field day with that little bit of painful poetic justice. When the judge spotted Maxie, she detected a look of vengeance in the judge's eyes. Even worse, Helen glared at her with reproach for her late arrival.

The city attorney read the charges, Penal Code section 415, disturbing the peace.

"What peace?" Maxie said. "There was no peace. It was pandemonium. Nothing to disturb."

"Ms. Dubois," Judge Sullivan-O'Leary said, "Will you ask your client to remain silent?"

"Where are the celebrities today?" Maxie asked. "It's only a question."

"Your Honor," Helen said, "may I have a moment to talk to my client?"

In the hallway during the short recess, Helen was livid. "Do you know how long the calendar is for arraignments? What a way to piss off an already biased judge. She was going to issue a warrant for you and I had to kiss her ass to hold her off."

"I'm sorry, Helen. Disturbing the peace. I'm having trouble letting go. The whole thing is so stupid."

"Maxie, we're going back in there and you will remain silent. Don't push me away, Maxie. How many friends do you have? No talking. Just show me." Helen held up a hand with five fingers extended. "Five friends? How many?"

Maxie held up her right hand with five fingers extended. Silently, she curved in each finger until the hand was balled into a fist. No fingers.

HELEN WAS A brilliant lawyer. When Maxie was called up, Helen took the case apart like a biologist dissecting a frog. The city attorney, acknowledging the absurdity of the case, proposed a minimal punishment for a no-contest plea. Sullivan-O'Leary was not having any of it. In the end, she sentenced Maxie to restitution, probation and community service. For maximum indignity, she added anger-management classes.

"If you were a nobody, I could have gotten the whole thing dismissed except for the restitution," Helen said as they left the courthouse.

"Just what I need, a criminal record because of a grudge verdict."

"We can expunge. Just do the penance. Look, L.A. is in such bad shape right now, we could be in a third-world country. Worse, I can't stop being angry at you."

"Do you want to take anger-management classes with me?"

"That's not funny."

"I'll wait to hear from you on how to set up my penance." Maxie waved as she turned and walked away.

It *was* funny. Helen was far too serious.

Maxie decided not to wait for Helen's help and called around to some buddies for advice. Teddy Kramer, the Ugly Lizards' drummer, recommended the shortest program qualifying for court-ordered anger-management rulings. He claimed to have cruised through the counseling without changing an iota.

It was a good time to be a convicted angry person in Southern California. With the tanked economy, almost anyone in L.A. could hang up a shingle and become an anger-management counselor. She called the place Teddy had recommended, New Dawn Clinic, and reserved a spot for the next week.

She felt almost hopeful, until the stalking phone calls started again. She deleted them from her voice mail without listening. Erasing them from her memory banks was something else.

Chapter Three

A New Dawn

NEW DAWN CLINIC was eight blocks from Maxie's house. She couldn't have gotten lost if she'd tried. She did manage to pull into the parking lot a few minutes late. Five minutes later a tanned woman leapt gazelle-like from a white Bentley.

"Hi." She waved at Maxie. "I'm Dr. Danielle Cutler, but I'm called Dr. Dani."

Maxie didn't bother with any cynical thoughts about the absent last name. None of the popular therapists had last names. Dr. Dani hosted a radio show called *Rage* where she administered advice on managing anger in the face of modern life's indignities. She lectured internationally. She appeared on *Dr. Oz* and *David Letterman*. Maxie figured that was why she was rumored to have the easiest court-approved program in Southern California. The poor woman was too busy with other pursuits.

Maxie trailed the therapist into a large airy room that faced out onto a magnificent walled garden. The décor was intentionally shabby chic, probably meant to reflect the disorganized but healing mind. Maxie took a minute to appreciate the framed posters on the walls. The place was a veritable gallery of women's art through the ages. A striking Georgia O'Keefe, a challenging Helen Frankenthaler and an obscure Artemisia Gentileschi masterpiece. At least Dr. Dani had an eye for good painting.

"I have to make a few calls," Dr. Dani said to Maxie. "Will you greet the arrivals?"

Maxie nodded, shamelessly sucking up. In the next few minutes, an assortment of screw-ups dribbled in, looking variously sheepish, resentful, cocky and guarded.

Dr. Dani popped her head in. "Two minutes, I'm on the line with *60 Minutes* about a post office rampage outside of Seattle."

"Does anyone give a shit about postal rage anymore?" a chick with spiked hair and a Gucci leather jacket asked. A few of the attendees chuckled.

Maxie guessed that the Gucci jacket was purchased used from a Melrose Avenue consignment shop. The color job on the hair looked discount, too.

Before any more inane commentary from the class, Dr. Dani burst in, carrying a stack of workbooks. "I have seven workbooks based on seven reservations and there are only six present."

"Seven," someone said from the entry.

Maxie's jaw dropped. Fisher Jacobs. Maxie watched her nemesis walk across the room and sit in a chair that faced Maxie in the healing circle.

The next half hour ranged from insulting to boring. The insulting segment consisted of Dr. Dani's self-introduction, which would have earned a chorus of groans at the Oscars. The boring entailed a tedious explanation of the curriculum, signing of contracts and other bureaucracy.

As far as Maxie was concerned, the more time wasted the better. Pretty soon, the entire first session would be over. Her stomach lurched as she learned what came next. Everyone in the group would be required to tell their story. Was this necessary? How about something like the old show *To Tell the Truth*? Everyone could make up their story except for one person, and then they could all guess who had told the truth.

Repentance and transformation were not on the minds of this bunch, in any case. The girl with the spiked hair, Chantal, had punched another girl in a bar during a heated discussion over Chantal's boyfriend. Only after being provoked. Too bad the judge didn't see it that way. Gee, wasn't it odd how many judges were incapable of listening to perfectly reasonable explanations for perfectly innocent attacks upon other people and property?

Maxie glanced over at Fisher. She had a feeling they weren't supposed to be in the same anger-management class. In fact, she was certain they weren't supposed to be in the same class. She distinctly remembered a no-contact order in the pronouncements at her court session. Fisher winked at her.

"You're next," Dr. Dani said to Fisher.

Fisher adopted a fetching look that Maxie supposed earned her passage into numerous bedrooms. "Unlike the others who've spoken so far," Fisher said, "I admit I may have lost my temper in a heated situation. I'm sorry for what I did. It was an isolated incident, but that's no excuse. It only makes me aware of something bottled inside I need discharged."

The class panted at the discharge reference.

"Here is a wonderful example of searching for buried motivations that trigger inappropriate actions," Dr. Dani said. "We all need to stop acting on automatic pilot in life."

The man next to Maxie snorted. The beefy guy had stomped into the room with a purple, mottled face, already on the edge of volcanic eruption. "What the hell is Ms. Jesus over here going to do for seven effing sessions, preach from the mountaintops? I've been through three of these effing seminars and there's always a goddamned Mister or Ms. Jesus preaching their effing insights."

Fisher lifted an eyebrow. "Three effing arrests and three effing seminars. Sounds like a guy to take advice from."

The guy's eyes bulged. "You better watch it, girlie." He waved a fist with callused knuckles in the air.

"You wish, brother," Fisher said without a trace of intimidation. Maxie was reluctantly impressed.

"Let's move on," Dr. Dani said.

"You didn't say what you did to get in trouble," Chantal said to Fisher.

"Our leader said you didn't have to," Fisher said, nodding her chin in Dr. Dani's direction.

"Probably put her girlfriend in the hospital," the guy said. "These tough dykes know how to mess up and get forgiveness."

"What's your name?" Dr. Dani asked.

"George."

"George, do you want to share why you're here?"

"I shot my mother in her bed."

The group gasped.

"Kidding. I got in a fight at my son's basketball game and broke some jerk's nose. My sports enthusiasm is a bad habit. If I don't cure this habit soon, I'll no longer get probation. I only got probation because I have a good lawyer and the court system is so screwed up."

"Thank you, George." Dr. Dani checked her watch. "The time is going so quickly. Let's move on with the introductions."

Maxie was the last one. George yawned. Chantal inspected her sharp nails.

"I don't have to speak," Maxie said stiffly.

Dr. Dani smiled at her. "Is speaking in a group something you fear? You think that no one has time for you?"

Everyone stared at her. She wasn't going to give them the satisfaction of a breakdown. She never had breakdowns.

"I'm like her," she said, pointing in Fisher's direction. "I lost my temper in a heated situation. I'm sorry for what I did."

"Oh, great," George said. "The Jesus Chicks."

"Let's take our break," Dr. Dani said.

"CAN WE TALK?" Fisher asked. They loitered by the fridge in the snack room.

"What do you want?" Maxie asked.

"Not here," Fisher said. "Let's go outside beyond the smokers."

When Maxie and Fisher pushed through the front door, the smokers eyed them suspiciously. The Jesus Chicks, their looks said.

"This way." Fisher took off in the direction of the walled garden area.

"I don't think this is no-contact," Maxie said to Fisher's back. "We weren't supposed to have any contact during our punishment." Fisher didn't reply. Maxie followed her.

When they crossed into the garden, Fisher moved toward a carved wooden bench under a crab apple tree. She motioned for Maxie to sit beside her.

"No funny business," Maxie said.

"Girl Scout's Promise."

"Ha ha. Were you a Girl Scout?"

"Yep. I received the Gold Award, the highest honor. You may think I'm bullshitting you, but I'm sorry for breaking your camera. It wasn't you. I had a bad day before I got to the Bad Mama. I had a bad summer. So, please, sit." She patted a place next to her on the bench.

Maxie sat. "Your restitution bought me a killer new Nikon. So, everything worked out great for me."

"Glad I could advance your life situation," Fisher said. "You're intriguing, Maxie. A sweet meaty walnut in a protective shell."

"I'm not into your charms."

Fisher smiled. "I have one of the best lists of athletes in the country. Because of my charms."

"Spare me. What do you want?"

"I want to take this class."

"I got here first," Maxie said.

"I have a plan."

"Forget it."

"Please?"

Maxie laughed. "Please?" Her amusement faded. "Don't pull that sad face on me. It won't work."

"We could both subject ourselves to jail time or we could take advantage of a bad situation," Fisher said. "Our probation officers are not the same ones we had in court. The new ones don't know who our victims are. It would be very easy to get through this without any trouble." She tapped Maxie's knee. "Besides, it'll be fun."

"Don't touch me," Maxie said. Fisher's suggestion intrigued her. The deception made the anger-management class more interesting. Otherwise, she'd be stuck alone with George and Chantal and the rest of the losers. Fisher struck her as a winner, but with a few issues. "Okay, I'm in. Break's over. We better get back inside."

She walked away without giving Fisher a chance to respond.

"WE WILL BEGIN our first exercise tonight," Dr. Dani announced when the group reconvened. "Everyone has a set of critical moments that can dictate their entire lives. We begin the healing process by finding three of these occasions. Not one. Not ten. Three. Three is a metaphysical powerhouse. The triad of the parents making a child."

"I hate this," George said. "The classes where they make us write about the effing past. This effing triad bullshit takes the cake."

"Do we have to share this?" Chantal asked.

"No," Dr. Dani said. She passed around pads, pencils and a folder. "You'll put your entries in your Memory Folder, which you'll bring to each session. Sharing is optional."

"First person or third? Chronological?" a woman named Penny who'd identified herself as an author asked.

"Your choice," Dr. Dani said.

The atmosphere swelled with a reluctant burgeoning concentration. Everyone in the circle bent over his or her pages, pouring out their hearts or at least pretending to do so.

Maxie doodled on the page. It wasn't that she couldn't think of three. Three? How about a million? Unfortunately, the doodle turned into a Hebrew star. With the clarity of a photograph, a scene appeared, then a sentence.

Maxie glanced up. Everyone stared at her. She had filled two pages and started her third. She set down her pencil.

"You can finish," Dr. Dani said.

"I'm finished," Maxie said. She put her secret history, or whatever it was, in her Memory Folder. She hadn't finished the assignment because she'd kept erasing and correcting. She had an urge to tear up the whole thing right in front of everyone. As soon as the class was dismissed, she jumped up and headed for the door.

She left the clinic in a mild panic. There were eighteen messages on her voice mail. She raced down Wilshire Boulevard toward downtown L.A., tearing into the parking lot of Jonah's Shack, a seedy whale-shaped diner with greasy windows. Once inside, she pulled the stupid journal entry sheets from her Memory Folder and began to scribble feverishly.

Chapter Four

Journal Entry Number One Yom Kippur in the Eighties
by Maxie Wolfe

IT WAS SIX o'clock. Maxie sat on a vinyl couch set against an exposed brick wall in the loft she shared with Judy Oyster in San Francisco. Her mother's minions ran around like insane squirrels, obeying her mother's commands, erecting a Hebrew star on a raised platform ringed by a circle of metal fire pits. Opening night preparations for Judy Oyster events were frenzied but nothing compared to the actual performances.

Maxie considered going to the kitchen where the caterers scooped mashed egg yolks into cooked whites, preparing one of her favorites, deviled eggs. No one, of course, asked her if she was hungry. She couldn't leave her spot no matter how much her stomach growled.

On opening nights, she had a ritual. If she scrutinized every moment of the activities, her mother would be safe. Sometimes, she imagined rescuing her mother from the performances. In these fantasies, her mother took Maxie in her arms and crushed her in a grateful hug.

Until she was seven, Maxie had not attended openings. Then Bobby Shepherd appeared. Bobby Shepherd was her stepfather. Her mother decided Maxie was old enough to attend her shows, under Bobby's supervision.

Now she was eight and Judy was into spanking. Not Maxie, but herself. Judy hardly touched Maxie. She touched herself. She beat herself and burned herself with cigarettes. She whipped herself and banged her head against walls. She was very inventive in her performance art.

Maxie caught sight of Bobby winding his way through the preparations. He seemed steady on his feet. That was good. He carried a plate of deviled eggs in one hand and a glass of champagne in the other. She cleared a space for him.

"Eat." Bobby slumped down and handed her the plate.

"Do you want an egg? They're good," Maxie said.

"Not hungry." Bobby took a large gulp from his glass.

"How many have you had?" she asked.

Bobby grinned at her. "You don't have to keep track of everything we ingest, Maxie. Judy and I are adults, we know what we're doing." The absurdity of his statement was clear to both of them. Bobby shrugged and she mimicked his sangfroid gesture before stuffing an egg into her mouth.

Bobby glanced at the platform. "Jeez. Fire pits. That's illegal."

"Yom Kippur is about being forgiven for all the bad things you did against God. I was listening to Judy's instructions. Judy's performance mocks the absurdity of atonement."

Her mother did not like to be called Mom, or even Mother. Maxie called her Judy.

Bobby whistled. "Aaah-tohh-mint. Peppermint. In mint condition, perfect. Just poi-fect."

Maxie laughed. Bobby liked to mangle words and then improvise poetry.

"Leave it," Judy screamed. One of the minions squeaked and dropped a candle. "Klutz," Judy said.

Maxie and Bobby studied Judy, who was doing what Bobby called her Sarah Bernhardt channeling. Judy tore from the room. All her admirers applauded. Maxie slid the plate of deviled eggs under the couch. Bobby stood up and rubbed his fingers over his bumpy face.

"Don't pick at your acne." That was probably why Bobby's face was pockmarked. He probably mangled scabs on his face when he was a teenager. Some people probably thought he was ugly, with his pockmarks and scraggly crew cut. She thought he was cute. "Where are you going?"

"To the bathroom, Miss Nosy."

"Bobby."

"Honey, Bobby needs his medicine."

She knew better than to beg him to stay.

The room filled up. For the seeming eternity that Bobby was gone, she did homework.

Maxie was enrolled in an alternative school filled with children of leftover Haight-Ashbury hippies, children of suspected drug dealers, children of radicals, and children of ex-radicals turned technological billionaires. The good part was that having a mother like Judy was not a really big deal. Most of the kids were too cool to bring it up.

She was solving a math problem when Bobby reappeared. Math was easy. All the subjects were easy, although Maxie pretended to struggle. Her mother was a genius. Maxie wasn't so sure whether being brilliant led to any good. Bobby staggered over and fell onto the couch. He embraced her. Maxie broke into two people. One felt the warmth in the hug. The other was nauseous, breathing in the smell of vomit that his careless washing hadn't removed. Bobby's medicine made him throw up.

"They're here," he said. "Our world as we know it is doomed." That was one of his favorite jokes, pretending the arriving crowd was a group of aliens from another galaxy. "Look, there's the Lizard Lady and the Robot Man."

Maxie did not laugh. Now that she was eight she no longer found some of the old jokes funny. "Here she comes," she said.

The Lizard Lady approached them, frowning. "I wonder how appropriate this showing is for a child."

Maxie and Bobby shared smirks. The Lizard Lady's lips smiled, but her eyes were yellow and mean. "Don't you have school tomorrow?" she asked.

"Of course," Maxie said. "I guess if you had kids, you'd know that."

"Maxie," Bobby said, "Don't be ruu-aaad. It's not nyy-aacce."

Maxie hid her smile.

They watched the Lizard Lady slink away. The room was packed now.

"Poem?" she asked.

Bobby recited: "The frightened children float up into the sky." He stopped, shook his head. "Ah, shit."

"That was good," Maxie said. "Keep going."

"Forget it," Bobby said. "Maxie, this is a bad time for white male heterosexual poets. We all suck."

"Judy says you dominate." Maxie meant this to be encouraging. "White men have all the power."

"That's why she's famous. She speaks the truth," Bobby said. "As Lightening to the Children eased/With explanation kind/The Truth must dazzle gradually/Or every man be blind."

He poked Maxie. "Now that's brilliance. Who?"

"Emily Dickinson, of course."

"Okay, Miss Smarty Pants. Now that we've established that women rule, it's your turn. You make a poem."

Maxie's stomach turned. "I can't."

"Aren't so smart, are you?"

"Can it, Bobby," Maxie said.

Bobby poked her. "Come on, Smarty."

"The frightened children float up, into the sky, explode like fireworks, and fall to the ground, broken into smithereens," Maxie said.

Bobby whistled. "That's great." He hugged her again. This time she minded the smell of vomit less.

"Look," she said. Her moment of happiness slipped away.

A group of white men with tight black pants, bare chests, black hats and fake curly sideburns carried her mother into the room. She was wailing and spanking herself. Maxie's face burned with shame. The deviled eggs curdled in her stomach. Her mother wore a loose white robe. Her breasts were exposed. Another man, dressed like a goat, pranced nearby. Fire leaped from the smoking pits.

Bobby groaned. "Maybe you shouldn't be here."

"It's too late now, isn't it?" Maxie said. The last thing she wanted was to be a part of the performance, a frightened child running away.

"You have sinned," the men chanted.

They carried Judy to the platform in front of the Hebrew star and hoisted her onto it. Somehow her robe's belt got tangled under one man's foot. As the robe pulled away, her mother slid out, like a sausage squirted from a casing. Her head slammed against the floor. Bounce, bounce, bounce. The robe burst into flames. Everyone screamed. Someone grabbed a fire extinguisher and doused the fire.

Bobby jumped off the couch, almost fell, and then staggered into the performance area. Maxie remained frozen on the couch. A woman ran to her mother from out of the crowd.

"I'm a doctor," the woman said. She knelt beside Judy Oyster.

Before the doctor could do anything else, Maxie's mother shook violently.

"She's having a seizure," someone cried.

Maxie gathered up her homework and walked to the stairs. No one noticed.

Seizure, she thought. See's-you-er. She's you-her.

She went to her bedroom, threw her homework on the desk and slipped behind the bed, nestled in the tight space between the bed frame and the wall. She crossed her arms around her knees and rocked, letting her head knock lightly against the wall. She's you-her. She's you-her.

Someone knocked on the door. She almost ignored it. But even she knew that would be dumb. Bobby Shepherd was all she had. "Come in."

"Where are you?" Bobby asked.

"I'm behind the bed, stupid."

"Stupid is right," he said.

The bed springs squeaked. Bobby tapped the wall above the bed. "She's going to be okay."

"See's-you-her. She's you-her," Maxie said. She heard a slapping sound. "What are you doing?"

"I'm spanking your teddy bear. I won't stop until you come out."

Maxie crept out from behind the bed. "I'm out."

"You should get some sleep. You have school tomorrow."

"I'm not tired."

"Honey, you have to sleep. You want to grow up healthy, for Pete's sake."

Maxie took the teddy bear from Bobby. "Did you hear that Pete?"

"I thought his name was Seymour. Seymour Glass, from the Salinger I read to you."

"I just renamed him. His name is For Pete's Sake. Pete, for short."

Bobby stood. "Now climb under the covers and go to sleep. For Pete's sake."

"If Pete says so," Maxie said. She let Bobby arrange the blanket over her. "Bobby?"

"What, honey?"

"Don't let Judy take Pete. I don't want him in the art work."

"I'll guard him with my life."

It wasn't that she didn't believe Bobby. But she wasn't less afraid.

When Judy wanted something, it was pretty hard to stop her.
The demise of Sneakers the Clown was a perfect example.

AND SO MAXIE Wolfe completed her virgin journal entry. She slipped the pages in her Memory Folder, planning to never look at them again.

Chapter Five

The Impressionists

THREE DAYS LATER, as Maxie cruised past a new tapas place on Beverly Boulevard, her cell rang.

"Maxie Wolfe speaking."

"Fisher Jacobs calling. Are you driving, Maxie? That's against the law."

"My hands are on the wheel. I'm on my way to an eating disorders clinic for teenagers."

"A scoop about anorexics?"

"These are children. Even I wouldn't stoop so low. I'm starting my community service gig. My lawyer got me one teaching photography."

"Teenage girls are tough customers, even the so-called well-adjusted ones," Fisher said.

"This is a piece of cake. Two sessions. I stole, oops, downloaded an entire curriculum from a museum web site. 'Turn your photos into Impressionist Art using Photoshop.'"

"You're over my head with the Photoshop stuff. I don't get how they erase wrinkles, do butt reductions and breast enlargements with those programs. However, I didn't call to discuss body perfection standards."

"Obviously."

"How'd you like to get out of the anger-management classes? They suck. I can't leave town and that pretty much ruins my job. I got an alternative."

"Are you kidding? That's impossible."

"Not if you have connections. You know the Oxymoron Brazil Café?"

"On East Third by Fairfax, next to the Urban Outfitter."

"Meet me there at one tomorrow. I have a surprise for you."

"I'll check my schedule and see if I can find the time."

"Sure. You do that, Ms. Jesus."

Sometimes silence was the best last word. She hung up on Fisher.

MAXIE CLIMBED THE stairs of a converted stone church, past the sign that previously announced sermons. Now it read, "The Amy Crenshaw Center For Eating Disorders."

Maxie crossed through an arched doorway into a hall with a vaulted ceiling. A utilitarian metal greeting desk and generic seating had been added to the front area. Beyond the reception zone, cheaply constructed walls hid the rest of the converted church.

As she entered, Maxie noticed everyone in the reception area staring at her. She fought an urge to flee. She asked for the clinic director. Almost immediately the director came out from behind the barriers.

Dr. Elyse Chandler looked like a short, plump African fertility goddess with expressive lips and analytical eyes. The clue to her hostility was in the eyes. The message came through clear. You're only slightly better than a cockroach.

Who cares? Maxie thought. What about Kafka's cockroach? He was one of the coolest dudes in the history of literature. Hooray for cockroaches.

"How is Helen?" Dr. Chandler asked. "My favorite lawyer."

"She's fine. Thanks for letting me do this."

The director allowed a small, tight smile. "I owe her husband multiple favors. He convinced me to take you on."

Maxie hid a smile. Husbands aiding clandestine flings. Maybe Helen had confessed to her psychologist hubby.

"Did you read the eating disorders material I sent you?" Dr. Chandler asked.

"I didn't know how intractable it was," Maxie said with an enhanced earnest tone. She'd glanced at the material in the parking lot.

"Unfortunately, there are no easy answers. Our girls are a complex group of young ladies." Dr. Chandler nodded with perceptive penetration. "Don't worry. You'll never be alone."

Maxie winced.

"I meant you'll always have help when you're with the girls."

"I knew that," Maxie said, trying to sound nonchalant.

"Of course. Let's get you a badge," Dr. Chandler said.

After Maxie was made official, she and the administrator traversed a long hall, arriving outside a room with a sign labeled "Art Therapy." Another woman was waiting for them.

"This is Ramona Lake, our art therapist," Dr. Chandler said.

Ramona reached down to shake Maxie's hand. She was at least six-five, built like an Amazon. She wore a short-sleeved polo shirt revealing bulging biceps. Maxie considered flirting. Ramona was a knockout. Even she knew better, however, under the circumstances. "Volleyball," she said. "I followed your team. USC Trojans."

"Was a volleyball player," Ramona said. "Good enough for Olympic trials, but I was starving myself to death. Quit competitive sports. Got help. Now I help others. It doesn't matter who I was. We all bring our self-talk cartoon balloons to this place. I'm working with my clients—and myself—to explore those balloons to maintain the healing skies."

Maxie's self-talk balloons floated into the atmosphere, threatening to cloud over any attempts to maintain the healing skies. Terminology bullshit, one of the balloons proclaimed. Maxie hated terminology. Most people used terminology like Ponzi schemers to inflate their egos at the expense of suckers.

"I'll leave you and Ramona to your lesson," Dr. Chandler interrupted, looking at her watch. "Time for a perpetual fund-raising luncheon at the Beverly Hilton. Helen will be there."

"Don't talk about me," Maxie said.

Dr. Chandler frowned.

"I was joking," Maxie said.

"I hope you learn something here today," Dr. Chandler said and turned away.

"I brought four cameras," Maxie said to Ramona.

"Only two girls signed up," Ramona said.

After a moment of feeling offended, Maxie decided she was relieved. The poor sign-up only made her punishment easier and that was the point, wasn't it?

WHEN THEY ENTERED the art therapy room, Maxie caught her breath. The two girls staring at her were thin. Really thin. They wore looks of curiosity mixed with antagonism.

The art therapy room smelled of ink and wet clay. Large paper panels stenciled with outlines of emaciated bodies plastered the walls. Bold block letters were scrawled on the stencils.

THUNDER THIGHS. LOVE HANDLES. UGLY. HIDEOUS. FAT.

"That's us on the walls," one of the girls said. "One of the stupid exercises we had to do."

"Why don't you introduce yourselves?" Ramona asked.

"Skye," said the girl who had just described the wall art. She was pasty-skinned, with straw hair. Acne mottled her cheeks. She appeared to be about five-eight and looked to weigh ninety-eight pounds. "My father is with a major aeronautics company and my mother was an airline hostess, hence the name Skye. I'm seventeen."

"At least they didn't name you Cloud," Maxie said.

Skye hesitated, and then grinned. "At least." She turned to the girl next to her. "You go."

"My name is Picassa." The girl had a nose ring, spiky black hair and raccoon mascara. Despite her eighties band appearance, she looked like a child in a Halloween costume. "I'm thirteen. My mother is a painter. She's a genius. She hates food. We both paint. We eat mostly broccoli and bananas with Splenda. We throw up."

Damaged artist mothers were not a topic Maxie wanted to pursue. She was surprised the girls were so blabby, but it was a self-selected group, probably the two show-offs.

"We know who you are," Skye said. "You got arrested

photographing Tiffany El. El used to be one of us. She's in recovery. Now she's fat."

"Are you gay?" Picassa asked.

Maxie shrugged. "Does it matter?"

"It's cool," Picassa said. "My mom is bisexual, but currently abstaining sexually, so she can focus on her art." Picassa touched a jewel piercing her left nostril. "We have matching studs."

Maxie looked over to the ticking clock mounted over an emergency exit door. If they didn't get started soon, she'd have to stay overtime. That wasn't going to give her any extra credits or relief from her punishment.

"So, give us the assignment," Skye said. "We know your time is valuable. Don't worry, you'll get out of here soon."

Maxie's hands shook a little as she pulled out her stolen curriculum. Dr. Chandler was right. These girls were like sonar depth finders in murky emotional waters. Their eyes bored into her.

Maxie held up a large photo of the Los Angeles skyline shot from Griffith Observatory. Then she held up a print that transformed the same skyline into a dramatic impressionistic night vision. "See what the artist did here?"

Skye yawned. "Altered the skyline with Photoshop adjustments. My father is a camera freak. He showed me how to Photoshop."

"Impressionism through computer manipulation," Picassa added. "My mom would puke."

Ramona was no help, sitting to the side watching Maxie's struggle with detached patience. Maxie pulled another set of photographs from her bag. "Can you have an open mind or what?" She set three images up on stands. "Know who this is?"

"Mary Cassatt," Picassa said. "She studied with Degas. Most famous female Impressionist."

"You are so right," Maxie said.

"Thanks," Picassa said. "My mother taught me. I'm the best at art history."

"Best at everything," Maxie blurted out. "Only thirteen. A skeleton. I'll bet your bulimic Mom is proud of you."

After a moment of shocked silence, the girls burst into laughter.

"That was so unbelievably inappropriate," Skye said. She turned to Ramona. "Wasn't that really, really inappropriate, Ramona? Isn't she going to damage us? What kind of therapy is this? Maybe she needs to do her community service picking up trash on the side of the road where she can't influence tender minds."

"Deal with it," Ramona said.

"Show us your stupid assignment," Picassa said. "You're weird. You fit right in."

Maxie held up the painting of a woman with a child on her lap. "The Impressionists changed the art world with their interpretations of reality. Cassatt brought her own female sensibilities to a predominantly male-dominated art culture." She glanced at the two girls. "What?"

"What do you think we'd see?" Skye said. "We have eating disorders and you bring us paintings of fat women with their fat children? Do you run around the world putting your foot in your mouth?"

"Pretty much," Maxie said.

Skye laughed. "You can be an honorary ED then, short for Eating Disorder. Our little insider nickname."

"Honorary ED. Okay," Maxie said warily.

Skye waved at the body tracings on the walls. "Now you have to do a stencil."

The girls clapped. "Stencil, stencil," they cried.

"No way," Maxie said.

"Then we won't participate," Skye said. "And you go to jail."

"For Pete's sake," Maxie said, turning to Ramona. "Get me a stupid panel." She didn't like the sound of her own voice. She sounded like she was regressing.

Ramona spread a blank sheet of paper on the carpet. Maxie lay down on it. Picassa took a marker and traced Maxie's outline. When she was finished she and Maxie hung it on the wall. Picassa handed the felt tip pen to Maxie. "Write something."

Maxie hesitated.

"Write!" Picassa said.

"Write! Write!" both girls chanted.

Maxie gripped the pen. She scribbled on the outline where the eyes should be, stood back and read her words. "Girls in ice houses/ cannot see/ crystals eyes like diamonds/ everything and nothing through eternity."

"That's cool," Picassa said. "Like a poem."

"It's definitely a poem," Skye said.

Maxie went back to the art table. "Enough, now. Let's discuss using Photoshop filters and layer masks."

For the next hour she and the girls took photos of one another and manipulated them into Impressionistic portraits, distorted bodies that were in turn disturbing and strangely beautiful.

After the session concluded, Maxie descended the church stairs feeling shaken. No matter what Ramona said, the girls were little emotional snoops. Still, they both had a certain charm, even Picassa with her artist mother fixation. They were right. She deserved to be a stencil on the damaged goods wall.

Chapter Six

The Ravaged Woman

THE NEXT DAY, Maxie woke up exhausted. All night long she'd tossed and turned, listening to the tick of a clock on the wall and the hum of the refrigerator's freezer. She almost stood Fisher Jacobs up, but her curiosity got the better of her.

Fisher was already there when Maxie arrived at the Oxymoron Brazil Café. The place smelled like damp earth after a storm, a scent pumped in through the air vents. Maxie wound through the towering tropical vegetation, juggling an organic espresso. She plunked down across from Fisher on a seat fashioned from a tree stump and adjusted her butt bones on the hard shellacked surface.

Two tables down Boyd Gruber sat with a gorgeous woman. He wore shades, cheap clothes and a floppy hat. Every star in town did the same thing. Don a funny disguise and appear in a public place. Everyone, including the star, knew they were instantly recognizable.

Fisher nodded in Boyd's direction. "That's not his wife, but who knows who she is? His sister? That was a raw deal, that story that went viral about him and the male prostitute outside the bodega. Turns out the guy's his accountant."

Before Maxie could reply, Boyd stood abruptly. Maxie cringed. He swelled into the Incredible Hulk. He headed right towards them, bulging through his silly outfit. As soon as he arrived, however, he shrank into normal size and adopted a neutral expression. He knew, as did Maxie and Fisher, that everyone in the room was pretending not to watch.

He bent down, his mouth inches from Maxie's left ear. "You're scum. Inescapable bottom-feeder. My accountant's wife walked out on him."

Maxie sipped her espresso and allowed him to blow off some steam.

If she hadn't taken the pictures, someone else would have. The wild speculations were part of the game, not her fault. She didn't feel guilty. Boyd wasn't exactly without sin. Reminding him about casting stones at this particular moment was not a good idea, however.

Boyd straightened up. A little boy in a space outfit had come up during his whispered insults. The kid held out a ray gun. His beaming parents watched from across the room. "Can you autograph this? I love you."

"So much for bad publicity," Maxie said.

AFTER BOYD AND the kid left, Fisher sighed. "Do you get tired of this?"

"Never," Maxie said. Not exactly true, but close enough. She hesitated. "What about you?"

Instead of answering the question, Fisher thrust a booklet at her. The cover read, *Cognitive Skills for Anger Management: A Home Study Course.* "How would you like to get out of Dr. Dani's ego show and do a home study alternative?"

"Home study courses are against the rules in L.A. County," Maxie said. "I already begged for one."

"You know who Abe Kraptow is?" Fisher asked.

"Are you kidding? Danny King's lawyer." A tiny burst of anxiety jabbed Maxie's gut at Danny King's intrusion into her life. "Lawyer of the century. Lawyer of the gods. Never-lost-a-case lawyer."

"He's my lawyer now," Fisher said.

"Don't you have to be really special to get him to represent you? Not just successful?" Maxie asked.

"It's a long story. Anyway, Kraptow cut us a deal. We're making amends by working together."

"Fisher, are you after me?"

"You're not my type. Kraptow said it was good karma, anyway. You and I resolving it together."

"I'm leaving California. Billion-dollar lawyers spouting karma."

Fisher opened the workbook. "It's the story of two families overcoming anger. The Poindexter family is dysfunctional and the Richfield family is functional. We answer questions about how the families react in a crisis. We explore inappropriate responses of the Poindexter family through the ages and give examples from our own dysfunction. At the end, we take a final exam. No sweat. It's eighth-grade level literacy."

Maxie took the workbook from Fisher and turned to the first page.

"This is the story of two families," she read aloud. She scanned the first few pages. "Here's the first quiz question: 'Family heritage can have a strong subconscious impact on our behavior. The subconscious can't tell truth from fiction. T or F?'" Maxie groaned. "Bullshit and more bullshit."

She flipped to the final exam. "We'll do what I did in college with open book tests. Just go backwards and find the right answers."

Fisher took the workbook from her. "Look at the first requirement. If you do this workbook as home study, you must do it with a coach. We coach each other."

"I don't want to coach you," Maxie said. "I don't want you to coach me."

"I have a mother, a father, and two older brothers. What about you?" Fisher asked.

"None of your business," Maxie said.

"When I was little, my brothers used me for sports practice. For soccer, they kicked balls at me. For football, they tackled me. We won't

get into ice hockey. If I cried to our mother, she shrugged and said
'Then don't play with them.' I would run out and do it all again. That's
why I am what I am. And you, Maxie? Do you have a mother?"

"Yes."

"How about a father?"

Maxie stood up. "I don't have a father."

"I'm sorry," Fisher said. "Did he pass away?"

"I don't want to talk about it."

"Maybe the next time we meet."

"I don't want to meet with you." Maxie was now convinced that
Fisher had a hidden agenda. She detected something strange in Fisher's
determination.

"What if I gave you the tip of the year?"

"Bribery." Maxie started to walk away.

"Since when are you opposed to bribery? Isn't that part of your
job?"

"You can't come up with enough to entice me."

"What if it was Donna Street?"

Maxie halted. A Street exclusive might make it worth playing along
with Fisher. Street had recently disappeared and no one could find her.
Her latest film was set to premiere in two weeks. In the last six months,
she'd been evading the press, although a few shots hinted that she
seemed to be growing in size, despite a lucrative contract with a weight-
loss milkshake product.

Maxie returned to the burl table and sat down. "Good-bye, Dr.
Dani."

"No kidding," Fisher said.

Maxie hesitated. "Stupid journal entries. Did you do them?"

"No," Fisher said. "Not after the first one in class."

"Why not? You apparently have a great family."

"What about you? I saw you writing in the class," Fisher said.

"I was doodling." Maxie leaned toward Fisher. "Give me the scoop
on Street."

"I have a contact. He'll be in the right place at the right time. You
won't be sorry about this, Maxie."

"I already am. But Dr. Dani is worse."

THE NEXT SATURDAY, Maxie was on her way to the eating
disorders clinic for her last required session, when the informant called.
She had no choice but to blow off the community service with a quick
call about having the flu. She drove as quickly as she could without
risking arrest, feeling the ambiguous buzz that was the most she could
muster regarding chasing celebrities. It was like sex. She had to keep
her metaphorical eyes closed.

When she arrived at the ultra-private Earthly Gates Spa in the hills above Malibu, she walked through a gate that the snitch had "accidentally" left unlocked. Street was going to relax in a Jacuzzi before a scheduled massage, all of this verified by the snitch. Unfortunately, the Jacuzzi turned out to be surrounded by a protective barrier of thick hedges. There was no way to get a picture without coming out in the open.

Maxie had no trouble with exposing herself. She was a hard-working paparazzo chronicling the meltdown of an egotistical bloated celebrity. The assignment was a no-brainer worth enough to pay several months of rent. She stepped past the hedge and fired off a succession of rapid shots of the fat, lumpy, cellulite-ridden body of the ravaged woman. Donna Street, completely nude, turned to face Maxie. Her features contorted into a look of humiliation and outrage. She bleated like a trapped animal. Maxie kept shooting.

The snitch shouted at her. He raced towards her and she took off like a cross-country runner. It was all part of the act. Good thing she was athletic.

Once she was down from the hills, she e-mailed the photos to Bruce Fein. Usually, she didn't feel much except accomplishment at mission achieved. Today, as she studied the images, she heard Street's awful squealing and it felt like psychic carnage. The paycheck, however, would be extravagant. Maybe she'd buy a video camera in addition to paying rent. Still photos weren't good enough, lately. She didn't like video, but the times they were a-changing.

THE NEXT DAY, she threw a few things into a duffle bag and climbed into the Porsche. She liked to avoid the 405, which was always a potential mess of accidents, police chases and puzzling construction. Instead, she hopped onto 170 and drove the twenty-some miles north to Granada Hills. Just off the freeway exit, she found a Ramada Inn and rented a room on the second floor in the farthest wing, facing the back parking lot.

In the morning, she dug out a worn pair of golf shoes, faded golf shirt and threadbare shorts and drove to nearby Old Hills Country Club. She looked out of place among the designer crowd climbing from their hundred thousand dollar cars.

The club's eighteen-hole golf course sprawled across the landscape—daunting bunkers, lake-sized water hazards, narrow fairways and elevated greens. A weathered man with a trim build greeted her in the pro shop. "How's my favorite golfer?"

"Life's a little complicated right now," Maxie said.

"That's the beauty of golf," Glenn Livvey said. "Takes you away from your problems."

Her former college coach had met with the same golf fate as Maxie. She'd been kicked off her college team and her scholarship rescinded.

Livvey was fired a few years later for alcoholism.

Livvey picked up the keys to the storage locker. "I'll get your clubs."

"Thanks, coach."

"Love to see you back into playing competitively again. Some little tournaments." He stopped speaking when he saw the look on Maxie's face.

For the next four hours, she played a pretty good game, considering how little she practiced. It didn't matter. She reveled in the absence of complications, like being in a monastery. Maybe she'd talk to Glenn Livvey about starting a monastery. They'd erect a palatial monastery with a five-star golf course.

When she got back to the clubhouse, she found Livvey. "What are the chances of letting me go another eighteen?"

"Things that bad with you?" He held up a hand. "Okay, okay."

Maxie golfed another round playing better with each hole. She eagled the last par five, chipping in from four yards off the green. A group of drunken men on the patio applauded. She bowed. Livvey was right. Golf could take a person away from the troubled world, at least temporarily.

BACK AT THE motel, her restlessness returned. The last thing she wanted to do was watch television or read magazines. She hesitated, and then pulled out the anger-management workbook. Might as well see how the two families were doing. She climbed into bed, twisting the covers around herself like a cocoon. She read out loud in a mocking voice. "List the qualities that make the Poindexters self-deceivers. List the qualities that make the Richfields good communicators."

She took the motel pen from the nightstand and filled in the blanks. She fell asleep curled in a fetal position, cradling the workbook.

Chapter Seven

Ice and Stones

"I'M LATE, BUT I'm coming," Maxie shouted into her cell phone the next morning.

"Thought you might bail on me," Fisher said.

"Something's wrong with my phone. You're breaking up on me. I spent the night in the Valley, getting away from it all," Maxie said.

"You're going to kill yourself." Fisher's voice crackled through the cell.

"It's part of the job." Talking on a cell phone while driving was an act of necessity for paparazzi. So what if it entailed potential mutilation or death?

Maxie entered a construction zone, steering with one hand. She reached a maze built of cones. The Porsche skidded on a patch of loose gravel and nearly rammed a concrete mixer. She pulled into a turn-off, heart beating rapidly.

"Are you okay?" Fisher asked.

Before she could respond, Maxie's phone battery went dead. It had been barely charging for a week. Another repair issue she'd ignored. She threw the useless phone onto the seat and pulled back onto the road. She was nearly back in town when she realized she'd left her workbook at the motel.

WHEN MAXIE ARRIVED at the Oxymoron Brazil Café, Fisher jumped up from her seat. "I was imagining you being extricated with a Jaws of Life from a squashed Porsche."

"Relax," Maxie said, settling into a burl seat. "My phone battery died. I had to stop at the Beverly Center Apple store and get a new phone. Maxie took in Fisher's pale face. "Are you all right?"

"What a great time for you to check out from the world."

"What are you talking about?" Maxie asked.

Fisher held out two photos. "I printed these out from the *People Weekly* web site."

One was of Donna Street standing at the edge of the Malibu Hill spa Jacuzzi. She stared directly into the camera with a look of abject outrage, hatred and humiliation on her gorgeous but puffy face. Her private parts were blocked, but not her loose flesh. The other was a shot of an ambulance wheeling a sheet-wrapped lumpy body into an emergency room.

"Uh oh," Maxie said.

"Street swallowed half her medicine cabinet, but her assistant found her and called 9-1-1. The paramedics got her to the hospital and the docs pumped her stomach. She's still alive."

"Oh, shit," Maxie said.

"Look, Maxie, no one imagined Street would go this far. Don't feel bad."

Maxie stiffened. "I don't feel bad."

"Have it your way, Ms. Poindexter. They fired the guy at the spa who ratted on her whereabouts and did such a poor job at security. I got him another hack security job, with a much bigger salary. That was part of the deal, of course."

"She'll lose her bazillion-dollar contract for that weight-loss milkshake crap," Maxie said.

"She would have lost the contract anyway," Fisher said. "She got fat."

"You look guilty," Maxie said.

"You should talk. You look messed up to me, even if you think you're hiding it," Fisher said. "I'm not the one who ran away."

"Oh, yeah?" Maxie reached for the photos and ripped them into pieces. Donna Street became a shredded pile of disconnected images lying on the table.

"I guess that takes care of that, emotional analysis-wise," Fisher said. "Where's your workbook?"

"I left it in the Valley."

"How convenient. I did the homework." Fisher held out her notebook.

Maxie scanned Fisher's answers. "List the qualities that make the Poindexters self-deceivers. List the qualities that make the Richfields good communicators."

"The point is trying to find out if the cycles can be broken. If you'd done the homework, you'd see that one of the Poindexter girls is making an effort to break the cycle. She's getting therapy and expressing her feelings. In fact, she's dating one of the Richfield girls." Fisher laughed. "All the latest workbooks are gay and lesbian friendly."

"Very touching."

Fisher stood up. "There's a copy place next door. I'll run over and make copies and you can put them in your workbook when you get it back."

After Fisher disappeared, Maxie sat staring at the torn pieces of photographs scattered on the table. After a moment's hesitation, she reconstructed the photos of Donna Street from the pieces she'd torn up, fitting the segments together like a jigsaw puzzle. When she finished, Street's hatred and humiliation stared up at her.

She got up and left before Fisher returned.

When she got back to her car, she got a call from Helen Dubois.

"Maxie, are you purposely self-destructing? You blew off your community service assignment. Do you like jail?"

"Sorry."

"I had to get my husband to call Dr. Chandler and convince her to give you a last chance."

"Thanks, Hellie. I appreciate it."

"Don't call me Hellie. Just make this right." Helen hung up on her.

Maxie dialed her cell. Marcello answered on the second ring. "Hey, professor," she said. "Did you catch all the Donna Street action?"

"*Nu?* Only the biggest scoop..." Marcello caught his breath. "You? *Bella,* how did you get that tip?"

"It's a secret."

"Of course. Good for the career. Ugly business, though, the suicide attempt."

"I didn't call to have you judge me."

"I wasn't judging you, *bella.*"

"Not in your words, in your tone."

"Don't interpret my tone," Marcello said. "People in ice houses."

"I told you. It's glass houses."

"*Bella,* Donna Street is a hellion. She's tougher than both of us put together. Attempted suicide is not suicide. You scored. I will come to your cottage and we will have an espresso to celebrate. I'll bring the coffee beans."

Maxie recalled the malfunctioning espresso machine. "I'm beat. Let me take a rain check."

There was a momentary pause. "Don't beat yourself up," Marcello said quietly.

"I've already forgotten about it." She ended the call and placed another. When the receptionist picked up, Maxie said, "Dr. Chandler, please."

A FEW DAYS later Dr. Elyse Chandler waited for her at the top of the steps leading to the clinic. Maxie climbed the stairs, mindful of Dr. Chandler's scornful gaze.

"There are times when I find my job to be the most stressful and least rewarding. This is one of them."

Maxie bowed her head.

"I considered signing off on your community service and sending you packing. I considered just sending you packing and letting you start over somewhere else, or go to jail."

Maxie awaited the director's judgment.

"Come inside," Dr. Chandler said.

"Thank you."

"Don't thank me yet."

Maxie felt like her soul was shrinking.

Maxie and Dr. Chandler entered the art therapy room where

Ramona, Skye and Picassa sat like magistrates at the arts and crafts table. With a single choreographed twist, they faced the space on the wall where Maxie's stencil had hung. The stencil lay in a torn heap on the floor. In its place was a mural of images. Women, fat and thin, caught in humiliating poses. In the center of the piece was a picture of Maxie, taken from her arrest outside the Bad Mama, fire burning all around her.

"What do you think, teach?" Skye asked. "Good Photoshop work, isn't it?"

"We showed this to my mother," Picassa said. "She thinks it's awesome."

Maxie felt a familiar shell forming around her. She wouldn't let these girls get to her. They were amateurs. She approached the mural.

"What if we wrote 'People like you did this to me?' across my face?"

"Redundant," Picassa said.

"It could work," Skye said.

"We won't know if we don't try it. Isn't that what art's about?" Maxie asked.

For the rest of the session, they improvised. When they were finished, the collage was pretty darn good. That was what art was all about.

ON MAXIE'S WAY out, Dr. Chandler handed her an envelope.

Maxie parked in an alley near the center. A pit bull barked ferociously from behind a chain link fence until its owner dragged the dog inside by its studded collar.

The envelope contained the completion form for her community service and a note. "I like to believe that you learned from this experience."

"It's not that simple," Maxie said out loud. She decided to look on the bright side. Maybe she was a jerk, but she'd provided those girls with a chance for catharsis.

Catharsis was not Maxie's deal, though. Catharsis was for other people.

Chapter Eight

Bad Publicity

"YOU LOOK TIRED." Fisher was already seated at a table at the Oxymoron Brazil Café.

"No kidding." Maxie sat. She was certain that people at the other tables were glaring at the evil Maxie Wolfe, suicide provoker. "I got three big assignments as a result of the Street incident. Street's movie came in number one at the box office on its opening weekend. I guess there isn't any bad publicity anymore."

"Almost no bad publicity anymore. There are still a few things that don't go over. Like cockfights or spousal abuse. I've had to do some damage control for one of my athletes, a man who thinks he has the right to do anything because he has a twenty-five million dollar contract."

"You see?" Maxie said. "I'm getting shit because of what I do best. You're good at what you do and it's not exactly charity work."

"Did you know there are about fifteen sports agents in the country who make big money? Do you know how many successful female agents there are? Hardly any. We all know what it takes. You insinuate yourself into people's lives. Sometimes you help good people and their families handle fame. Sometimes you rescue bad people from behavior they should pay for. My clients know I can be counted on, no matter what."

"You don't seem morbid. How come?"

Fisher shrugged. "Believe it or not, I got into this business because I love helping people realize their dreams."

"Say, you got yourself arrested instead of Petra and Tiffany El to protect them, didn't you? Amazing. That's loyalty." Maxie reached over and flipped open Fisher's workbook. "You answered all the test questions already. I love your Girl Scout responses."

"I took the test for both of us. I didn't think you'd bother."

"You really think I'm a lowlife, don't you? I had a little on my mind. Give me a break." Maxie held out her workbook, which she'd recovered from the Ramada.

Fisher took the booklet and looked it over, then glanced at Maxie. "You answered the questions."

"I took the streamlined approach. I looked over a few chapters and then went to the final exam. It was ridiculously easy. I'm sure I got a hundred per cent."

Fisher sighed. "I'm going to fill out the coach's evaluation of our process and how much we both learned. See here? I sign and indicate my relationship to you." She held out her workbook. "You do the same for me."

"I didn't read the questions to you. I didn't coach you. I didn't even read the damn workbook the whole way through."

"In the spot where they ask my relationship to you, I'm going to put good friend," Fisher said.

"Don't be mean."

"I'm not being mean. I like you. Despite myself," Fisher said.

"You're something else." Maxie sipped her espresso. "How do you like what happened to the Poindexter girl and the Richfield chick?"

Fisher smiled. "Poindexter and Richfield get married in a state where gay marriage is legal. They adopt twins and start an organic garden in suburbia."

"What a crock." Maxie glanced down as her cell phone rang. "I have to take this." She rushed outside and around the corner from the café. She took the call from her mother's nurse, Susan, at the convalescent center.

Maxie knew she was pale as a ghost when she came back. "I gotta go."

"You look like someone just got murdered."

Maxie busied herself checking plane flights on her phone. "I need to go up north in a couple of days."

"Can I help?" Fisher asked.

"That was the care facility where my mother lives. They need to see me."

"I'll go with you," Fisher said.

"No way."

"You want to do it by yourself?"

"I always do it alone."

"Maxie Poindexter."

"Don't tease me."

"If you don't let me go, I'm scratching my coach signature off your completion affidavit," Fisher said. "Then you can't just take off anywhere on impulse without violating your probation."

"What is your problem? I don't even like you that much."

Fisher stood. "I can use frequent flyer miles. Call me with the flight information and I'll book my seat."

"Suit yourself." Maxie slipped from her seat and headed to the door. She didn't intend to look back, but she turned around and found Fisher watching her. Maxie waved and mouthed Marcello's phrase, *Ciao*. He had told her it was a saying that meant either hello or good-bye.

MAXIE WASN'T SURPRISED when Fisher wasn't at the departure gate at LAX a few days later. Still, she kept an eye out for her until the crew bolted the passenger doors. She settled back and gloated after the jet lifted off the ground. Have a nice life, Ms. Richfield. Thanks for nothing.

She wrapped a set of Bose earphones around her head and switched on her iPod. Nina Simone, one of her mother's favorites, sang about Daddies and sugar bowls. She noticed a kid in military fatigues sitting in the window seat was staring at her. His head was shaved. His pink scalp matched his rosy cheeks. He had big ears. He was emanating needy vibes. She would have ignored him, but the battery in her iPod picked that moment to die.

"We're extremely proud to have a young man aboard shipping out to an unspecified war zone," a stewardess announced over the intercom. "Let's give him a show of appreciation."

The full flight responded with applause, while the kid tried to hide his pleasure.

"We wish you the best, Private First Class Lloyd Hacker, of Needles, California, in helping to keep our country secure," the stewardess said.

Even Maxie tingled. What was it about uniforms?

When the drink cart rolled up, she turned to Lloyd Hacker. "Buy you a drink?"

"Not old enough," he said. "Anyway, I'm a Seventh-Day Adventist. We don't drink."

"I'll buy you a snack." Maxie reached for her bag from under the forward seat, unzipped it and pulled out her wallet.

Lloyd pointed at her camera equipment. "Are you a photographer?" he asked.

"Sort of," Maxie said.

"A professional?"

"More or less."

"You busy?" His expression seemed haunted.

"No," Maxie said warily.

Lloyd pulled an envelope from his backpack. He withdrew a bundle of photographs bound with a rubber band. "My dad took these during Desert Storm. Made me look at them, wanted to scare me away from enlisting."

Maxie studied the photos. Carcasses piled along dusty roads. Charred shreds of flesh, bone and blackened tatters of cloth that she assumed had once been men, women and children.

She'd seen shots like this before. Amateurish and horrifying, like tourist shots from hell. Usually, she could dismiss them, but Lloyd in his fatigues carrying his dad's tormented photos and radiating determination to go to war unnerved her. The kid would probably wind up on the side of the road like the people in the pictures.

"How about a lunch box?" she asked. "Let me buy you a sandwich."

Not waiting for a reply, she ordered three lunch boxes and extra chips. She hadn't eaten anything since the previous evening.

Lloyd produced more photographs — of his virtuous family, his wholesome friends and his boring hometown. She murmured appropriately at the thick stack of touching Americana, resisting any commentary about the shadowy evils that lurked beneath the cotton candy surface. She warmed up to Big Ears. Whatever else, he was sincere.

By the time they got to the chocolate chip cookies she had the history of his life spread out on her pullout tray. Before she knew it, she confessed the Donna Street debacle to him.

Lloyd responded with an old soul acceptance. "You made a mistake," he said. "You gotta move on."

"Easy for you to say. You've never done anything this reprehensible in your whole life."

Lloyd picked up a chocolate chip cookie and shoved it into his mouth. A sprinkling of cookie crumbs fell onto the photos. "I will, though." He gently dusted off the photos. "I will."

Chapter Nine

Petaluma

THE FLIGHT ARRIVED at the San Francisco airport and as Maxie and Lloyd exited the plane she caught sight of Fisher standing in the waiting area. Maxie thought about how she already trusted Lloyd more than a lot of people, including — especially — Fisher Jacobs.

"My client Noah Brady had a crisis. Had to talk him down, so I couldn't make the flight. He's a bad boy multi-million dollar quarterback and he owes me, big time. He had me flown here on his private jet," Fisher said.

Lloyd gave Maxie a brief, awkward hug. "I get lessons when I come back." He spun around and charged away. "You promised," he called over his shoulder. "I'm counting on you. Then I'll come home alive."

"Cradle-robbing?" Fisher asked. "Black widow spells on juveniles?"

"Shame on you," Maxie said. "He's probably going to be a hero and come back in a casket. Let's go, we need to rent a car."

FISHER INSISTED ON driving the rented Escalade. "You don't have good driving habits, Maxie. You can ride shot-gun and tell me the way."

They were mostly silent as they drove through San Francisco, crossed the Golden Gate Bridge and headed north on Highway 101 through Marin County. After passing the exit to Novato, Fisher squeezed the car onto the two-lane freeway that stingy Californians had never widened, crossing into beautiful Sonoma County.

Less than a mile from the exit to Petaluma, Maxie pointed to a ramshackle white clapboard structure with broken windows bordering the west side of the highway. Half of the building had collapsed into a pile of rubble.

"That used to be the Garden House, owned by two gay men named Derek and Sammy. I was a bus girl there. I made milkshakes for ranchers, gay leather boys going up to the Russian River, radical feminists and Republicans. I assisted a waitress named Tanya whose husband, Dutch, was an oil rigger. Tanya and Dutch went to nudist colonies."

Fisher laughed. "We went to the Saint Paul Grill for brunch. There weren't any nudists. Or leather boys."

Maxie exited on Petaluma Boulevard South.

"I came up here a few years ago to observe a scary good tight end at

Montgomery High School in Santa Rosa," Fisher said. "Chappie Hill.
Chappie went on to Penn State on a full athletic scholarship. Think he
failed all his coursework. Drug rumors. Probably living up here selling
sporting goods. Hopefully not overdosed in some alley." Fisher sighed.
"A lot of bad injuries these days. A lot of drugs."

"You're addicted to the thrills," Maxie said. "Like me. You'd never
quit."

"Maybe I'll go home to Minnesota and sell shoes."

Maxie laughed. She glanced at Fisher's expression. "Sorry."

"My family is in the shoe business. I love shoes."

"I didn't mean to be insulting. You wear really nice shoes."

They passed the charming city plaza, with its expensive antique
stores, new multiplex theatre and chic restaurants. Petaluma had
transformed from "Egg Capital of the World" to a yuppie stronghold
where most of the eggs sold were artists' renderings emblazoned on
expensive tourist gear.

Maxie turned onto Ninth Street and crossed C and B Streets. She
parked in front of a large three-story pale violet Victorian with purple
and maroon trim.

Fisher nodded at the discrete sign. "Spirit House. My brother spent
a year rehabbing at a place called Hope Center in the Twin Cities."

"Your brother?" Maxie asked.

"He lost part of a leg in an accident when he was nine. A story
maybe I'll share with you sometime."

Maxie stared at the multi-denominational statuary populating the
front lawn. The cement gods and goddesses brought back memories of
past visits. Several wheelchair occupants were enjoying the sun on the
sprawling front porch. "I'm going to say we're engaged," she said as
they walked up the path.

"Lovely. What brought on this change of heart?"

"Don't tease. I want to make sure they allow you in the meeting."

WHEN MAXIE AND Fisher entered the building, a nurse met them
at the reception desk. She wore a tie-dyed nursing smock over blue
scrub pants. Her graying hair was cut short and functional. Maxie took
a deep breath and tried to let the babbling of the water chimes calm her.

"Maxie."

"Susan. This is Fisher Jacobs. She's my fiancée." Maxie's
introduction of Fisher elicited a curious look from Susan. Maxie had
never brought anyone with her, much less a spouse-to-be.

Susan turned to Fisher. "I've been taking care of Maxie's mom since
she arrived from the hospital after her injury. Seventeen years. Maxie
was fifteen when the accident happened." Susan hesitated. "Would you
like a few moments in the meditation garden before we go to the
meeting?"

"Not really. Are Roy and June coming?" Maxie asked.

Susan shrugged. "Technically, they don't qualify. You're her legal guardian, so it's your decision on whether or not they are informed of the current circumstances."

"On second thought, we will take a minute in the meditation garden." Maxie took off leaving Fisher to follow.

The meditation garden wasn't as impressive as the Hollywood version at Dr. Dani's New Dawn clinic, but not too bad for a group home. Maxie led them to a bench surrounded by lavender bushes. She shivered. Every time she smelled lavender she was brought back to this garden. A huge cloud passed over the sun.

Fisher waited.

"Ever here of Judy Oyster?" Maxie asked.

"Are you kidding? We studied her in college." Fisher's mouth fell open. "Judy Oyster is your *mother*? I got a C plus in art history. I slept through a lot of the lectures. Eight a.m., bad time for viewing slides in a gloomy lecture hall. Still, I remember Judy Oyster. My instructor was a nut for radical performance art. She idolized your mother."

"My mother idolized artists like Forest Bess. To meet his artistic and spiritual destiny, he performed surgery on himself in an attempt to become a pseudo-hermaphrodite. Died in a nursing home, an alcoholic basket case." Maxie shuddered. "That's what I grew up around, until..."

"She went too far," Fisher finished for her.

"Damn her. It's one thing to smear your breasts with pig blood. What did she think would happen if she balanced on top of a pyramid of slippery nude men?"

Because of the tension, because of whatever, they both burst out laughing. Then it wasn't funny.

"She was going to recite the Declaration of Independence. She fell and hit her head on the floor for like the tenth time. This time there was too much impact." Maxie stood. "Let's go."

THE MEETING ATTENDEES consisted of Judy's primary doctor, the supervising social worker for the home and Susan. All of them looked pained.

"Maxie, we'll get straight to the point," Dr. Schindler said. "Your mother had an outburst and verbally abused an orderly for the eleventh time, all documented. We believe it was the result of a seizure. She's been seizure-free for quite a while."

Maxie's heart sank. Seizure. She's you-her.

"We want to put her back on seizure medication and add tranquillizers. As her legal guardian, we need your consent and for you to understand that we are not doing this as a result of her aggressive behavior or as a chemical restraint. We won't use any restraints, if we can help it."

"My mother loves restraints," Maxie said.

No one laughed. Maxie held out a hand. "What do I need to sign? Give me the papers."

She finished all the required document signing and then she and Fisher set off to Judy's room.

MAXIE ALWAYS FORGOT how ravaged her mother looked like until they were together again. She was startled when they entered Judy's room.

The outrageous Judy Oyster was a human eyesore with tattoos on her shoulders and forearms, piercings on ears, nose, left eyebrow and a coating of blood-red lipstick on twisted lips. Surgical scars laced her skull.

"Hi, Judy," Maxie shouted over the mayhem coming from the television.

Judy Oyster did not acknowledge the greeting. She stared at the television cartoon images screaming their outrage.

"Take that!"

"Ouch! I have no arm now!"

Susan went to the table next to Judy's chair and used the remote control to lower the volume.

"I was listening to that," Judy said.

"Maxie is here to see you."

"I know." Judy glanced in their direction. "Who's the stranger?"

Fisher walked up to the La-Z-Boy and looked into Judy's eyes. "Nice to meet you," she said. "My name is Fisher."

"I like that name. It goes with the ocean." Judy gestured at the television. "Do you know SpongeBob?"

"He lives under the sea."

Judy's attention drifted back to the commotion, as SpongeBob SquarePants severed the legs of a pinkish, vaguely starfish character. "It's all right," Judy said. "They grow back again."

Maxie approached Judy. Although she made no attempt at an embrace, Judy recoiled. "Don't touch me." She pointed to the screen and laughed. "The boulder fell on Bob. He's flat as a pancake."

"This is her passion," Maxie said. "A senseless cartoon that poisons children's minds."

"You don't know what you're talking about," Judy said.

Fisher found a chair and scooted it next to the La-Z-Boy. "That's Patrick Star's sister." She indicated a large, brutish female version of the pinkish starfish character.

"She's stupider than he is and she doesn't know it. Oh, look." Judy gripped Fisher's arm. "Patrick and Sister Sam just wrecked Squidward Tentacle's house. He's a crab. He's crabby." She laughed at her own pun.

"Ha ha," Fisher said.

"Oh, brother." Maxie stood alone noting how far away the door was, in emotional yardage.

"Maxie, pull up a seat," Fisher said.

"I'll get one." Susan rushed out and returned with a folding chair, which she expanded and placed next to Fisher.

"Here's Sandy Cheeks to the rescue," Fisher said.

"Damn right," Judy said.

Maxie closed her eyes. The last thing she wanted to do was watch television.

"Look," Fisher said. "It's very interesting, actually. Everything takes place in Bikini Bottom, a town under the sea. Sandy Cheeks is a squirrel from Texas, a karate expert who has to wear a protection suit when she leaves the dome she lives in, because she can't breathe underwater."

Judy nodded approvingly. "She died, but no one ever really dies. They always come back." She frowned. "I don't remember the episodes, but it doesn't matter. Everything always starts all over again."

"All very archetypal," Fisher said. "Death and rebirth. Life under the water in a mythical Atlantis."

"How did you get to be such an expert analyst of SpongeBob?" Maxie asked.

"You know that client Noah Brady who had me jetted up here? I hang out with his wife and kids while he's out cheating on her. We have a whole bunch of SpongeBob DVDs. The kids love them."

"SpongeBob," Maxie said. "You meant it about taking care of your athletes."

Judy turned to Susan. "Can they go now? They talk too much."

Maxie jumped up, grateful for the excuse to bust out of there.

"Where are you going?" Judy asked.

"I'll be back," Maxie said.

"That's what you always say."

"I always come back."

"Bring her with you." Judy pointed at Fisher. "She's smart."

"Sure, Judy." Maxie glanced over at Fisher. She was surprised to see what appeared to be a compassionate expression on Fisher's face. She had a brief, irrational flash of how much easier it would be to have someone in your life to buffer your wretched family obligations. She shook off the fantasy, reminding herself that Fisher Jacobs made a living exuding benevolence.

Judy's voice lowered. "He comes to see me, you know." She squinted at Maxie with a conspiratorial look. "He comes to see me in the middle of the night, right out of the television."

Susan touched Judy's shoulder and looked over at Maxie. "I told your mother, if SpongeBob comes in the night, it's okay."

Maxie knew it wasn't SpongeBob her mother was alluding to.

IN THE RENTED Escalade, Maxie informed Fisher of their next stop.

"I'm here to serve you," Fisher said. "Tell me the way."

"You are the mother hen type, aren't you?"

"I refer you to chapter three of the anger-management workbook. 'Taunting words come from wounded people,'" Fisher said. "I'm not listening to your jabs, I'm listening to your need."

"Did you memorize that damned workbook?"

"I'm relentless when I'm on a mission."

Maxie frowned. "What's your mission?" She watched Fisher's face, and wondered at the varied expressions. Guilt? Affection? Perhaps sincerity? Whatever was going on Maxie decided to go along with it. "Go four blocks and turn right."

Chapter Ten

Trophies and Tragedies

THEY PULLED INTO the drive of a canary yellow house with blue trim on English Street, around the corner from Petaluma High School. A trim elderly woman and man popped out, like figurines in a cuckoo clock. They raised their arms simultaneously in greeting.

Maxie approached the couple with Fisher trailing behind. By the time Fisher caught up, Maxie had finished with hugs. "Roy and June Shepherd. This is Fisher Jacobs, a friend of mine."

Everyone shook hands and then trooped inside. In no time, Roy and June had Fisher and Maxie arranged on a loveseat facing a plate of fresh cookies and a coffee carafe and mugs. Maxie considered the possibility of cookie overdose. She'd already had at least six cookies on the plane with Lloyd, but that seemed like a lifetime ago.

"I know you like your coffee strong," June said to Maxie. "I can make tea, if you like," she said to Fisher.

"I like strong coffee," Fisher said. "I love cookies, too." Cookies were passed around and beverages were poured, followed by exclamations from Fisher about the cookies, and then silence.

"Maxie, we already talked to Susan. She told us about the situation. We know you'll make the wisest decision," Roy said.

"There weren't any decisions. I just signed the papers. It's bureaucratic bullshit to prevent lawsuits." She shrugged at their pained faces. "Sorry."

Fisher's gaze flitted around the room and landed on a large trophy dominating the fireplace mantelpiece. Roy noticed her interest and jumped up to retrieve it. He handed the trophy to Fisher, who read the inscription and burst out laughing. "No way."

Roy pointed to a glass case lined with trophies next to the fireplace. "The inconsequential ones are mine, from various silly tournaments. The rest are Maxie's."

"Maxie Wolfe is a champion golfer," Fisher said.

"She was one of the highest-ranking high school golfers ever to come out of Sonoma County. Full college scholarship, could definitely have been a pro." A troubled look passed over Roy's face.

"I got kicked off the college team." Maxie placed the facts on the table to end the rhapsodizing.

"Roy is the golf coach at the high school," June said. "He taught Maxie everything. She used to come for summer trips when she was little. She came to live with us permanently when she was fifteen, after Judy's accident."

June rushed over to a wall lined with photographs and removed one with a blue ribbon attached to its frame. She thrust the photo at Fisher.

"I taught Maxie photography," June said. She sounded disheartened.

That's what I do to people, Maxie thought. Create disappointment.

The photo captured a hummingbird sucking nectar from a blossom. It was very pretty.

"Maxie took top honors at the Petaluma Art Festival when she was a junior in high school. She was a prodigy. She absorbed the principles of aperture, f-stops, light metering, dark room techniques—we used film cameras then. She was remarkable in the dark room." June stopped to take a breath. "Maxie has an eerie talent for framing subjects, a genius she was only beginning to explore. Her specialty was portraiture."

"That's enough," Maxie said.

"I never knew Maxie was so talented," Fisher said. "She's so modest about her achievements."

June took the photograph back to the wall. For a moment she faced the wall, back rigid. Roy was staring at the carpet. June removed another photograph from the wall and brought it to Fisher.

"This is our son Bobby," she said.

"Bobby Shepherd." Fisher studied the photo. "The poet."

Maxie could see Fisher was putting two and two together, recollecting the sorry tale related by her art history instructor of the tragic romance of Bobby Shepherd and Judy Oyster. "I'm sorry," Fisher said to June.

Maxie closed her eyes. The photo was burned into her brain. A baby-faced, acne scarred adolescent Bobby before the heroin ravished him. Maxie was sure that June was about to pull out some of Bobby's high school poems and his awards. She stood. "I'm sorry, we have a plane to catch."

"We thought you'd have time to stay for dinner," June said. She turned to Roy, who finally looked up from the carpet.

"Maxie, we love you," he said. "No matter what you're up to in Hollywood. We learned with Bobby. We didn't accept him." Roy hesitated. "We didn't accept his relationship with your mother and we should have. We watch over her, like we promised we would. Each day we pray for strength to practice forgiveness."

Maxie nodded, face neutral. It was the best she could do. About a thousand emotions battled inside her.

Fisher stood. "I'd love to stay. To learn more about Maxie and, of course, your son."

"No," Maxie said. "We have a plane to catch. We can't stay." She turned to the door to avoid the crestfallen looks on Roy and June's faces.

When they climbed into the car, Maxie groaned.

"I know, no conversation," Fisher said.

"At least not until we're on the plane," Maxie said.

WHEN THEY REACHED cruising altitude on the Delta fight to LAX, the pilot came on the intercom. "Ladies and gentlemen, please remain in your seats with seatbelts fastened. We will be experiencing some turbulence ahead." He had barely spoken when the plane lurched violently. A lady across the aisle cried out in fear. A stewardess almost toppled over.

Fisher, unfazed by the bumpy flight, insisted on nagging her. "Time for conversation?"

"Don't rock the boat, Fisher. Aren't you queasy?"

"Call me Ishmael. Speak."

"Judy Oyster had me instead of an abortion. I was her experiment in motherhood. Not all experiments are successful."

"That's succinct."

"I don't dwell on my mother. She deserves to remain an enigma. That's what she always wanted."

"But you don't have to be an enigma."

Maxie hesitated. "Okay, just shut up and listen." She closed her eyes and leaned back against the seat. In her imagination, she could see every word of her Journal Entry Number One. She didn't need the pages and she didn't want Fisher to see them anyway. As though speaking in a trance, she related the entire opening night incident from the entry.

She opened her eyes. "I have a thing about deviled eggs. They make me nauseous."

"Thank you, Maxie."

Maxie shrugged. "Just don't spread it around. Or make too much of this. It was an impulse. I have trouble with impulse control."

Fisher gripped the armrests, but persisted. "Your real father?"

"Don't ask me that question."

"You must have some thoughts about him, whoever he is."

"I said don't ask me."

"I thought we were going to talk."

"We did. Now we're done." She was grateful for another lurch so severe that someone in the rear screamed. They rode out the rest of the bumpy flight in silence.

WHEN THEY EXITED the terminal, Maxie noticed a throng of press lined the sidewalks outside the sliding doors. She glanced around, feelers alert, searching for celebrities. As soon as the swarm spotted Maxie and Fisher, the shouting reporters and photographers surrounded them.

"Maxie! Maxie! Are you devastated?"

"Hey, guys, I don't have a clue what you're talking about," Maxie said.

The paparazzi looked startled and delighted. Maxie caught sight of Marcello. She pushed her way to him. "What's up?" she shouted, because the noise level had grown intolerable.

"Donna Street *è venuta a mancare*," he said. "She died an hour ago. She blamed you on her deathbed."

Chapter Eleven

Repercussions

STREET'S CONDEMNATION OF Maxie lit up the gossip skies. Everyone on the planet gleefully expounded upon her evil ways on national television. Maxie fought to stay strong in the face of adversity, but she weakened. She spent the next two days watching the Donna Street memorials, along with analysis of the suicide note and the devil incarnate, paparazzo Maxie Wolfe. When her cell rang she let all the calls go to voice mail.

On the third morning of Maxie's self-imposed confinement an explosion of breaking news blew the Donna Street elegies off the airwaves. The day began with a call from Marcello. Maxie was getting isolation jitters. She answered on the second ring.

"*Bella*, meet me in Van Nuys. *Pronto*." He rattled off the address and ended the call.

MARCELLO WAS WAITING for her outside a modest suburban bungalow. He hid behind a large fuchsia bush in the neighbor's yard. "You know who Noah Brady is?"

"Bad boy football player. I know his agent."

"He killed his wife a couple of hours ago."

"Yikes," Maxie said.

An older Buick Regal pulled into the driveway of the bungalow. An elderly couple emerged and helped two confused-looking kids from the back seats. "Those are the children of Noah Brady with the maternal grandparents." Marcello started to come around from the bush. He was getting focused and she knew he expected her to do the same.

Maxie grabbed his arm. "Don't. We'll scare those little kids. Let's use telephoto."

Marcello squinted at her.

Maxie took a shot of the little boy. He clutched a SpongeBob against his chest. She and Marcello took as many shots as possible before the grandparents and kids disappeared into the house.

"I'M SORRY, FISHER," Maxie said into her cell.

"Noah says he went temporarily insane. I don't believe him. I want to be in SpongeBob's world under the sea. I want the wife to regenerate."

"That would be great. Donna Street, too."

"I'm sick of all this, Maxie," Fisher said. "Aren't you?"

Normally, Maxie would have lied. "I might be a little tired of it," she said.

"I'm leaving, Maxie."

"Are you kidding me? For good?"

"My parent's are having their fortieth wedding anniversary. I want you to come with me to Minnesota to help celebrate with my family."

"I don't even know where Minnesota is on the map. I can't tell it from Wisconsin or Michigan."

"Don't say that when you're in Minnesota. I have a nice family. I want you to meet them."

"They wouldn't want to meet me."

"If I bring you, they'll welcome you. That's what they're like."

"Fisher, is this a trick?'

There was a loaded silence. Then Fisher spoke. "Come with me. You won't regret it."

"No," Maxie said. "It's a trick. I know it."

"Great," Fisher said. "I'll start making the arrangements."

"Didn't you hear me?" Maxie asked.

"I listened to your words and I listened to what's under the sea of words. You're coming."

Maxie didn't protest. She was going to Minnesota, which was neither Wisconsin nor Michigan.

Part Two

Chapter Twelve

Princess Kay of the Milky Way

WHEN MAXIE AND Fisher reached baggage claim at Terminal One, Maxie caught sight of a wiry woman with an electrified mass of sandy-colored hair texting madly on her cell phone. When the woman noticed them, she reacted with a high-octane karate chop. "I was trying to reach you!"

"Where's Trapper?" Fisher asked.

"Performing surgery as usual."

Fisher turned to Maxie. "This is Honey Zucker, my brother Trapper's significant other. Honey, this is my friend, Maxie Wolfe."

"Your *friend*," Honey said with a teasing tone.

"My *friend*," Fisher said with an impatient tone.

Honey had sharp features and a furrowed brow. Her appeal increased when she smiled, which she did now with affected resignation. "Your entire family had inescapable commitments, so Honey to the rescue."

"We could've taken a cab," Fisher said.

"No, Ma'am. Anyway, I had to pick up a lithograph at the DHL terminal." Honey studied Fisher. "You look good."

"So do you."

"I mean it," Honey said.

A silence laced with old history hung in the air.

Well, well, Maxie thought. We've been here four minutes and already interesting hints of subplot in the family story.

Honey grabbed the handle of a suitcase and started to roll it away. "I have a meeting in two hours with a West Coast artist who does political statement pieces using deactivated weapons of destruction. She's already attracting the museums. I'd be lucky to get her at the gallery."

"Nancy Swan," Maxie said.

Honey stopped. "You know her?" she asked.

Maxie groaned inwardly. At least in L.A., snobbery was so clueless that it was easy to ignore. She suspected she was about to be engulfed in a clan of super-achievers armed with ivory tower enhanced weapons of emotional destruction. "Nancy and I studied photography together in college," she said.

"You studied photography? I thought you were a paparazzo," Honey said.

"Amazingly, paparazzi come from all walks of life," Maxie said.

"Sorry. I have a way of putting my foot in my mouth."

"It's okay," Maxie said. "Same here." She glanced at Fisher.

Caught in an unguarded moment, Fisher quivered like a

traumatized child.

Maxie felt a twinge of pity for Fisher. Did everyone have meltdowns going home? She liked to think so. It made her feel more one with humanity.

They wheeled the luggage to Honey's Toyota Highlander, loaded their stuff in the rear and took off for whatever dramatics might unfold. Maxie watched out the window from the back seat as they merged onto the highway.

"We're crossing the majestic Mississippi River," Fisher said.

Maxie caught a quick glimpse of the wide expanse of water flowing with languorous self-confidence as it traversed the continent. She admired the Mississippi River. Maybe she'd take a few scenic pictures. She couldn't remember the last time she'd snapped a scenic picture. She'd send copies to Roy and June. She was feeling bad about their last encounter.

IN LESS THAN ten minutes, they exited on Edgcumbe and climbed a hill to a charming neighborhood of single-family homes. Trees exploded with brilliant fall colors, shimmering reds and yellows, leaves made translucent from the sun in a cloudless sky. Mothers with toddlers in high-tech strollers sprinted past hearty old people walking ecstatic little dogs. Entire families raked fallen leaves and hacked at perennials. The collective primal enthusiasm was exhausting.

Fisher turned to face her from the front seat. "This is Highland Park, a neighborhood of Jews and Catholics with a healthy dose of Scandinavians. Down the hill, we passed the Jewish Community Center. Dad's family paid for a third of it." She pointed to the north. "We have four colleges and universities in the area. It's an upscale college town crossed with a melting pot village in the middle of a metropolis. Sushi meets Guinness Stout, bagels and Jello."

Poor Fisher, Maxie thought. Ms. Richfield was apparently narrating a segment of the *Travel Channel* to ease a troubled mind. Okay, if that made her less strung out, then fine, because Fisher was strung out, no matter what she was pretending.

At the moment, the world outside looked fantastic, as far as Maxie was concerned. No helicopters chasing fleeing cars. No eardrum-blasting sirens, stretch limos or gawking tourists. No damaged celebrities or wife-abusing NFL players.

Maxie was tempted to grab her camera and capture the delirious autumn revelers. Big Ears Lloyd, the boy soldier, had infected her. She had some kind of pretty picture flu. Meanwhile, Lloyd was probably defusing bombs in an unspecified war zone by now and taking pictures of emaciated little kids sucking lollipops that he'd given them.

They turned onto a winding road bordering the Mississippi populated with a row of eclectic, majestic houses. Honey turned onto a curved private road lined with flaming maples. A three-story flagstone house towered at the end of the drive. *Leave It to Beaver* on steroids, Maxie thought.

A battered rusty Jeep parked in front of the house marred the idyllic scene. "Whose backwoods piece of junk is that?" Fisher asked.

"That's Charles's statement vehicle," Honey said. "He's the family's new celebrity chef-nutritionist and personal trainer. The rust-bucket is for transporting his hunter's kill. He catches his own fish to use in his recipes. He shoots pheasant and roasts them over flames."

"What happened to Francisco?" Fisher asked.

"I don't get involved in the comings and goings of the health gurus and their lifestyle regimens." Honey glanced back at Maxie. "Do you have a personal trainer?"

"No."

"I thought everyone in L.A. had a personal trainer."

"There are a dozen or so of us who don't," Maxie said.

"How about a chef-nutritionist?" Honey asked.

"I dated one. Does that count?" Maxie said.

"You sound like Fisher. Didn't you date a chef?"

"This is boring." Fisher opened her door. "Are you coming to dinner, Honey?"

"Definitely, but first I'm taking the deactivated weapons of destruction artist to Saigon Village for pho, then a tour of my gallery. I have to seduce her. In the business sense, of course." Honey turned to Maxie. "Don't let them overwhelm you."

"I can take care of myself," Maxie said.

Honey gave Maxie a final look-over. "I'll bet." She backed down the driveway at a fast clip.

Fisher's face paled. "Damn her. She knows not to do that."

"Go backwards?" Maxie asked.

Fisher shuddered. "Back up too fast. My mother hit my brother going backwards. He was on his bike and she didn't see him. He was nine, I was seven."

"Oh, no. I'm sorry." Maxie hesitated. "Did you write about it?"

"What?"

"Dr. Dani's assignment in that stupid anger-management class. Three incidents from the past that formed you. The magical transformation triad, remember?"

"Maxie, I can't believe you're bringing magical transformation up now. No, I did not write about it. We escaped that class. We did the workbook instead. Did you write three things? Come on, it's not likely. Did you?"

"No. Well, maybe."

Fisher expelled a breath. "Maxie, you are truly a puzzle. I don't get you."

"Ditto."

"What? You don't get me or you don't get yourself?"
Maxie shrugged. "Both."

AS SOON AS they got inside the house, a pack of tiny dynamos on muscular legs hurtled towards them barking nonstop. Their alarm turned to glee when they realized it was Fisher. The bunch bounded up and down vertically like metal springs, yelping with joy.

"This is Lady Rowdy and her two sons, Ruckus and Racket."

"They look like shrunken Dobermans."

"Miniature Pinschers. They have a lot of energy, as you can see."

Maxie squatted down. The trio licked her outstretched hand, their little tongues emitting as much wattage as electrical generators.

"Awesome," Maxie said. "Wish I could do that."

Fisher groaned. "What are the Midwestern conversational rules I drilled you on?"

"Chill. I remember. First, avoid the f-word and sex jokes. Second, don't interrupt people when they're talking. Last, say 'thank you' as much as possible."

"So, how would you classify that reference to tongues?"

"Relax, I won't say anything like that in front of your family."

By now the three dogs were trying to climb into her lap. Maxie held them off and stood.

"That's a good sign as to your inner character," Fisher said. "They can be nasty to newcomers."

"I had a thing with a vet. She had six dogs, four cats, a bird and a turtle. She lived on a goat ranch. All the creatures loved me, even the turtle. I wish it was like that with people." Maxie yawned. "I do miss that turtle."

"I'll show you to your room. Take a nap. You're going to need your strength for when you meet the family. You think the dogs are hyper wait until you meet their owners."

"Can't wait," Maxie said.

MAXIE ENTERED A bedroom straight from a Pottery Barn catalogue. The first thing she did was to unpack the new Nikon she'd bought with the insurance money. It was a beautiful thing. She ran her fingers over the controls. Marcello was right. Who was she? She took adequate pictures with the settings locked in automatic. She hadn't played with manual settings since college. She was a hell of a lot better than Nancy Swan back then.

She traipsed around the room, experimenting, framing shots, and getting familiar with the controls. It was arousing, disturbing. Then she climbed between the linen sheets with the camera tucked securely on the pillow next to her.

"Sneakers the clown fell down," she said. "He bounced back up with hardly a frown."

It was the line the TV Man had said to her so many times when she was little.

A LOUD RAPPING on the door penetrated her consciousness.

"Door's unlocked," she called from the bed.

Fisher opened the door and stood at the entry. "I didn't think you'd want to miss dinner."

"Dinner?" Maxie glanced at her watch. "How do you like that?" She struggled to a sitting position. "What should I wear?"

"We're a casual family at home." Fisher wore a preppie plaid skirt and a wool cardigan decorated with pine trees. "But not too casual." She looked like an Eddie Bauer model framed in a Pottery Barn world.

"Relax, I left the stinky overalls and shit-kicker boots back at the vet's goat ranch," Maxie said.

"I'll meet you downstairs," Fisher said.

"Wait for me. I don't want to go down alone."

"Maxie Wolfe, are you nervous?"

Fisher's amused tone annoyed her. "Wait."

When Fisher was back in the hallway and the door was closed, she got out of bed and dressed. She came out into the hallway a moment later wearing a black Pima cotton turtleneck, beige slacks and walnut leather ankle boots. Maxie Wolfe could pull an Eddie Bauer if she had to.

"You look great," Fisher said. "Nice shoes. Blundstones."

Maxie shuddered. "I hate compliments when I'm agitated."

"It's okay," Fisher said. "My family won't admire you or pester you. They're not going to be that attentive. They have other things on their minds." She hesitated. "One more thing."

Maxie sighed. "I know. I know. Can the paparazzi impulses."

"I don't care if Prince or Bob Dylan come to dinner."

"Does your family know Prince? Oh my god, Bob Dylan?"

"I have an uncle who knew Dylan in Hibbing. Went to a Passover at his parent's house. Prince buys shoes from us."

"You're killing me. Let's just hope Jesse Ventura doesn't drop in."

AT THE BOTTOM of the stairs, Lady Rowdy, Ruckus and Racket charged at them. Ruckus gripped a leather sandal in his mighty little jaws. "Uh oh," Fisher said. "Someone's not going to be happy."

Ruckus wagged his tail without remorse. He and Racket proceeded to engage in a tug of war with the sandal. "They're great dogs," Fisher said, "but they'll eat anything."

"Some have accused me of the same," Maxie said.

"Maxie!"

"Okay, okay. I'll behave."

THEY REACHED THE dining room. It was a large, well-lit space dominated by an enormous Scandinavian table surrounded by blond wood chairs. The only occupant of the room was also Scandinavian blond. She fussed with a huge bouquet of fall flowers and grasses in a glass vase.

When she saw them, she clapped her hands and marched over to them. She glanced down at Ruckus and sighed. "Another sandal. It's a good thing we own a shoe empire. I love these guys, but this breed will eat literally anything if you don't watch them."

"That's exactly what Fisher said," Maxie said.

"This is my mother, Artemis," Fisher said.

Artemis? Maxie thought. Well, it was no odder than having a mother named Judy Oyster.

Artemis shook hands with a vice-like grip. She was tall and powerfully built, with nice, white teeth.

"My friend, Maxie Wolfe," Fisher said.

"*Friend*," Artemis said. Her tone was guarded and polite.

"*Friend*," Fisher said.

"We're *friends*," Maxie said. Her ironic comment was wasted, however, as two men burst into the room. The Pinschers barked with joy.

"My prodigal daughter," the older of the two men said. He squeezed Fisher in a full-body hug. Fisher squirmed, initiating a subtle wrestling match until she freed herself. "My father, Leonard," she said. "This is my friend, Maxie Wolfe."

Leonard looked like an ageing lion with a muzzle-like nose laced with red veins. "Maxie Wolfe," he said and took her in his arms. He wasn't much taller than Maxie, probably an inch shorter than his wife. Maxie didn't struggle. She liked Leonard's warmth and his retro smell of Old Spice. The hug was going on a little too long, however. Maxie squirmed and pulled away.

Leonard gestured in the direction of the other man who seemed to be hiding discomfort with a tight smile.

"This is my oldest son, Hunter," Leonard said.

Artemis, Hunter, Trapper, Fisher. Maxie noticed a theme.

Hunter was short and compact, like his father. He had an athletic build and straw-colored, short-cropped hair. His handshake was strong, but not any stronger than his mother's.

"*Friend*," Hunter said.

"I lied. She's actually a lesbian prostitute," Fisher said.

"Actually, a high-end lesbian escort," Maxie said. She abandoned squelching ironic repartee. There was too much bait being thrown out by this family.

"If she's your friend, she can be anything, including a lesbian call girl. You know this family welcomes all walks of life if one of us drags them into the fold," Hunter said.

"I think we can sit for appetizers," Artemis said. "Honey and Trapper are in traffic. We don't need to wait."

A Greek god type crossed the threshold, holding a silver tray. His black T-shirt appeared to be spray-painted onto his etched granite chest. The dogs bounded vertically in front of him. He thrust the tray up in the air. "Keep those beasts away from my food!" he screeched with drama queen fervor.

"Go to your beds, the three of you," Artemis said.

The dogs slunk over to a trio of pet pillows along the wall.

"My son Trapper rescued the Pinschers from a puppy mill. He's a committed animal-rights activist," Artemis said. "We tolerate much acting-out in our pets." She turned to Charles. "I'm sure you followed our food preference guidelines."

"Everything is of organic vegetable, fruit or whole grain origin." Charles inspected Maxie.

"Try some no-salt kimchi," he said, batting his eyes. He definitely had the prettiest eyelashes in the room.

"I didn't know you could make kimchi without salt," Maxie said.

Charles puffed up with pride. "I have my ways."

"We'll serve ourselves," Leonard said to Charles. Their gazes lingered on each other.

Flirty vibes between chef and family father, Maxie noted. Everyone else seemed oblivious. She resolved to avoid looking for skeletons in closets.

"Every item on the menu is tailored to optimal pre-race sustenance," Charles said. "Based on research and my intuitive connection to a spiritual plane."

Charles would have fit nicely in Hollywood. Maxie selected a spelt cracker and bit off a dense hunk. Spelt shards ripped down her throat. Trying not to choke, she grabbed a glass of green fluid. After a large gulp of what tasted like pond scum, she felt a wave of nausea. Fortunately, Honey and a tall man burst into the room, giving Maxie a few precious moments to stabilize. Despite her queasiness, she noticed that the arriving brother could have been Fisher's fraternal twin. He was gorgeous with longish dark hair and expressive eyes.

Honey picked up a cracker. "I'm ravenous." She gagged. "Yuk! This tastes like used sandpaper."

"I don't need this kind of treatment!" Charles tore out of the room, waving his arms in disgust.

Honey glanced around the table. "Sorry. I'll go and apologize. Trapper, introduce yourself to Maxie Wolfe, Fisher's *friend*."

Trapper inspected Maxie. "You sure don't look like the other ones."

He grinned at Fisher. "What happened, sis? Did the Barbie and Ken Agency go out of business?"

A moment of silence ensued.

"I was kidding," Trapper said. His body language emanated seduction. People just didn't realize how much they gave away with body language, Maxie thought. That's why photography was so cool. You could rip the phoniness away with the right shot. A picture is worth a thousand words, to use a worthy cliché.

Honey returned, carrying two martini glasses. She brought one to Leonard. "Maxie, I'm sorry, would you like to join us in a cocktail? I'll get it."

Maxie refused the offer. She was already intoxicated with family drama.

Fisher was right. The family didn't grill her. They were too caught up in their impending triathlon the next morning. While they ate, Hunter pontificated on the carbo-loading controversy. Next came race strategies. Maxie let her mind wander, until a strange pronouncement brought her back.

"I will beat the Enemy Butter Queen's son," Trapper said. "Or die trying."

Artemis turned to Maxie. "Our perpetual rivals. Mother Joyce was crowned Princess Kay of the Milky Way at the Minnesota State Fair many years ago. She and her obnoxious son operate a working dairy ranch and train for triathlons at the same time. I thought this family was overachieving. We call her the Enemy Butter Queen."

"The Butter Queen is crowned in counties throughout Minnesota," Leonard explained with a serious tone, although his eyes glittered. "She must come from a dairy farm or business, she competes locally, then regionals, and then on to the State Fair. The grand winner is crowned Princess Kay of the Milky Way. The Princess and her royal court all have their heads carved in ninety pound blocks of butter, sitting six hours in a freezing room in the Dairy Barn while nearly all of Minnesota watches. The same woman has been carving forever."

"Too weird," Maxie said.

The family glanced at her with a faint air of wounded censure.

"That's really amazing. What happens to the butter heads?" she asked.

"Eaten on crackers at community celebrations," Leonard said. "Symbolic cannibalism."

"Dad, stop it," Fisher said.

Leonard beamed. "I wasn't pulling her leg. They do eat the heads."

"I should have Maxie pull *my* leg," Hunter said. He stood and pulled up a pants leg, revealing a prosthetic attached just below his right knee. "Now wait," he said and left the room. He returned with a slick metallic gizmo with ski-like footings at its base. "This running leg costs a fortune," he said. "Fortunately, we're rich."

"Hunter is one of the top physically challenged amateur athletes in the country," Artemis said.

"Tomorrow's event is a fun day for me," Hunter said. "We go as a family. We're Team Footsie."

"Team Footsie?" Maxie asked, back to earnest questioning, as straight-faced as she could manage.

"For the family involvement in the shoe business." Hunter's chest swelled with pride. "Heard of Talerius Boots?"

"Brad Pitt and Angelina Jolie wear them to Africa," Maxie said. "Bono has six pairs."

Hunter laughed. "Before they became an international craze, they were the choice for serious workmen in demanding physical jobs in difficult environments. Oil rigs, nuclear power plants, and cattle ranches, to name a few. We have a special contract with Talerius at our chain of shoe stores, Home Sole Shoes."

Honey motioned to Charles. "Guru, could Leonard and I have another cocktail?"

"I think you and Dad might have had enough," Trapper said to Honey.

"Let them drink," Hunter said. "As long as they don't drive, they're not hurting anybody."

"Are you in the shoe business, too?" Maxie asked Trapper.

"I detest retail," Trapper said. "I couldn't escape the family foot fetish, however. I'm a podiatric surgeon." He flushed with pride. "Today I repaired the fractured heels of a man who jumped from a second story window after belting his wife. He was arrested, but he needed to be repaired before being shipped to jail."

"It sounds like he was the heel," Leonard said. Polite groans followed. Leonard's comments were getting increasingly slurred. Everyone, Maxie noted, was ignoring this fact.

"It's tricky," Trapper continued. "I had to put all the pieces back together and screw a plate into place to hold it all. Calcaneal fracture is also known as the Don Juan fracture, imagining a cheater who jumps from a bedroom window to avoid his lover's spouse. So, I inserted..."

"Isn't that a great metaphor?" Honey said. "My foot doctor boyfriend is fixing fucking lover's fractures. One fucking bad heel deserves another."

Maxie glanced around. She was quite sure Honey had just broken several of the Midwestern conversational rules.

Honey giggled. "Excuse me. I've been under a lot of pressure recently." She waved a hand. "I need another cocktail."

"You really have had enough," Trapper said.

"No commentary from you," Honey said. "Why don't you go back to your story about cheating? I bet you could say a lot about that topic." She turned to Maxie.

Maxie squirmed. The last thing she needed was to be the dinner guest at a remake of *Long Days Journey Into Night*.

"What do you think about monogamy?" Honey asked.

"Hypothetically, it's great." Maxie knew maybe twenty people who actually practiced it.

Honey burped and giggled. "Trapper and I have always proclaimed that we would never get married until same-sex couples could get married in this state. Then, out of nowhere, it's legal in Minnesota. However, my beloved foot surgeon has behaved in ways that make me wonder about marriage at all."

Trapper launched a peach pit at Honey. It glanced off her shoulder and fell to the carpet.

"That was passive-aggressive." Honey took another sip of her drink. "Fisher, tell the story about peeing in the closet."

"Oh my god," Fisher said. "I will not."

"Peeing in the closet?" Maxie asked. Now that sounded good.

"Fisher was taking a medication that had diuretic side-effects when she was little. She sleepwalked into her closet and peed on her new shoes. Rushed out wailing and scratched her ankle. Blood everywhere."

"Leonard went to her," Artemis said. "I can skin a deer, but I can't see my children bleeding."

"Mother, you know I'd prefer if we didn't talk about hunting at the dinner table," Trapper said. "Or ever, really."

"I wish we had a picture of that peeing incident," Hunter said. "But we all had a good laugh about it, anyway."

"Speaking of pictures, I got a new camera," Honey said. "It's a point-and-shoot." She moaned. "But I still suck. I don't want to take the pictures at the triathlon."

"You have to," Trapper said. "Mother, Hunter and I need shots of our victories. No one else can do it."

There was an expectant silence.

"I can take the pictures," Maxie said.

"She's very good at getting action shots," Fisher added with a smile.

Honey shrieked, interrupting the conversation.

Lady Rowdy shuddered on the carpet, choking violently, her little eyes bugged out.

"I think she swallowed the peach pit," Honey cried.

No one moved. Maxie ran over to the pathetic dog. She lifted Lady by the back legs and rapped on the dog's back. Lady expelled the peach pit. Maxie leaned down and listened. No breathing.

Maxie got Lady Rowdy on her right side. She positioned the torso and legs. She placed her mouth over Lady Rowdy's nose and lips and blew air into the lungs. Nothing. Maxie started doggie CPR, counting calmly as she compressed. Lady Rowdy's lips quivered and she began to breathe in little whimpers.

"Oh my god," Trapper said. "I cannot believe I froze. Good thing

I'm not a disaster relief physician."

"I dated a vet once," Maxie said. "She showed me resuscitation techniques. We should probably have her checked out. Must be an after-hours animal hospital nearby."

Fisher jumped up. "Maxie and I can go."

No one protested.

IN THE CAR, Maxie held Lady Rowdy in her lap. The dog licked her hand and stared gratefully at her. Fisher gripped the wheel too hard and stared straight ahead.

"Your father drank a lot, I noticed," Maxie said.

"He's upset. His best friend died recently."

"Sorry. They were all very welcoming to me."

"Maxie, make your point."

Maxie squirmed. "What do they really think of us? I hope they don't think we're involved."

"They might be talking behind our backs, it's human nature. In the end, we support each other in my family. That's the bottom line. Didn't Roy and June do that for you? They seemed like really nice people."

Maxie waved her hand. "Enough. I'm feeling nauseous. I think it's the analysis."

AT THE ALL Points Animal Hospital on West Seventh Street, they were led into an examining room. A woman in scarlet scrubs entered. "Fisher Jacobs," she said, looking startled.

"Erica Brekke," Fisher said. "You were going to be a brain surgeon."

"I discovered I like animals better than people." Erica looked puzzled. "I saw your arrest escapades on *TMZ*. What are you two doing here together?"

"It's a long story," Fisher said. She turned to Maxie. "Erica was the Prom Queen. I was one of her attendants. We had crushes on one another, until..."

"Until she got hooked-up, in secret of course, with the star golf player on the girls team and trailed her to Stanford," Erica said. "What became of Shelby?"

"She was my first client. She struggled in the Symetry League for a couple of years and burnt out. Burnt out on me, too."

Fisher had that star-crossed young love look, Maxie thought. She felt like wrapping her arms around her. The feeling was fleeting. Maxie hardened. No wonder Fisher was such a chick-magnet.

The vet finished examining Lady Ruckus and handed her to Maxie. "Good job," Erica said to Maxie, but she seemed to be sending judgmental vibes in Maxie's direction.

You would think a place that took dairy queens with butter heads seriously would be a little more forgiving. Maxie and Fisher thanked the good doctor and made a quick exit back to the car.

Chapter Thirteen

Competition

WHEN SOMEONE RAPPED on her door at four in the morning, Maxie staggered out of bed, stumbled across the room and flung open the door. She found a distraught looking Fisher at the threshold. Fisher's eyes were bloodshot. She wore a kitschy nightie speckled with calico kittens unraveling balls of yarn.

"Why aren't you dressed?" Maxie asked.

"I'm not going."

"Are you sick?"

Fisher wrapped her arms around her middle and hugged herself. "I'm experiencing Perfect Family Reaction Disorder."

"See? I told you," Maxie said. "Things beneath the surface. Secrets and surprises."

"Maxie, please, I hurt."

"Great. Now I have to feel sorry for you. You're making me go alone with your family. At least let me gloat a little about the shadows we both see around here."

"That's really not very supportive."

"Okay, okay. I'll try harder." Maxie cleared her throat. "Fine. I'll go without you. Get some rest." It was all she could manage in the way of comfort.

"YOU GUYS ARE four minutes late," Hunter said. Everyone was doing jumping jacks at the bottom of the stairs.

"My watch says two minutes late," Fisher said.

"It's wrong." Hunter did a quick kickboxing sequence. Punch, jab, sidekick.

"Your brother is nervous." Artemis glanced at her watch. "He's right. It's okay, cookie. We love you anyway."

"Can we stop with the baby-girl love fest?" Hunter looked around wildly. "Where's my whey-fortified oatmeal? Where's Dad?"

"He isn't feeling well," Artemis said. "It's his ulcer."

Most likely his hangover, Maxie thought. Leonard and Honey had downed five cocktails each at dinner. Messed-up, messed-up, her demons chanted, but she felt a stab of guilt. It wasn't like she wished anything bad on the Jacobs clan. She kind of liked them.

Trapper shrugged. "He just dozes in his lawn chair anyway." He glanced at Maxie. "Got your camera?"

"All my equipment," Maxie said.

Up to now, Maxie noted, everyone had been ignoring Fisher. Now they turned in unison and silently regarded her kitty nightie attire.

"I don't feel well," Fisher said. "I'm going back to bed."

The room seemed suddenly airless.

Honey interrupted the nosedive. "She doesn't have to come. We have Maxie. Pull out the metaphoric adoption papers." She turned to Maxie. "You're officially in the fold now. The Jacobs family loves strays. I know. I was one. You don't even have to be a particularly good person. I'm not."

Maxie had been a stray once upon a time. Look at what she'd brought upon her rescuers, Roy and June. Let's see how this one played out.

MAXIE RODE TO the triathlon with Honey in her Highlander. The event was held in a small town about an hour north of Saint Paul. Artemis, Fisher and Hunter followed them in Hunter's van, probably chanting affirmations and consuming power foods. Honey passed slow drivers on the right, checked her phone, screamed at careless bicyclists and carried on a running conversation about the difficulties of the art world. Finally, she paused and directed her attention at Maxie. "What's up with you and Fisher?"

"Friends, we told you," Maxie said.

"Looks like more to me. That's what happened with Trapper and me. We were attracted to each other forever, but couldn't be together for reasons I can't go into. I left town, then came back because of him. What do you think of Trapper? He's hot, isn't he?"

Maxie blinked. "He's attractive."

Honey frowned. "A little clueless emotionally, to be frank. I know I may not be one to talk. But at least I keep up my end of the bargain."

This was, Maxie realized, the moment where she could be socked with some kind of revelation that she didn't want to hear. They were interrupted by Honey slamming on the brakes.

"Get out of my way, fool," Honey screamed at a semi that was weaving across the lanes. Then her cell phone rang. Honey carried on a lengthy conversation with a marketing executive.

Maxie sighed with relief, spared the secrets. Her pulse quickened as they pulled into the race day parking lot outside the village of Saint Michael. She began framing her shots.

Volunteers directed the oncoming hoards. According to Hunter, the race had 700 participants, supporters and spectators, probably more people than the population of the entire host town. She took a Marcello's Way breath. She could channel the Way in a war zone, if she had to. She nearly floated, feeling like her feet were two inches off the ground, to Hunter's van and took a quick succession of shots as Team Footsie jumped out. They looked at her with startled expressions.

"Do your thing." Maxie closed her eyes. When she opened them, she felt herself dematerializing, not invisible, but a part of the fabric of the environment. Her subjects proceeded with their agenda, oblivious to intrusion. No matter what else, this was the one thing she knew would never fail her. If she wanted a shot, she found a way. Sometimes she had to be the ultimate best friend and other times she became an apparition.

When she exhausted all possible shots of Team Footsie, she took off amongst the crowd, camera in hand.

Honey trailed along, lugging two folding lawn chairs, two insulated mugs, a thermos and a small lunch bag. "I'll go stake out a good spot to watch the action," she said. "All I want to do now is nurse my hangover."

"Uh huh," Maxie muttered. "I'll find you."

AS THE JACOBS athletes registered, Maxie stationed herself nearby. Race workers branded the athletes' legs with numbers and laced electronic devices around their ankles. The ritual had a freaky livestock air to it, which Maxie felt sure she'd caught. She ignored the pleas of a few volunteers to stay out of the pre-race area, until she was booted out.

She used the telephoto lens after that, although she preferred close shots. Something happened when she got close, like the pull of subatomic particles, but she could get a great picture from any distance, if she wanted to. She *really* wanted to today.

AS DAWN BROKE, sunrise cast a carrot-colored glow on the virile participants penned in the transition area. They were obsessively organizing athletic shoes, sustenance, helmets, sunglasses and water bottles in the tiny allotted squares next to their bikes.

Maxie felt a quickening at the play of colors, of light and shadow. Photography was all about light and shadow. Light and shadow rendering pretty portraits, cellulite, hummingbirds or corpses on the side of the road.

At the announcer's edict, the athletes exited the transition area and gathered on the sandy beach. She located Hunter in her viewfinder. He had removed his prosthetic leg and hopped on the sand, hand resting on the shoulders of a buddy, both emanating man-love. Next she located Trapper and Artemis, who wiggled, doing ritualistic pre-aquatic warm-ups, looking like sexy seals in their slick black wet suits.

As race time approached, the sun came up in a clear sky. A light wind brushed the lake, sending benign ripples along the surface. Minnesota weather, Artemis had explained to Maxie, was fickle, especially in spring and fall. They were lucky today.

An official announced the beginning of the waves of entrants.

Trapper's wave was earliest. He surged into the water. Hunter's wave edged to the start. The crowd roared. He hopped towards the lake with the group, balancing on one leg, supported by his friend. Then he dropped to the sand. When the buzzer rang, he crept into the water and pushed himself into the depths, swimming as soon as he could. A few waves later, Artemis pushed into the water. Maxie got it all with her telephoto, including a close-up of Hunter scrabbling through the sand, ringed by a sea of legs. Nice shot, Maxie Wolfe.

The swimmers would circle around marked buoys in the lake and arrive back a few hundred yards up the beach. Maxie spotted Honey up near the reentry point. Honey clutched Hunter's prosthetic leg. Even Honey looked caught up in the excitement. "I'm allowed to hand this to him when he gets out of the water."

The mass of bobbing heads and stroking arms traversed the lake. Hunter emerged to the cheers of the crowd. Maxie captured his joy and concentration, a close shot of his face, then widening out to his one-legged hop from the water. Honey thrust his prosthetic leg at him. He attached it and charged up the path. Maxie raced to the transition area. Hunter laced up his bike shoes and ran his bike to the exit. He'd lost time to a man in Trapper's division, but he wore a fierce, focused look. Maxie finished her shots and raced back to the lake.

In a few minutes, Trapper appeared. He was apparently a slow swimmer. He sprinted to the transition area. His bike shoes were already attached to the pedals of his bike. He exited the staging area and leaped on. As he attempted to navigate the crush of cyclists, his bike clipped another biker. Trapper crashed to the pavement. His right ankle tangled through the bike's frame. As the other bikers veered around him, he climbed back on, grimacing in pain. By this time, Honey was at Maxie's side.

"Give it up, Trapper," Honey said. "Just throw in the towel for a change."

"Is he badly hurt?" Maxie asked.

"Probably," Honey said.

A few minutes later, Artemis completed a smooth transition and raced on. She looked like a goddess through Maxie's lens. Maxie's heart raced with a thrill of accomplishment. She took a deep breath. Her sudden passion was unsettling.

"What's going to happen with Trapper?" Maxie asked.

"Don't get involved with it all, that's my advice. Let's go sit and drink coffee. Hunter keeps an 18 mph pace. We have a little while to relax before he gets back to the transition area."

"Obviously Hunter doesn't let his disability affect him."

"Don't patronize him. He gets to preach about disabilities, but he hates personal comments from others. Besides, they protect him."

"What do you mean?"

"Never mind." Honey made a show of zipping her lips shut. "I have such a big mouth."

By now, they'd settled in their lawn chairs and nursed warm coffee in insulated mugs.

"Did Fisher tell you about me?" Honey asked.

"Not really."

"I lived up the block when we were kids. My parents are Orthodox Jews. I had to follow their archaic, misogynist rules. When I was seven, I started hanging out at the Jacobs residence. I didn't do anything at first but play over there. Then I began cheating." Honey shivered. "Cheeseburgers. Shrimp. I was in non-kosher euphoria." Her look darkened. "More things happened." She shuddered. "I thought Trapper and I could overcome it all. Why can't things just work out?"

Maxie cleared her throat. "I'm not the person you want to be trusting with your secrets. I'm a *paparazzo*."

Honey laughed. "All right, snoopy. I have a challenging assignment for you. Get to the bottom of this."

"Bottom of what?"

"Fisher and Artemis are scheming."

"How do you know?"

"That's all I'm going to say. Here comes the golden boy."

Hunter tore into the transition area and leaped from his bike. Maxie focused on his legs, then his face. One of the keys to action shots was to keep in the moment, judging when to close in and when to go for distance, what to put in sharp focus, what to blur. Hunter removed his regular prosthetic, attached the carbon-fiber running sled leg and was gone in a flash.

Maxie took a deep breath. Screw Honey and her innuendoes. Maybe she'd take Honey's challenge, maybe not. Honey had confirmed, however, Maxie's gut feeling that Fisher had dragged her on this trip for some hidden purpose.

Hunter had been gone several minutes when a young Norse god with golden hair rolled into the area, levitated off his bike, changed shoes and sped out of view. "Uh oh," Honey said. "Trapper's rival, the Enemy Butter Queen's son. No Trapper in sight."

Five minutes passed. Artemis rode in and switched shoes. She glanced back at a woman with graying braids who was seconds behind her. The Enemy Butter Queen according to Honey. Artemis sprinted out with a determined look.

Maxie could see where Fisher got her tenacity.

AN ETERNITY PASSED. Finally, Trapper cycled jerkily into the transition area. He toppled off his bike. He threw on a pair of running shoes and stumbled out of the transition area.

"And now we face another bout of grouchy injury recovery. The last one was rotator cuff repair after a rock climbing incident." Honey shrugged. "Hunter should be finishing his run soon."

Maxie positioned herself behind the barriers in the final stretch. Her new camera was a gem. She was falling in love with her new darling. They were becoming one.

Hunter surged up the last stretch, grimacing. Maxie could see an ugly red raw spot where his prosthetic attached to his stump, but he increased his pace. She shot a close-up.

The crowd chanted, "Go! Go!" as he crossed the finish line, pumping his fist. Maxie caught it all, in a series of short and long shots, a few beauties focused on the prosthetic racing leg in time-lapse.

She pushed through to the finish area. Hunter turned to her. The rest of humanity was a blur. Maxie captured the triumph on his face and raced back to the final stretch.

Artemis bounded up. On her tail was the Enemy Butter Queen. With only a hundred or so yards to go, the Enemy Butter Queen surged. The mothers jostled like roller derby thugs. Artemis revved into a superhuman sprint and crossed the finish line a breast's length ahead of her rival. Maxie raced back to the finish area. Artemis spotted her and raised both her arms in triumph. Her elated expression faded. "Where's Trapper? He should have been ahead of me."

The Enemy Butter Queen and her golden son approached them. "I won my division," the son announced. "Where's Trapper?"

"Good question," Artemis said.

By this time, Honey and Hunter had reached them. They went back to the observation area just before the finish line and waited. The over-seventy women arrived to loud cheers. Young stragglers with failed strategies struggled on weary legs. The walkers strolled along, looking pleased with their intentional slowpoke progress. The time limit was approaching.

"There he is," Honey said.

Trapper was third from last. He dragged his right leg like it was a lead anchor. His ankle was the size of a grapefruit. Just before the finish line, he fell to the ground and crawled the last four feet as the crowd shouted, "Go! Go!"

Maxie raced to the other side of the finish line. Trapper caught sight of her as she raised her camera and captured his pain. Maxie shot as the paramedics raced over. Maxie brought her camera close and took a shot of his eyes. "Get out of my face," Trapper said.

Maxie had heard a lot worse than that. She kept shooting. Trapper's eyes were windows into a hurt that was older and much deeper than a sprained ankle or a lost race. Maxie shivered with the moment of unintended connection. She was behind her camera, but she wasn't as shielded as usual.

"Get out of here," one of the paramedics shouted at Maxie. "What's wrong with you?"

Maxie retreated. No matter. She'd gotten the images she wanted.

Chapter Fourteen

The First Show

DINNER WAS SCHEDULED late. Even the Intense Perfect Family was exhausted. Trapper and Honey went back to their place, Hunter to his. Artemis and Maxie returned to the Jacobs hacienda.

Instead of napping, Maxie spent two hours staring at the triathlon images called up from her camera's memory card. Her inner critic longed to fix the mistakes beyond the capabilities of her Nikon's editing functions, but she had no computer and she had no Photoshop.

She traipsed down to the main level and meandered into the family room hoping to escape the longing to do editing wizardry and no tools to do it. Leonard sat slumped in a lounge chair, with a huge cocktail on the table next to him and a stack of newspaper clippings on his lap.

Leonard drained his glass. He motioned for her to sit. "Can I show you something?"

No way could she say no to this man. Not with his sad eyes. Leonard was a broken guy, no matter how much this family was in denial. Her stepfather Bobby Shepherd had taught her how to handle broken father figures, the ones that deserved to be handled.

Leonard held up a clipping. "In July, my best friend died out of the blue, too young and too soon. He was one of the most respected men in Minnesota. I won't read the whole article. Only the parts that describe how Ned Burdock negotiated peace in a political storm others would find impossible to navigate. He was a nonpartisan administrator at the Minnesota House of Representatives for many years and was revered by everyone." A tear ran down Leonard's cheek. He read in a choked voice. "The governor has officially declared next Monday as Ned Burdock Day. A bronze sculpture has been commissioned in his honor." Leonard couldn't go on, he started sobbing. He thrust the article at her.

Maxie studied the clipping. She could see Ned Burdock's essence from the photograph fused with Leonard's love. "He was exceptional," she said.

Leonard sobbed harder, rocking back and forth, hugging his arms to his chest. "Why was he taken from me?"

"My darling." Artemis stood in the doorway.

"I'm not babbling. Just explaining the facts." Leonard stuffed the clippings into his folder.

Artemis marched into the room and held her hand out. Leonard took it and allowed his wife pull him up. Artemis turned to Maxie. "It's time for dinner."

AFTER DINNER, MAXIE approached Artemis in the hallway. "I was wondering if you have a computer I could use."

"We have many, including my own. Hunter and Trapper keep installing programs for me that I can't figure out."

"Any photo editing programs?"

"Christmas last year, Hunter bought me a camera and put some kind of a program on my laptop." She gestured toward a doorway. "Come with me."

Maxie followed Artemis down a flight of stairs into a lower-level family room boasting a tournament level billiard table and a handsome full-sized oak bar. "Party joint?"

"The kids loved this hideaway when they were teenagers."

"I like to shoot pool," Maxie said. "I have to. It's part of being a lesbian."

Artemis laughed. "We'll have a game some time. My father taught me."

Maxie had a strong suspicion that Artemis could beat the pants off her at billiards. "I won't bet my rent money."

"If I win your rent money, you can come live with us."

Artemis's offer left Maxie temporarily speechless.

She followed Artemis down a hallway to another room. A laptop computer and a cheap inkjet printer dominated the center of the room, sitting on an otherwise empty office table.

Maxie switched the computer on and waited for the inadequate screen to populate. She searched through the applications. Her heart leapt as she located the latest version of Photoshop. Good god, no wonder Artemis was flustered. Who spent a trillion dollars on a complex editing program for their mother who hated technology, on a computer that could barely handle the energy sucking application? And who cared, because now Maxie had what she wanted. It was all she could do not to run up three flights of stairs and get the memory card from her camera.

"I'm sure you'll make better use of it than me," Artemis said.

"Thanks," Maxie said. She remembered the Midwestern conversational rules. "Thank you, thank you, thank you."

THE NEXT MORNING, she throbbed through breakfast, drinking a big glass of pond scum and ingesting a large bowl of oatmeal fortified with flax.

Fisher approached her in the hallway after breakfast. "I promised Dad and Hunter I'd drop by the corporate office. You can come if you like."

"I'll chill around here," Maxie said, her heart racing. "You go. Have fun with the shoes."

As soon as Fisher was gone, Maxie flew down the stairs to her new underground retreat and worked furiously, trying not to get frustrated when the wimpy laptop froze in the middle of a complicated series of filtering commands. She dragged herself back up the stairs for lunch.

Everyone was gone except Charles and the Pinschers. Charles made her a roasted zucchini sandwich, which she shared with the dogs when he wasn't in the room. She hoped zucchini wasn't on the dog no-eat list. Charles complained that the entire family was coming to dinner. That inspired her to rush back to her work.

By now, the dogs loved her. They trailed her to the workroom and curled up in three doggie beds she'd found by the billiard table. Maybe she'd get a pet when she got back to Hollywood. She might start with a turtle.

By nearly dinnertime, she had to do two hundred jumping jacks, a hundred bicycle crunches and fifty push-ups to relieve the stiffness induced by hunching over the computer for so many hours. She ate dinner mostly in silence, participating only to exclaim in a polite manner at the boring conversation. Everyone was on good behavior, even Honey.

Just as dessert was served, Maxie clinked her water glass with a knife. "I have a confession." Maxie glanced around at the expectant faces. She couldn't tell if they looked excited or nervous. What did they think she was going to say? "I made a slide show from the triathlon."

"How splendid," Artemis said.

"Give me ten minutes," Maxie said, rising.

She ran downstairs and brought up the laptop. She carried it to the entertainment room and set it up, attaching it to the mighty fifty-inch projection television. She prayed as she fired everything up. "Hallelujah," she said when the first image appeared on the screen. Fuzzy, but it would have to do.

"This is exciting," Artemis said, after the family trooped in and settled on the couches.

Maxie timed the electronic slides to move elegantly from one shot to another, just enough to allow emotional impact, then moving to the next. When the images of Trapper crawling across the finish line appeared, a collective gasp rose up. The agony of Trapper's collapse brought groans. She had worked for an hour on that shot, dodging and burning to bring sharp focus on his eyes.

I'll be damned, Maxie thought. I'm good.

She glanced around the room, trying to see if the family had picked up on the hidden pain revealed on Trapper's face. As far as she could tell, no one was having any epiphanies.

"I love the shot of me on the podium with that bitch the Enemy Butter Queen," Artemis said. "Maxie captured the phony look on her face. Good work."

"Makes me feel like I was there," Leonard said. "Better. Maxie concentrated the action and emotions for me."

"That was awesome." Hunter tossed a hacky sack he'd been squeezing at Trapper. "Sorry, bro. You're a fallen hero. The pictures showed it. Gotta be hard, though."

"I'm over it." Trapper threw the hacky sack across the room. "I'm not over it! I have eight surgeries scheduled next week. And what about the golf tournament?"

"I can play for you," Honey said.

The family burst into laughter.

Honey turned to Maxie. "The Intense Family has a charity golf tournament tomorrow. Trapper is their best player. Their rivals make the Enemy Butter Queen family look like invalids. I suck at golf, worse than photography."

"I'm going to hobble," Trapper said. "I'll self-medicate and ignore the consequences."

"Forget it," Honey said. "For once, I'm putting my foot down."

Leonard giggled at the pun. "Good one. Putting your foot down. Let Fisher play."

"I wouldn't pick up a golf club if someone held a gun to my head," Fisher said. "I hate golf."

"You represent three of the top LPGA players on the tour," Maxie said. "Do they know this?"

"It's a preposterous sport. I won't play. I suck."

Honey smiled. "Let Maxie play. She's the new go-to-girl."

"Ever played?" Hunter asked.

"I played a little," Maxie said. "Many years ago."

Fisher stared at her. She refused to meet Fisher's eyes.

"I would love it if Maxie took Trapper's place," Artemis said. "We'll cope. We'll be less competitive."

Hunter laughed. "We're incapable of not competing. Sure you want to join, Maxie?"

Maxie shrugged. "Sure."

"Then we'd love to have you," Artemis said. "Leonard is playing and he's a social golfer."

"Social is a polite term for total hack," Leonard said. "You can't be worse than me."

Artemis clapped her hands together. "We're Team Footsie. Now Maxie is an honorary Footsie."

Maxie stood up. "I'd better get some sleep. I'm not as tough as the rest of you."

"You seem very tough. And talented," Artemis said.

Maxie blushed.

"The photographs were amazing. You're an artist."

Honey snorted drunkenly.

Trapper glared at her. "Don't be rude, Honey."

Honey's eyes narrowed. "I'm sure no one here wants to get into a discussion of what's art."

"Not if some of us insist on being elitist snobs, darling," Trapper said.

"Not if some of us are incapable of judging art from above the waist up," Honey said with pugnacious obscurity. She turned to Maxie. "I get frustrated when people who don't know anything about art make pronouncements outside of their league, so to speak."

"What did you think of the show?" Maxie asked.

"How many shots did you take?" Honey asked.

Maxie hesitated. "A lot."

"Why so many?" Honey asked.

Maxie sensed a trap. "Because you need a hundred to get a few good ones."

Honey smiled, like a prosecuting attorney cross-examining a hapless criminal. "You have a lot of chutzpah, wouldn't you say?"

"You don't have to answer," Fisher said. "Honey, leave her alone."

"I know how to get in people's faces."

"Did you Photoshop the pictures?"

"Yes."

"So, you took an okay series of journalistic pictures because you shot a lot of rejects and have a lot of nerve. Then you Photoshopped." Honey glanced around at an imaginary jury. "It's tricky photojournalism. Real art is more demanding, challenging, soul-searching."

"You think it's not art unless it's ugly and mean," Trapper said.

"I think art isn't pretending life is a bowl of cherries, cliché intended," Honey said. "Maxie's photos manufacture a feel-good ending. That's neighborhood art. That's art to please the masses, not to challenge them."

Trapper stood up. "All right, Honey. You've made your point."

Honey held up her arms in surrender. "Maxie asked me to critique her."

"I loved Maxie's show," Artemis said.

Honey groaned. "Oh my god, I didn't say I hated it. I actually think it's wonderful. It just isn't art."

Maxie didn't flinch. "I've had worse criticisms than that." Beyond her nonchalance was turmoil. She knew she'd taken State Fair blue-ribbon winners for this family. She'd created a feel-good story, except for that one moment of Trapper's defeat, which no one acknowledged. Screw Honey. It beat exposing Donna Street's cellulite and inspiring her suicide.

A loud snore interrupted the conversation. Leonard's chin fell against his chest. A stream of drool trailed out of his mouth and down his chin.

"I think the party's over," Fisher announced. She took Maxie's arm. "Let's go."

JUST OUTSIDE THE guestroom door, Maxie paused. "That was fun. *Long Day's Journey into Night* crossed with *Cat on a Hot Tin Roof.*"

"What's that supposed to mean?" Fisher asked.

"Weird family undercurrents. Intrigue masked as conversation. Too much alcohol."

"I don't get you. You volunteer to play golf acting like you're a novice. Why didn't you tell them about your golf history?"

"I like games as much as your family does."

"Don't make this into a game," Fisher said.

"It's all a game. I've been telling you that all along."

"All right about the golf scheme. I don't like when you slight yourself, however. You let Honey bully you."

Maxie tried to slip into her room, but Fisher grabbed her shoulder. "Don't do that," Maxie snapped, pulling away.

"Sorry," Fisher said, recoiling. "I wasn't going to hurt you."

"Never grab me like that."

"Forget Honey. She has a narrow definition of art and it seems to have to be angry or brutal or absurd or best of all pretentious to qualify."

"I don't care. I don't want to be an artist."

"I think you are in a major case of denial," Fisher said.

"People in ice houses."

"What?" Fisher asked.

"Don't get on my case for toxic denial," Maxie said. "Examine your surroundings."

"I don't know what you're talking about," Fisher said.

"That's what I'm saying, girlie." Maxie slipped into her room.

Chapter Fifteen

Under Par

MAXIE'S SPIRIT QUICKENED as they pulled into the parking lot of Sleepy Haven in Mendota Heights, an exclusive club that looked like a Scottish royal castle. They parked and Artemis pulled out a bag of hats. She fitted a TEAM FOOTSIE hat on Maxie's head. "Don't you look like a champ?"

A horn honked as Honey's Highlander screeched into the spot next to them. Honey jumped out and ran over to the passenger side to help Trapper from the SUV.

"Do not tell me I shouldn't have come," he announced with a determined grimace. "I am going to sit on my ass under a nice tent and sell auction tickets, high as a kite on pain pills."

"I'm driving one of the beverage carts," Honey said. She glanced at the assembly. "Cute hats."

"There's one for each of us," Artemis said.

"I don't want a hat," Fisher said. "I don't want to be a family advertisement." She glanced at Maxie. "Where's your camera?"

"I didn't bring it." Maxie had decided that she was getting obsessed with photography. She'd forced herself to leave the camera behind. Now she felt like she'd left a limb behind.

"Why not?" Fisher asked.

"I just want to enjoy the occasion," Maxie said.

"I hope this isn't about that cockamamie discussion of art," Fisher said.

"I really didn't mean to insult you," Honey said. "It's cute, though, Fisher defending you."

"Okay, enough," Fisher said. "I'm going to spend my time in the clubhouse on the phone with L.A. until the awards dinner."

"For god's sake, can we cut the blabber?" Hunter said. "We have a tournament to play. Get your game heads on, people. Let's go get the carts. Chop chop."

AS THEY UNLOADED the equipment from the cars, Artemis and Hunter debated strategies given their weak team members. Artemis loaded two sets of bags into a cart, her newest set and a cast-off set for Maxie. "Let me drive."

"Just don't crash," Maxie said, then instantly regretted her joke as Artemis winced.

"What did Fisher tell you?" Artemis asked.

"She told me about Hunter's accident. I'm sorry, what a stupid remark."

"We all have our secrets. They do tend to come out, though, don't they? For instance, you do know a little about golf, don't you? Maybe more than a little."

"Fisher is a tattle-tale."

"I'm curious, what are you up to?"

"No real plan." Maxie blushed. "I wanted to impress you guys. Maybe a few good holes."

Artemis touched Maxie's arm. "We'll see what we can come up with. This puts some extra spice into the day."

"You are a schemer, aren't you?"

Artemis glanced away, but before she did, Maxie saw the troubled look in her eyes. Artemis was definitely up to something and Maxie suspected it wasn't about golf.

AT THE WELCOMING station, an ecstatic volunteer wearing a red carhop outfit pointed to their place in the cart lineup.

"It's a fifties theme," Artemis said, as they were engulfed in a swarm of rock-and-roll crooners and diner waitresses handing out water bottles and goodie bags filled with balls and tees. They joined Hunter and Leonard in the lineup. Hunter came over to them. "It's a best ball scramble. At each hole, whoever hits the best ball, that's the one we play."

"Hey, Jacobs family, is that your ringer?" a red-faced man with a large potbelly shouted at them.

"Dream on, Mahoney," Hunter shouted back. He turned to Maxie. "A ringer is a top-notch player you bring in secretly. The Jacobs family doesn't need ringers. We actually play decently. Except Dad." Hunter kicked the tire of the cart. "I don't know, without Trapper, Mom and I will really have to step up our game."

The Mahoney foursome, two males and two females, in matching Irish green golf gear emblazoned with cocky elves riding bulldozers, were downing large cups of coffee and arranging their pro-level clubs.

"We hold the tournament record," Artemis said. "Eight under par. So what if we win and we happen to be one of the biggest charity sponsors?" Artemis gave Maxie a secret look. "Maxie, don't feel any pressure to be anything but who you are."

Maxie put on her innocent face. "I'll do my best."

"Good sport," Hunter said. "Mother and I will rise to the occasion. We always do, don't we, Mother?"

"Or die trying," Artemis said.

There was an uncomfortable silence.

MAXIE'S PULSE QUICKENED as they lined up for the first hole. The four men in front of them had apparently already indulged in a few pre-round beers. They weaved to the men's tee and hit ugly drives into surrounding trees and bunkers.

"Which is the best ball for those guys?" Maxie asked.

Hunter laughed. "Now you see what I mean about hacks."

"This first hole is a killer," Artemis said. "Par five with a downward slope to the right. Dogleg left to the green."

Hunter wore shorts, exposing his walking prosthetic with a golf shoe attached. He hit a clean one hundred and eighty yard drive into the fairway. He had already made sure Maxie knew that he was in the top twenty of physically challenged golfers in the country. "A little short. I'll get better after I warm up."

Leonard hit from the senior's tee. The ball plopped fifty-five yards into the rough before the fairway. "That's pretty good, Dad," Hunter said heartily.

Leonard looked pleased. "At least it wasn't in the water."

Artemis's ball soared a good twenty yards past Hunter's. Maxie whistled softly. She felt all eyes on her. She picked up the borrowed driver and executed an ugly swing across her body. Her ball plopped into the water hazard.

"You hit it," Hunter said. "Let's go. It's mother's ball."

As they carted down the course, Artemis grinned at her. "Ugly start. I like it."

For the rest of the hole, Maxie arranged to be the worst ball. She repeated her awful performance on the second and third holes.

"Fore!"

Everyone ducked as a ball nearly beaned Hunter. A gleeful couple carted past them, waving.

"Hacks," Hunter said. "Let's go, people. We're not going to win making pars."

ON THE FOURTH hole, a par three, an Elvis impersonator in a snug white sequined jumpsuit waved a three-iron at them at the tee box while gyrating his hips provocatively.

"That's our golf pro," Artemis said. "Prize goes to anyone who beats Elvis on this hole."

The hole had a reedy water hazard blocking the approach to the green. Hunter's tee shot flew completely over the green. "Water jitters," he said. "Took too much club."

Elvis teed off with grace. His ball landed eight feet from the hole. He rotated his hips and belted out a few lyrics. It was a priceless opportunity crossing sports photography with Diane Arbus. Maxie agonized over the absence of her camera.

Leonard took his shot with the same calm he'd displayed for all his lousy shots. This time, miraculously, his shot landed on the green. After a shocked moment, everyone applauded. "Lucky," he said.

No kidding, Maxie thought.

As Hunter had, Artemis teed off with a seven-iron. Her shot flew past the green, too.

"Trying too hard like me, Mother," Hunter said.

Maxie approached the tee box with her driver.

"Too much club," Hunter said.

She shrugged. Not for her purposes. She topped the ball. It landed in the middle of the water hazard. In mock frustration, she threw her driver to the ground, causing a burst of sympathetic laughter from her companions.

Maxie flubbed her next shot. Hunter and Artemis were playing neck and neck. Each made nice chip shots, landing close to Elvis's ball on the green.

A silence ensued as Elvis approached his ball. He one-putted it into the hole, for a birdie. Artemis and Hunter each made par. Leonard approached his ball. He took a deep breath, bent over his ball and sunk a thirty-footer into the hole for a birdie.

"Tie goes to the amateur. You won, Dad," Hunter said. "You tied the golf pro, for god's sake." He grabbed his father and enveloped him in a bear hug. Elvis came over and joined in the hug.

My camera, my camera, Maxie's mind chanted.

Just then, a cart rolled up. A young man with a camera climbed out. "Group shot."

Maxie darted over to the photographer. "I'll give you thirty bucks if you let me take a few shots."

The young man hesitated. "I have a contract."

"Fifty. No one has to know. Just send me what I take. Seventy-five bucks."

The guy handed over the camera.

"Line up," Maxie said.

The Jacobs family and Elvis mugged and embraced while Maxie captured them. She felt whole again.

AS THEY PROCEEDED to the seventh hole, Honey motored up in the beverage cart. "Drinks, anyone?"

"I'll have a vodka tonic," Leonard said.

A hush fell over the group.

"It's a fun tournament," Honey said. "Let him have some fun. You guys can be so uptight." Honey handed Leonard his drink.

The hole was a four hundred and ninety yard par five. Hunter took a powerful swing on his tee shot, landing off the fairway in a stand of trees. "Damn," he said. "Up to you, Mother."

Artemis hit a beauty. Her ball launched two hundred yards, into the fairway, five feet short of a deep bunker, good length but terrible angle. Maxie proceeded to the tee box. She looked at Hunter. "I know this is probably rude, but can I borrow your driver?"

Hunter blinked. "Why?"

"It's got a much fatter bottom than mine," Maxie said.

Hunter shrugged and handed her the club. She lined herself up and took a breath. Her drive landed in the middle of the fairway, on the other side of the bunker.

"My god, that was probably two hundred and thirty yards." Hunter's eyes narrowed. "Okay, what's going on here?" He turned to Leonard.

Leonard shrugged. "No idea."

Hunter turned to his mother. Artemis smiled, but refused to speak, so Hunter turned to Maxie.

"I did play a little in college," Maxie said.

"A little?" A slow grin spread on Hunter's face. "We have a real ringer." Then he frowned. "Look, Maxie, this is just for fun." He paused and smiled again. "Maybe this adds even more fun."

ON THE EIGHTEENTH hole, a par five with a severe left dogleg, the green was completely out of sight. Hunter sliced his ball over the trees into the next fairway.

Artemis, in a rare moment, topped her ball. It landed ninety yards up on the fairway. "Only four hundred to go," she said. In unison, the group turned to Maxie.

Maxie grinned. "Should I?"

"You know this family hates to lose. I'm sorry, I can't help myself." Hunter held out his driver.

Honey roared up in her cart. "Doing okay drink-wise, everyone?"

"Shhhh," Hunter said. "Let her concentrate."

"What's going on?" Honey asked.

Maxie approached the box. She visualized her crucial shot against LSU in her freshman year. The ball sailed over the water hazard, over a towering tree, and took a slight arc to the left.

"What was that about?" Honey asked.

"Probably two hundred and twenty right in the fairway," Artemis said.

"Can I eagle the hole?" Maxie asked

"Too obvious," Artemis said. "Hunter can get us close to the green. You get us on. I'll putt it in."

"You didn't witness this," Hunter said to Honey.

"My lips are sealed."

AT THE CLUBHOUSE, Maxie found Fisher with a gorgeous woman

in the bar. "I thought you stayed up here to catch up on your work, my darling," she said.

"I found this delightful person," Fisher said, projecting her Hottie Magnet vibe at her new companion. "This is Shannon."

The hottie smiled at Maxie.

"Nice to meet you. Are you an actress or a model by any chance?" Maxie asked.

"She's an engineer and systems analyst at Medtronic," Fisher said, glancing with feminist empathy at Shannon. "This is Maxie, my fiancée. She can be a little conventional at times."

"I got engaged to her for her money," Maxie said. "I lack serious career goals."

Shannon looked from one to the other of them. "I see," she said wryly. "I'm engaged to a Minnesota Vikings defensive end with a homicidal jealous streak."

"Is that true?" Maxie asked.

"What's truth?" Shannon asked. "Are you really her fiancée?"

"No, actually I'm not." Maxie noticed Shannon's Canon Rebel. "I didn't bring mine. I'm missing some great shots."

Shannon held out the camera. "Use it. I take four lousy pictures and wind up erasing them."

Maxie took the camera as if she was being handed someone's arm. "Thank you."

"You can put it on auto and push the button on the top," Shannon said.

"I can probably figure it out." Maxie fiddled with the settings, then took a shot of Shannon's face framed by a rack of incandescent bottles.

"Let me see," Shannon said.

Maxie brought up the image.

Shannon turned to Fisher. "You should marry her. She makes a person feel interesting when she takes a picture."

AS THEY HEADED back through the dining room, they bumped into phony Elvis, the golf pro. "I saw your approach shot from the terrace on the last hole, Maxie. Ninety yards with a sand wedge." He wagged his finger. "I *hope* they didn't hire you."

Maxie tried to look aghast.

He laughed with unctuous false sincerity. "I love the Jacobs family, but they would probably be in a doping scandal, if they were Tour de France cyclists." He reddened. "Kidding."

As soon as Elvis was out of hearing range, Fisher shook her head. "What did you do?"

"Won a few holes for the team."

"Okay, you had to play out some funky scheme, didn't you? Was it fun?"

"You should talk. You and your mother are scheming, aren't you?"

Fisher blinked. "I have no idea what you're talking about."

Maxie felt satisfied. She'd hit a nerve, she was sure of it.

AT THE END of the evening, Maxie found Shannon standing next to a humongous man wearing a Minnesota Viking's pullover. She held out the camera. "Can I take the memory card? I'll send it back."

"Take the camera. You're the one who should be using it." Shannon took the giant's arm. "But only if you'll do your magic on us."

Maxie stepped closer. "Your fiancée is great," she said to the guy, who adopted a stiff posture. "How long have you been engaged?"

"Six months," he said with a guarded tone.

"Nice ring," she said. "What's your name?"

"Domino Sanducci." Domino took Shannon's hand, caressing the ring.

"Tell me about that lovely diamond."

"It's my grandmother's," Domino said.

"Tell me about your grandmother."

"She was my idol. Shannon is her successor." Tears rolled down Dominic's cheeks. He stroked Shannon's face. He was absorbed in timeless love as Maxie took her shots.

Maxie was in a photographer's heaven on earth.

ALTHOUGH SHE WAS exhausted, Maxie considered downloading her photos before she went to bed. Fisher stopped her in the hallway. "Don't stay up all night. We're going to the lake country tomorrow with mother. Bring your nightie."

"Fisher, I don't own a nightie. Don't go getting freaky with me."

"Okay, but pack up for a couple of nights."

"Do I get an explanation?"

"I guarantee you some photo ops."

Maxie shrugged, but she knew Fisher could see past the nonchalance. "Then count me in."

"Good. I'll supply the strong coffee and warm doughnuts, too."

"Stop! You're killing me. I said I'd go."

Chapter Sixteen

Ishpeming

TRUE TO HER word, Fisher supplied half a dozen warm doughnuts from Inga's, a Scandinavian joint on Randolph Avenue, and a large thermos of Sumatra from Dunn Brothers on Grand. They headed north, Fisher at the wheel, Artemis beside her and Maxie consigned to the backseat, which suited her just fine. She had strong coffee to savor and sticky fingers to lick clean of glazed sugar during the three-hour drive.

About ten minutes north of a town called Pike Haven on a winding road along a large lake they passed a wooden sign as large as a billboard with letters carved elaborately: ISHPEMING LODGE.

"It's Native American," Fisher said. "Ishpeming in Ojibwa dialect means Heaven."

"Wait." Maxie rolled down the window and took a picture.

They drove a quarter-mile up the private drive. At its end, the Great Lodge loomed before them, a towering four-storied chalet with windows framed by green shutters.

As they pulled up under the covered portal, a middle-aged man in a green Ishpeming Lodge coat and a green Ishpeming Lodge cap rushed up. "Welcome back, Mrs. J. Welcome back, Fisher. How good you look. California is treating you well."

The man held out his hand to Maxie. "Leroy Preston. Assistant Manager. Friends and family call me Bunty." He hesitated. "Shall I call the folks?"

Artemis grinned. "No, we'll surprise them."

A bellhop arrived with a rolling cart and unloaded their luggage. Maxie grabbed her camera bag. "I'll keep that."

Artemis retrieved a bulky package from the back compartment. "I promised to guard this with my life."

IN THE LOBBY, an entire army of sycophants descended on them, getting them registered with elaborate ceremony. Artemis refused to part with her mystery parcel.

They proceeded down a hall lined with photos and glass cases of historical artifacts. Maxie had a quick eye. In the short time they traversed the passage, she'd absorbed much of the history of the Lodge. She caught sight of quite a few shots featuring Artemis as a toddler, child and teenager.

At the top of a stairway, Artemis set her package down and tiptoed to a doorway. She pushed the door open. "We're here!"

A strapping old man jumped up from a dark wood desk. A silver-haired woman stood from her matching desk. They rushed over with euphoric expressions. The man gripped Artemis in a bear hug, released her, then pulled Fisher into a tight hold and rocked her back and forth. "Good god, gal. It's great to see you."

He turned to Maxie. "Gunter Hagan. Ring a bell?" He rose to full height and pumped out his chest.

"Football? You still have a powerful build." The quick way to win an old pro's heart. Tell them they still looked like players.

"Hockey," Fisher said. "One of the best goalies in Minnesota sports history. Grandpa's got a network like you wouldn't believe. He got me my job in L.A."

Gunter threw up his hands. "Nepotism. Still, she was a lackey at first. Had to prove herself." He frowned. "Wait a minute. Aren't you the paparazzo that attacked my granddaughter? Saw it on *ESPN Sports Talk*. What are you doing here?"

"It's a long story," Fisher said.

Gunter shrugged. "Fisher, you've always been a girl with good judgment. You inherited that trait from your grandmother."

"This is my grandmother, Ilsa," Fisher said.

Ilsa inspected Maxie and seemed to approve, or at least she was going to ignore any of Maxie's shortcomings. She held out her hand and shook with Maxie.

Artemis addressed her mother. "Is Dad taking his medications? He looks pale."

Ilsa wrapped an arm around Gunter. Aside from being about a foot shorter than her husband, Ilsa looked like a tough broad to Maxie.

"I cut the pills myself and hand them to him." Ilsa turned to Maxie. "My husband thinks he's invulnerable."

Just behind the old couple, a painting of the resort in a gilded frame formed a background. Maxie pulled her camera from her bag. "Mind if I take a picture?"

"As long as you don't sell it to the tabloids," Gunter said in a grave tone.

There was a moment of silence.

"That was a joke," Gunter said.

"Could you all stand over there?" Maxie asked. "Maybe you can put this on your wall."

"The walls are full, Maxie. Every once in a while, we put up something extraordinary." Gunter stopped speaking, but his silence said it all. *Not from some paparazzo.*

What made this man think she couldn't be good enough for his walls? Maxie shrugged it off and took the pictures.

AS THEY HEADED back down the hall, Maxie inspected the crappy photos on the second-floor walls. She could do better with drugstore camera.

Artemis pointed to stairs. "I want to go down to the souvenir shop. Nostalgia. We'll meet up at dinner."

When Artemis was gone, Fisher turned to Maxie. "Are you tired?"

"Why?"

"I want to show you around. Some of the photo ops I promised."

"Too bad they'll never make the walls," Maxie said.

"Are you still stressing about the fine art thing?"

"No way," Maxie said. "Let's move."

She and Fisher went down a back flight of stairs and exited from a rear door. Vehicles that looked like miniature galactic explorers sat in a row in the parking lot. "Far out. *Star Wars.*"

"Street legal high-end all-terrain vehicles. Climb in."

THEY BUZZED AROUND what seemed like a thousand acres, with Fisher in tour guide mode. The whole damned place was enchanting. There were three charming lodges and a slew of delightful cabins. They roared past the spa and fitness building, the tennis courts, the boating docks and the sandy beaches along the shores of East Tick Lake.

"My ancestors bought three bankrupt resorts that go up the road for about a mile. As a kid, it was like coming to paradise. Not to mention grandparents who idolized me," Fisher said.

"Another example of what makes you a Richfield."

"Poindexter, you're an honorary Richfield now, don't resist. You sealed it with the golf tournament."

"Then, what's up with Grandpa Gunter?" Maxie asked. "He's too exuberant. What's his story?"

Fisher tugged at an earring on her left ear. "Grandpa Gunter is one of the kindest men on earth, but he has a splenetic side."

"Fancy word for an anger-management candidate," Maxie said. "Runs in the family, then?"

"Maxie, please, no snide remarks. When Grandpa was playing for the North Stars, he went to a bar. Some dunderhead was abusing his girlfriend. Grandpa threw one sucker punch. The guy's head snapped the wrong way and he died soaked in beer on a sawdust covered floor."

Fisher stopped the ATV near the edge of the lake. Ash trees shimmered with golden light. A black-headed bird with a white breast skimmed the water's surface. It flapped its enormous outstretched wings, caught an air current and sailed up into the sky.

Fisher leaned back in her seat. "Grandpa Gunter was exonerated in the courts, but he was never the same. He lost his edge and gave up hockey."

"Look," Maxie said. A fish twisted up from the water, performed an aerial ballet and sliced back into the lake. "I hope the bird doesn't eat it."

"Creatures eat one another," Fisher said.

"I know," Maxie said. "Ever watch those documentaries where the lady praying mantis eats her husband? Hunger trumps relationships, even for bugs."

Fisher pressed on the accelerator. "This discussion is making *me* hungry. Too bad for the husband praying mantis, though."

A MEDIEVAL-SIZED FIRE blazed in the fireplace when they showed up for dinner. Along a wall, stuffed animal heads condemned their executioners with glassy eyes. Fisher led Maxie to a linen-covered table near the wall of beasts. Maxie could feel the heat from the flames of the tree-trunk sized logs crackling and sending sparks up the flue.

Artemis, Gunter and Ilsa sat at the table. They looked up with the expressions of people who'd been gossiping.

"Mother, what have you been telling them?" Fisher asked.

"Bragging," Artemis said.

"Sit down and have a cocktail," Gunter said. "Then you can tell us your version."

"First a few pictures," Maxie said.

Fisher joined the family and Maxie took a round of shots. She looked at their faces. No matter what they'd heard about her, they were open and relaxed. They were accepting her into the fold. She felt a twinge of belonging then shook it off. She was letting the clan get to her. She was supposed to be sucking her victims through photography, not getting sucked into them.

Maxie ordered an IPA from a local brewery. Fisher got a Hendricks martini. Artemis was drinking white wine and the grandparents were drinking red. As was her habit from childhood, Maxie completed her assessment of potential intoxication disasters. No one looked overly soused. She returned her attention to the conversation.

"When Artemis and her brother were growing up, we ate most of our dinners here in the Lodge," Ilsa said. "I never liked to cook."

"I got your genes in that respect," Artemis said. "We have a personal chef."

"Your brother is the one who could be a chef," Ilsa said.

"Our son Roman is a homosexual," Gunter said. "Homos often cook gourmet food."

"Dad," Artemis admonished.

"I wasn't criticizing. I've made peace with all that." Gunter glanced at Fisher. He had tears in his eyes. "It's all right, my granddaughter. We know about you. Homosexual. Maybe it's in the genetics."

"At least say 'gay,'" Artemis said.

"It's a stupid euphemism." Gunter gestured at Artemis. He swelled up, as though he'd just been injected with emotional prednisone.

"My daughter got my genes." He pointed to a deer head on the wall. "Twelve-point buck she bagged. My daughter and I are not antler addicts, but that fella is a dream. The antlers are gorgeous, heavy main beams, a tight spread and perfect tines. By the way, bow season is open."

Ilsa frowned. "Gunter, you can't hunt until your medication issues are resolved."

"Not me. Artemis can go. Maxie can go with her."

"She won't go," Fisher said.

"Why not?" Maxie asked.

"Hunting? You didn't want the loon to eat the fish," Fisher said.

Maxie turned to Artemis. "Can I bring my camera?"

"I knew it," Fisher said. "You're getting crazed about the photos."

"I'd love for Maxie to go," Artemis said. "I hadn't planned on hunting, but why not?"

Gunter cleared his throat. "My darling, I am thrilled that you came, but Ilsa and I were wondering about the visit. Is it about that girl, the artist?"

"She's a most peculiar young lady," Ilsa said. "Of course, since you asked us to let her stay here, we were happy to do so."

"For free," Gunter said.

"For free," Ilsa echoed. She hesitated. "She is not the most grateful guest."

"What is all this about?" Fisher asked.

Maxie studied Fisher's face. She appeared genuinely puzzled.

"The artist is a genius, according to Honey," Artemis said. "We asked my parents if she could stay up here to work on her show. She needed the package I brought to finish her project."

"Honey," Gunter said. "The girlfriend of my grandson who refuses to marry him or have grandchildren." He grunted.

"I kicked him under the table," Ilsa said.

"Never mind," Gunter said. "Let's get a bottle of nice champagne to celebrate Fisher's return, not to mention the addition of Maxie to our lives."

After a heartwarming toast and pleasant appetizers, they settled into a main course of stewed venison with boar bacon, wild thyme and morel mushrooms. Maxie thought the dish tasted like dirt.

"What do you think?" Gunter asked.

"It tastes earthy," she said. "Flavors of the soil and wilderness caress the palate."

Gunter laughed. "She's a poet as well as a photographer."

Maxie blanched. "Not really."

"Sounded like poetry to me." Gunter turned to Fisher. "How's business, gal?"

"Very good," Fisher said, staring at her plate.

They're not eating you up out there?" Gunter asked.

"Not yet."

Gunter gestured a fork at Maxie. "She was such a good kid. I worried that the sharks would consume her when I set her up at the agency. I never understood why she wanted to be a sports agent, but it didn't matter." He spit out a piece of gristle. "Better than selling shoes."

"Dad," Artemis said.

"Don't blame me if I can't see selling shoes as an adventure in life. Fisher followed her passion. I wasn't sure she could take the heat, though." He turned to Ilsa. "Tell Maxie about the retarded boy."

"We don't use the word 'retarded,'" Ilsa said.

"Not that story again," Fisher said. "Please."

"Have you heard about the retarded boy?" Gunter asked Maxie.

"No, just the one about peeing in the closet."

"When Fisher was a girl, she came here in the summers. Our most loyal guests at the time were a couple from Minneapolis with a — what's the right word again?"

"Mentally challenged," Ilsa said.

"A mentally challenged son," Gunter said. "The boy was terrified of water. All of a sudden he's swimming. Turns out Fisher taught the boy. When we asked her why she'd kept it a secret, she said she didn't see any reason to boast about it."

There was a collective sigh of appreciation.

"She did it out of kindness," Gunter stated.

"I got *those* genes from *my* father," Fisher said. "Kindest man on the planet."

Maxie detected another peculiar silence. Ilsa glared at Gunter.

"Heard Leonard's best friend died. Ned Burdock," Gunter said. "That man was a pillar of Minnesota politics. Confirmed bachelor, isn't that right?"

Artemis's shoulders tightened up toward her ears. Fisher twitched.

Ilsa frowned. "Let the dead rest in peace, Gunter."

"We keep the dead alive for a reason," Gunter said. "That's why we take pictures, isn't it, Maxie? We'll have a slide show of the pictures you take here."

Maxie hesitated. "A show? Well, why not?"

"Probably still won't make the walls, though," he said with a twinkle in his eye.

"We'll see," she said. The man and his damned walls were going to be a challenge.

Chapter Seventeen

The Hunt

MAXIE WAS DREAMING when a knock came at her door. The dream faded, leaving vague images of slaughtered fish lying in a pool of blood on the shower floor of the bathroom from Hitchcock's *Psycho*.

"Here's your gear," Artemis said. "Meet you downstairs."

Maxie stared at her new attire with full-blown Hollywood liberal snobbery. Still, if it meant getting some good pictures, she'd dress like a walking bush. She arrived in the lobby decked out in camouflage and blaze orange from head to toe.

The lobby was deserted, except for Artemis, who looked fabulous in her gear. The dim lighting and ominous shadows reminded Maxie of her dream.

Artemis patted the chest of her jacket. "Everything's very high-tech these days. These garments were washed in a special detergent to eliminate human scent."

"Coffee?" Maxie asked. "I need caffeine."

"It's in the thermos." Artemis shivered. "My blood is racing. I always get this anticipatory surge before hunting. Better than caffeine."

"Like sex," Maxie said. "Thinking about it before is almost better than doing it."

Artemis looked taken aback, then smiled. "Good analogy." She stooped down and picked up the package she'd brought from the Twin Cities. "I have to deliver this after the hunt."

"To Honey's artist," Maxie said. "She must be worth the effort."

Artemis smiled. "Your artistic genius is far more important to me."

Maxie could feel the warmth of a blush on her cheeks. "Don't," she said.

GUNTER'S MUD-SPATTERED FORD 250 waited for them in the driveway. Maxie climbed a short flight of stairs and struggled into the passenger seat of a cab the size of a man cave. Gunter had glued an eight-by-ten wedding picture onto the dashboard. The sun had baked it with a crackled glaze that meshed past with present, the youthful couple burnished with age, a rather nifty piece of imagery, Maxie thought, something that might be fun to play around with.

Artemis guided the pickup onto the route headed north. "We're going to a resort my parents bought from a widow named Torkelson. We own everything for a mile or so on both sides of the road."

"Fisher told me," Maxie said. "She gave me an extended tour."

"I think she was happiest as a girl, coming up here. She never hunted or fished. She liked to park cars with Bunty and help clean rooms wearing an apron." Artemis laughed. "Honestly, I wondered if she was going to become a hotel maid." She waved a hand. "Not that it would have mattered. We'd have embraced it."

"Well," Maxie said. "She became a force of nature, like her mother."

"Yes, from what I've heard." Artemis gunned the accelerator. The pickup roared down the road at eighty. The cab reeked of WD-40 and clandestine cigars. Maxie shivered, absorbing Artemis's energy. Artemis drove like a crazed teenager. Maxie and Artemis looked like pumpkin-tinged terrorists. Deer season was way more intense than chasing celebrities.

In a few minutes, Artemis pulled into the barely visible entrance of a gravel parking lot. She hauled equipment from the back of the pickup bed. She pulled out a plastic bottle and sprayed Maxie's boots.

"Ugh," Maxie said.

"A scent to mask your human odor. A smell the bucks like."

"I smell like rancid piss."

"Doe urine, to be precise. During mating season, male deer use their sensitive sense of smell to check out where a receptive doe has urinated. This might be overkill, but I like to increase my chances."

"Now that's a weapon of destruction," Maxie said as Artemis removed a weapon from the pickup bed. Maxie had her camera ready.

"It's a compound bow with 55 pounds of pull-back."

"Show me what you do." Maxie circled Artemis as she demonstrated her technique.

"I have a trigger release for a steadier shoot. These are the peeps. They glow for different distances. I use carbon arrows with titanium broad head tips that could practically penetrate cement. You're right. The anticipation may be better than the kill."

Maxie shivered. "What if you hit the wrong spot?"

"If I'm not certain I can kill, I don't shoot. I practiced for two years before I attempted a single shot. Let's go, I'm feeling...precoital." Artemis grinned. "I hate to say it, but that's what it feels like."

Maxie clamped her lips shut to avoid comment.

ARTEMIS LED MAXIE along a broad path, lighting the way with a high-beamed flashlight. They trudged past two sagging cabins surrounded by scrubby brush. "Our guests who crave a rustic experience love these shacks."

"I'll take the Lodge," Maxie said.

At the third cabin, Artemis paused. "That's where I'm delivering the package later."

"The mystery parcel," Maxie said.

"Honey is convinced this artist, Mallory Doyle, is a genius. Trapper worships her, too. He and Mallory Doyle are on the board of directors of the Twin Cities chapter of P.E.T.A. Do you know what that is?"

"People for the Ethical Treatment of Animals," Maxie said. "We love them in California. I once got a great shot of Doris Day at an anti-fur demonstration."

"If Mallory Doyle is a genius, she's an unpleasant and ungrateful one." Artemis hooked her arm through Maxie's. "You're my kind of genius."

Maxie withdrew her arm. "Please don't condescend to me."

"I wasn't condescending."

"I'm a hack. Ask Honey. Ask Doris Day."

"What does Honey know?" Artemis hooked her arm around Maxie's again. "Or, for that matter, Doris Day." She smiled at Maxie. "Honey says you're supposed to give artists more leeway than normal people, especially the geniuses."

Maxie was tempted to mention Judy Oyster but couldn't get the words out.

They proceeded through the darkness along the increasingly rugged path. In about a quarter mile, the woods opened up into a meadow. They crossed the meadow and stopped in front of a massive thick-limbed tree. About eighteen feet up, a sturdy wooden structure sat on a massive branch. Maxie's heart lurched. "I'm not big on heights."

Artemis pointed to the ladder. "Deer don't look up. That's why hunters like tree stands. This is the luxury model. We had it built for Dad for his seventy-ninth birthday. Before, it was a rope ladder dangling from a metal platform about five feet wide."

Maxine climbed the ladder, feeling woozy. She felt better as soon as they were safely inside.

The tree house had a couple of swiveling bucket seats bolted to the floor. The floors were carpeted with tough industrial material. A propane heater occupied one corner and an icebox another. Hinged windows allowed a panoramic view of the meadow.

"Dad complains it's too bourgeois, but he loves it."

"What happens now?" Maxie asked.

"We wait. After dawn, the deer come out of the woods to eat in the meadow. Be silent once they appear."

"What do we do until they come?"

"We appreciate the wonders of nature. Didn't you get into the wilds when you were a girl?"

"I got into the wilds, all right." Maxie took a deep breath. She knew how to wait. She'd learned to wait for her human prey, behind bushes, in parked cars and crouching beside stinking dumpsters in back alleys.

The sun was just beginning to rise. A red glow spread across the horizon, as magnificent as anything rising over the Pacific Ocean. A flock of pheasant ran full tilt across the browning meadow grass. They matched the meadow's colors, looking like creatures that had broken off from the earth to run freely.

Artemis sat up. "Look," she whispered. "They're early."

Four pretty doe, two adorable fawns and a magnificent buck with a crown of horns sauntered into the open meadow. Artemis picked up her bow. "Come out, big boy." She breathed in short gasps. "Big, handsome Daddy."

Maxie listened to Artemis's quickening breath. After what seemed like an eternity, the deer crossed the meadow, advancing towards the tree stand, noses and ears twitching. Artemis raised her bow.

Maxie's nose twitched. No, no, she thought, but she couldn't help it. "Aaaa-chooooo!!!!!"

As a unit, the deer bounded out of sight.

"I'm sorry," Maxie said.

Artemis appeared calm. "Why?"

"You didn't get to kill anything. I messed up."

"It's all right, Maxie. This is your first time."

Maxie grinned. "No one expects their first time to be perfect."

Artemis set her bow down. "My father and I watched the pheasants and the beaver and the clouds in the sky. If we shot a deer, fine. If not, then so be it. This is what parents do if you let them."

"What's that supposed to mean? I don't have parents. Not functioning ones." Maxie said. She watched the struggle on Artemis's face.

"Never mind," Artemis said.

"You won't tell about the sneeze, will you?"

"No," Artemis said. "It will be our secret."

WHEN THEY GOT back to the pickup, Artemis pulled out Mallory's parcel. They trooped back to Cabin Three and climbed the creaky steps. Artemis banged on the door.

A woman in a paint-smattered smock flung it open. "Give that to me." Her aggrieved royalty posturing was celebrity level. Mallory Doyle had flawless skin, beautiful cheekbones and startling red hair, a Gaelic beauty marred by her distorted features. "If it doesn't get in the show, it's not my fault." She grabbed the package and slammed the door.

"She seems like a lot of fun," Maxie said, as they headed back to the parking lot.

AT DINNER THAT night, Artemis related their time in the tree stand, emphasizing Big Daddy and his narrow escape, which did not result from Maxie's sneeze, according to Artemis's slightly altered version of the morning. "Maybe I'll get him some day," Artemis concluded.

"You will," Gunter said. "I probably bagged his father." He clapped his hands together as the waiter approached. "Pan-fried walleye tonight, girls. Minnesota's favorite fish. With wild rice pilaf."

The meal included a detailed discussion of deciphering deer body language, which Maxie was led to understand was an art that required many years of study. At one point, Gunter jumped up and performed a series of postures, calling for Artemis to guess their meaning.

Gunter froze, alert, head high. He held his ears forward with his hands and stared.

"Alarm pose," Artemis said.

He simulated a tail, which he wagged from side to side.

"All is safe," Artemis said. "That's a subtle one, shows the other deer that the threat is gone."

Deer charades, Maxie thought. She didn't think it would go over well with Doris Day in Hollywood.

Gunter returned to his seat. "No matter what you learn, the deer still get away."

Ilsa turned to Maxie. "They love to discuss the ones that got away."

"The older I get, the more I root for the ones that get away." Gunter turned to Maxie. "How's the walleye, girl? Fresh caught this morning."

The fish was delicious. Sorry, Doris Day. Maxie was glad someone had killed and gutted the creature.

Chapter Eighteen

A Little Buddhism

IN THE MORNING, Fisher left before breakfast, without explanation. Maxie had the best blueberry pancakes she'd ever eaten, soaked in Minnesota maple syrup and butter possibly churned by a Butter Queen.

After breakfast, Artemis approached Maxie. "Come with me on an errand?"

"No hunting," Maxie said. "I need to ease into the killing mentality."

"No, much more benevolent," Artemis said.

They hopped into one of the ATVs, rumbled up the driveway and turned onto a small road weaving through an isolated patch of the resort. They arrived at a ramshackle cottage. A vegetable garden withered in the yard near a large stack of firewood. Artemis pulled a small package from the back seat.

Bunty answered at the first knock. He was dressed in faded plaid and denim, looking more drained than he had at the Lodge. He held out his hands. "I appreciate it."

"I found them in an antique store on St. Clair," Artemis said.

Bunty removed a pair of small brass figurines. "Thank you, thank you, thank you."

"Fu dogs," Maxie said.

"Guardians of the temple," Bunty said. "You know them?"

"A friend of mine has studied a little Buddhism." Maxie made a small bow. One of Marcello's many ex-girlfriends was a Buddhist.

Bunty threw on a canvas jacket. "Would you accompany me?"

"We would be honored," Artemis said.

"Can I get my camera?" Maxie asked.

Bunty's face lit up. "Pictures. I want copies."

Maxie ran to the ATV. She returned to find Artemis and Bunty heading around the cabin. A marble monument loomed in the middle of a small meadow. Bunty approached the pillar clutching his fu dogs. A cremation urn sat on the hard ground in front of the pillar. Bunty placed the little statues on a shelf carved into the stone. With a wail, he collapsed to the ground and lay there, racked with sobs.

The memorial read, "To My Beloved Greta, you are my all and everything. No one will ever take your place."

Maxie recorded it all. She shivered at the last shot of Bunty lamenting, face buried in the wilted grass.

They waited, but Bunty didn't move. Artemis steered Maxie away.

When they were out of earshot, she said, "He's heartbroken, although it's been over three years since Greta's death. Some people have a hard time letting go of their loved ones."

When they got back in the ATV, Artemis scowled. "Greta was shot by a careless hunter, probably a fool from Minneapolis. The coward was never found."

"Nice comment on humanity," Maxie said.

Artemis slapped the steering wheel. "I fantasize doing some vigilante work on the perpetrator if I found him."

"Bunty never remarried, I take it."

"Remarried? Maxie, Greta was Bunty's *hunting dog*."

"His *dog*? Now *that's* sad." Maxie laughed. She held her hand out to squelch any reproachful responses. "It's sad. But it's funny."

"It does have a certain comic element," Artemis said. "Maxie, let's not mention the fu dogs at dinner tonight." She hesitated. "I don't want to get into any discussions of prolonged mourning. My father doesn't need more ammunition about Leonard's grief."

"Then we have another secret. A lot of secrets around here." Maxie watched Artemis squirm. She hadn't meant to be a creep, but she wanted to let Artemis know that Maxie Wolfe wasn't a sucker.

AT DINNER GUNTER brought up the Bunty excursion. "One of the fellas saw you on an ATV going up the road to Bunty's place."

Artemis adopted her commanding general veil. "We did go by to say hello."

"The man is still broken up over that hunting bitch. See? The old bucks should go first. Women are stronger than men, let's face it, even hunting bitches." He glanced over at Fisher. "Wouldn't you agree, granddaughter?"

"What?" Fisher asked. "Sorry. I'm a little distracted."

"Women. The stronger sex."

"A law of nature," Fisher said.

"If it isn't, it should be." Gunter said, glancing fondly at Ilsa. "Women are the stronger sex."

"Tell me that when I'm trying to get you to take your medicine," Ilsa said.

"I eventually obey," Gunter said with a grin.

They'd probably been doing the same routine forever, Maxie thought, but it was still cute. She was more concerned about Fisher, who looked like a broken spirit. "Where were you today? Scouting community college athletes?"

"I visited the Home Sole outlet in Brainward and did the 'we-are-family' routine. Dad and Hunter are going to be thrilled."

Maxie laughed. "Pretty soon they'll be expecting you to move back and sell shoes."

Fisher poked at her scalloped potatoes. "Would that be such a bad thing?"

"Ha ha," Gunter said. "My super-agent granddaughter selling shoes."

"It's not that funny."

"Of course not, my girl. I have nothing against shoe salesmen. You're just meant for better things."

"It's an honorable profession," Fisher said.

Maxie interrupted the uncomfortable conversation. "I have a little show I'd like to present during dessert." With a little help from one of the obsequious assistant managers, Maxie had prepared an alcove adjoining the main dining area with media equipment from the resort's cache.

"We'd love it," Ilsa said. She poked Gunter's arm. "Wouldn't we darling?"

Gunter yawned, looking devilish. "Better be good. I'm feeling drowsy."

"Better than caffeine," Maxie said with a bold tone, though she was jittery.

AFTER DESSERT WAS served in the alcove, Maxie got the slide show going, thanking the audiovisual gods for working their magic on the outdated equipment. She projected the images from the collection she'd amassed on the first day during Fisher's animated tour. She delighted in Gunter's grunts of approval. Ilsa and Artemis displayed appropriate bursts of enthusiasm at the tribute to Ishpeming Lodge. Fisher, on the other hand, slumped in her chair and barely paid attention.

Halfway through the show the glass doors protecting the alcove flew open. Mallory Doyle charged in, clutching a large Raggedy Ann doll. "Is Honey trying to sabotage me?" She held out Raggedy Ann's torn arm. "Rebecca was wounded in transport. Now I'm going to destroy her in Honey's honor." She turned to Artemis. "You'll come by tomorrow and get the results."

They waited for Mallory to leave, but instead she studied the slide on the screen. "Having a show?"

"It's Maxie's work," Artemis said.

"I love shows." Mallory took a seat and set Rebecca next to her. "Can I get a piece of that pie?"

"Of course you may," Ilsa said.

"Rebecca will have a fudge brownie." Mallory smiled at their looks. "We'll take it to-go."

During the rest of the show, Mallory forked pie into her mouth and glanced cursorily at the screen, until they came to a shot of Artemis holding her bow. Mallory threw down her fork.

"Hunters," she spit out, turning to Artemis. "What does your son Trapper think about you killing defenseless animals? I think we both know the answer. Murder."

Mallory jumped up and headed for the door cradling Rebecca. She'd gone perhaps ten steps, when she slowly turned around, a playful look on her face. "Excellent pie," she said. She waved Rebecca's intact arm at everyone and sauntered out.

"She forgot Rebecca's brownie," Ilsa said.

"Very peculiar girl." Gunter wiped whipped cream from his mouth and stood. "I'm tired." He turned to Maxie. "Not good enough for the walls. I'm sorry, Maxie."

She hated the looks of remorse on everyone's faces. Screw them. She would be on those walls if she had to kill a guest wearing an I ♥ ISHPEMING T-shirt and then photograph the corpse to do it. Maybe she'd consult with Mallory Doyle.

Chapter Nineteen

Big Daddy

ARTEMIS AND FISHER intercepted Maxie outside the dining room before breakfast. She could tell from their looks that they were conspiring. They made her nervous. Still, she agreed to go with them after the meal for whatever scheme they had cooked up. Better to be a part of it than left out in the cold.

The three of them drove up the road and turned into one of the decrepit resorts. No one had bothered to remove the evergreen-shaped sign that read, "Hidden Pines."

A grizzled man in stained overalls waited for them outside the former registration office. He disappeared momentarily and returned with a box.

"She's a little fighter," he said, setting the box down at their feet. "But I don't want her. Don't have the patience."

Artemis opened a blanket and lifted a struggling creature, cradling it against her chest. At first, Maxie thought it was a very large rat, but realized it was a very young, very sickly puppy.

"This is Tom Welsh, one of our caretakers. He used to breed hunting dogs. Whoever dumped this poor thing probably thought Tom would take her in."

"Little gal needs a home where she's loved," Tom said.

Back on the road again, Maxie asked, "Why didn't he just take it to the animal shelter?" She was in the backseat with the whimpering puppy.

"Because Fisher and I have a better plan."

They drove back to the Lodge and halted under the entry portal. Bunty was just finishing with a couple of new guests in a Jeep Grand Cherokee. He saw them pull up and waved.

Maxie got her camera ready. Bunty approached them. Artemis and Fisher set the box at his feet.

Bunty pulled back the blanket.

"Look at you," he said, picking up the runt. He held the puppy against his chest and stroked its emaciated torso. "Such a tiny gal."

Maxie almost got caught up in the moment, but the camera was between her and the antics. The finale featured Bunty planting a kiss on the puppy's nose.

LUNCH CONVERSATION CENTERED on the Bunty scheme and its success, meeting with the approval of both Gunter and Ilsa. Maxie was distracted, thinking of the photos. Potential wall material, but she'd have to work on them.

After lunch, Maxie and Artemis climbed back into Gunter's mighty pickup and rumbled up to the road back to the gravel parking lot near the path leading to Mallory's cabin.

"You brought your camera," Artemis said.

"I'm thinking of taking a few shots of Mallory."

"Think she'll let you?"

"You watch."

When they arrived at the cabin, Mallory flung open the door. She held Rebecca, who had a bandaged arm and bruises painted on her face. "Stay here. I don't like people coming into my workspace." She glanced at Maxie. "What are you doing?"

Maxie stepped closer. "Documentation of your creative process."

She saw Mallory's wheels turning. She knew how the mind of an attention-craving artist worked.

Mallory hugged Rebecca, slapped her, hugged her and shook her. It was spooky and fantastic. Maxie took a series of shots.

Mallory whimpered. "You wait here." She slammed the door. They waited for ten minutes. Mallory reappeared with a crate that resembled a casket, apparently bearing the remains of mangled Rebecca.

"I don't care how late this is," Mallory said. "Tell Honey I want Rebecca prominently displayed. Tell her the point of the show is in this doll."

Maxie and Artemis lugged the casket down the path. They passed the first cabin when Artemis came to an abrupt stop. Someone must have left food on the cabin deck. A large buck glanced at them and returned to nibbling scraps.

"Big Daddy," Artemis whispered.

Maxie felt an urge to shout a warning to him.

"Quick," Artemis said.

They bumbled down the path, joggling the casket. Artemis retrieved her bow from the pickup. "Foolish Big Daddy. It's rutting season. He was getting ready to go into the woods for the night, found a treat and is feeling cocky."

"Rutting?"

"Mating season. Their hormones overcome their sensibilities."

"I've been there," Maxie said.

WHEN THEY GOT back to the cabin, the buck was still there. Maxie longed to photograph Artemis's swelling rapture, but she knew the noise would mess everything up.

Artemis waited until the buck moved. Maxie aimed her camera at Artemis. As soon as Artemis released her arrow, Maxie went to work. The arrow struck the deer near the right shoulder, but he didn't go down. He took off through the vegetation near the gravel path, staggering.

They raced down the path, trailing the blood tracks for about fifty yards. They found him behind a stand of scrubby bush. He was on his side, legs collapsed underneath him, twitching. Artemis shot him in the heart.

Big Daddy started a round of seizures. After what seemed like an eternity, he sighed a rattled breath and died.

"Bless you, Big Daddy," Artemis said. "Well, the good news is he's closer to the pickup. I'll go get the dressing stuff. You can wait or come with me."

"The dressing stuff?"

"We have to gut him," Artemis said.

"I'll come with you." The last thing Maxie wanted to do was plop next to Big Daddy. His swelling tongue hung out his mouth and his eyes were still open.

ARTEMIS DONNED A double set of gloves. She tugged the arrows out from where they had pierced the hide. From her kit, she removed a razor-sharp knife. Then she started at the buck's chest and began slicing. Blood leaked from the carcass.

"Slicing just under the skin," Artemis said. "I'm getting it out of the way. We don't want holes." She sliced all the way down, past the belly, past the genitals, until she reached the leg bones. "This is the 'H' bone."

She sliced deeper into Daddy, through the windpipe and down. She reached into the deer and pulled out the guts, a thick mass of quivering slimy, oozing tubes and organs.

Maxie gagged. The only thing that kept her from vomiting was the camera between her and the bloodshed.

Artemis's arms were covered in blood up to her shoulders. Splatters dotted her chest. When she'd finished she stood. "Now comes the hard part. Good thing you're a strong girl."

"Wait." Maxie set up the camera on a tree stump for a group shot. She knelt down next to Artemis and the eviscerated deer.

"You're one of us now," Artemis said. "This photo proves it."

"The family or you and the deer?"

"Everything," Artemis said.

They turned the buck sideways and let the blood drain out. Artemis and Maxie grabbed the antlers. Maxie glanced down at the guts. "What about those?"

"A gift for the carrion eaters," Artemis said.

They dragged the carcass to the pickup and hoisted it into the bed. By now, Maxie was splattered in blood, too. In the pickup bed a gutted deer and a casket entombing a mutilated doll nestled together.

Artemis drove about three miles to Manny's Gas and Supplies. A huge pike replica on the roof twisted in fishy grandeur. Manny was a huge man with thick glasses who beamed when he caught sight of Artemis, then whistled with admiration when they all traipsed back to the pickup with the registration tag.

"You're the best, girlie," he said. "City living hasn't ruined you."

Maxie knew passion when she saw it. Manny looked at Artemis with profound incurable love.

"The city makes a person stronger, Manny," Artemis said.

"Wouldn't me," Manny said.

"Mind if I take your picture?" Maxie asked.

Manny stood stock-still, a human tree rooted to the spot with suppressed desire. "Can I put my arm around you?"

"All right," Artemis said.

He draped an arm over her shoulder, adopting the self-conscious expression of people posing.

"Do you have a loved one?" Maxie asked.

"I have a dog." Manny whistled. "The old man's getting hard of hearing."

A bag of bones in a dog hide stumbled from a kennel next to the blue dumpster on the side of the store. Artemis had tears in her eyes. "Grizz is still alive."

"Barely," Manny said, his voice catching.

Grizz, when he finally arrived, sniffed Artemis's leg, looked up at her with cataract-clouded eyes and wagged his arthritic tail. Manny sighed. "He still loves you."

Manny hugged Artemis with one arm and laid his other hand on Griz's head. He smiled at the camera with seemingly unaffected joy. Maxie took pictures.

Artemis grinned at Maxie as they left. "You are amazing. Manny is notoriously camera-shy."

"Were all men around here in love with you?"

"Probably. Speaking of local men, we're not done yet."

"Oh my god, where now?"

"To the locker."

"We're going to lock up the deer?"

"No. We're going to have our friend made into dinner."

Maxie, needless to say, captured the whole meat locker experience, a place called Big Bear Processing, where men in bloody white aprons posed and proclaimed Artemis's goddess qualities.

AT DINNER THAT night, Artemis provided a blow-by-blow description of the hunt and Maxie's participation, while Gunter exclaimed with delight. He turned to Maxie. "Girl, you are becoming a Midwesterner. Maybe we'll get you here long enough someday to teach you how to use a bow."

"We'll see," Maxie said to avoid rudeness concerning such a ridiculous notion.

Gunter poked a finger at Fisher. "I'd like to see you convince your new friend to stick around." He grunted.

"I kicked him," Ilsa said.

"Maxie's got spunk. She'd make somebody a good wife, or whatever they're calling it now," Gunter said.

Fisher turned red, which puzzled Maxie.

After dinner, Fisher walked Maxie up to her room.

"I think Gunter is having delusions about us as a couple," Maxie said.

"Is that such a nightmare?"

"Oh for Pete's sake," Maxie said. "Ishpeming has put a spell on you."

"What about you?"

"Don't know. Seems like a place of spells."

MAXIE TOSSED ALL night, dreaming of deer with her own and Fisher's faces dancing a lesbian rutting tango while homophobic deer hunters aimed arrows at them. By morning, she was worn out.

Both Artemis and Fisher looked a little worn out, too, as they said their farewells to Gunter and Ilsa.

"I expect you back here," were Gunter's last words.

"I'll be back," Maxie said, though she knew it wasn't true.

Once on the road, Artemis turned back to Maxie, who nursed a cup of coffee and ate one of the Lodge's signature white chocolate chip scones.

"Maxie, don't show the hunting pictures to the family. Sorry, I'm involving you in more subterfuge. Please don't judge."

"People in ice houses."

"Isn't it glass houses?" Artemis asked.

"Not in Minnesota," Maxie said.

THEY WERE BACK at the Jacobs' home by late afternoon.

On the way to their rooms, Artemis intercepted Maxie. "I have a surprise for you."

Artemis led Maxie down the stairs to the lower-level workspace. On the desk was a new iMac with a 27-inch display. Next to it was a high-end printer. "I had Hunter choose the equipment while we were gone. He said this model had lots of RAM, whatever that means."

A dark cloud dampened Maxie's initial euphoria. "Why are you doing this?"

"I want to see you make something of your talent."

"Okay," Maxie said. "Thank you."

Artemis smiled. "Just one? Where's the Midwest gratitude?"

"Thank you, thank you, thank you."

AFTER SHE AND Artemis parted ways, Maxie went in search of Fisher, who was in the dining room feeding strawberries to the Pinschers.

"Are they supposed to eat fruit?"

"Berries are okay, I looked it up on the Internet."

"Thank god for the Internet." Maxie popped a strawberry in her mouth. "Why is Artemis being so nice to me?"

"You deserve it?"

"I don't and you know it."

"Don't glamorize your depravity. If love and generosity were based on purity, we'd all be doomed."

"I know you and your mother are scheming."

"Can I have a little time? You won't regret it."

"Oh, brother," Maxie said.

"Is that a 'yes'?"

"It's not a 'no.'"

"Double negatives, I can accept that. By the way, you and I are making another trip tomorrow."

"Let me guess. An execution."

"We don't have the death penalty in Minnesota, smart aleck. Bring your camera."

Fisher had her number. They all did. She didn't know if she was more frightened or electrified. A dark voice warned of all the bad things to come.

Chapter Twenty

Rodeo

THE NEXT MORNING Hunter and Fisher waited for her in the front entryway. Her mouth fell open. "What now?"

Brother and sister wore boot-cut stiff Levi's jeans, Western shirts, cowboy boots and wide-brimmed hats. Hunter held out a third hat with a feather in its band.

"No way."

"Wear this. I swear you'll get some great pictures."

Maxie took the hat and settled it on her head.

"You look fetching," Hunter said. He picked up his briefcase. "Road trip indulgences?"

Maxie sighed. "The Scandinavian place for doughnuts and coffee from Dunn Brothers. You're the devil of temptation."

"You seem to be an easy target," Hunter said.

"Not really. Ask your sister."

"She's actually a pretty tough nut to crack," Fisher said.

After the purchases, they headed south on Interstate 35E, then exited onto a state road twenty miles below the Twin Cities. They were quiet, getting a buzz from the caffeine and sugary fats. Gentle slopes burst with lingering autumn greenery. An endless string of lakes populated the terrain, interspersed with hamlets selling bait, gas, convenience foods and religion.

Hunter broke the silence.

"Do your homework, sis?" he asked.

"No nagging," Fisher said.

"Just give me facts."

"Manager Wayne Powell is a bible banger. Probably an anti-abortion homophobe who condemns stem cell research."

"Wayne Powell is our bread-and-butter. Can be as prejudiced as he likes, long as he keeps it out of the store. Give me the rest."

"In 1994, this unit was the first to take in a million dollars. The store was mediocre until Wayne was promoted to manager."

"Fisher Jacobs. You *are* studying the shoe business," Maxie said.

"Why not?" Fisher asked.

"She would have to start out on the selling floor, just like everyone else," Hunter said. "Then she'd have to earn her promotions. Not too many women executives in the corporate office. Makes us look progressive, even if she is a family member."

"I guess it can't hurt Fisher to consider her options, however boring they are," Maxie said.

She thought how horrified Grandpa Gunter would be, but didn't think it was the appropriate time to bring up that particular tidbit.

"Maybe boring is tempting," Fisher said.

"Whoa," Hunter broke in. "Sis, if you're doing this to be bored, we don't want you."

"I meant no adrenalin rushes circulating among the superstars," Fisher said. "Normal corporate greed versus overwhelming sports industry greed."

Fisher Jacobs, shoe salesperson. Maxie smiled to herself. Maybe *Life of a Shoe Salesman* was Fisher's karma. Marcello had once told her that karma was a metaphoric garment worn under a personal storm cloud until you could find a way into the sunshine. Maybe Fisher had a date with drenched feet and karmic rain boots.

Maxie wondered about her own karma. She was pretty sure interfering with other people's delusions wouldn't force the sun to come out.

They arrived at a shopping mall at the eastern end of a decent sized town called Mankinko. Hunter watched Maxie pull out her camera bag. "We'll use your stuff for marketing. Steer clear of exposing rotten human nature, okay?"

"Rotten human nature in a shopping mall? How could that be? People worshipping material possessions? Eating their way into morbid obesity? By the way, have either of you ever thought about karma?"

Hunter placed his hands over his ears. "No deep talk. At least take some nice ones at the store."

"I'll try," Maxie said.

A YOUNG MAN in a pressed shirt, creased slacks and gleaming shoes greeted them at the entry to Home Sole Shoes. His nametag read *Toby White, Sales Associate.* "We've been expecting you," he said.

A man with sculptured gray hair emerged from around a tall shoe rack. He limped over, arm extended. His nametag read *Wayne Powell, Manager.* He took Hunter's hand and shook it vigorously. "We're happy that you're carrying on the family tradition."

"This is my younger sister, Fisher," Hunter said. "She's thinking of joining the business."

"I'm Fisher's beloved fiancée, Maxine," Maxie said, holding out her hand. She ignored Hunter and Fisher's shocked looks.

Wayne Powell didn't miss a beat. "Nice to meet you, Maxine." He glanced at her camera. "Are you a photographer?"

"We were hoping to get some shots for training and publicity," Hunter said.

"Absolutely," Wayne said. He waved his arm around the store. "A tight ship with a dedicated crew all pursuing one goal: customer service." He glanced at Maxie's battered sneakers and suppressed a shudder. He seemed more distraught by her footwear than her sexuality. "All who step through our portal are offered a shoe shine. Unless their shoes can't be polished."

"I think we'll purchase a pair of shoes for the fiancée," Hunter said. "Ones that can be polished."

Maxie spied some boots. "What about those?"

Wayne turned to Toby. "Start from the beginning."

For effect, the trio re-entered the store.

"Welcome to Home Sole Shoes. My name is Toby. How may I serve you?"

"Do you sell shoes for dead people? My father died. I couldn't bring him with me," Maxie said. She couldn't help it. She was ashamed of herself.

Toby didn't miss a beat. "Gladly."

"I was joking," Maxie said.

"Ha ha," Toby said. "What can I show you?"

"Notice how Toby greeted the customer as though they were the most important person in the world," Wayne said. "We drop everything when a customer arrives."

Maxie marched over to the Talerius Boots display and pointed to a chunky leather shit-kicker with steel toes. "These."

"We have oil rig workers in Alaska who depend on that boot, which features metatarsal guards. The young people love them as well, both boys and girls. They'll last forever. The shoes, not the boys and girls." Toby waited.

"That was a joke," he said.

"Ha ha," Maxie said.

She turned to Wayne Powell. "Does anything last forever, Mr. Powell? Does heaven exist for the saved?"

"Call me Wayne." The manager stroked his chin. "Very interesting questions. Toby, what's next?"

Toby led Maxie to a bench. He knelt before her, undid her laces, removed her tattered sneakers and set her foot into a quaint metal item stamped with lines and numbers.

"I haven't seen one of these since I was a kid," Maxie said.

"A Brannock Device," Toby said.

She noticed Toby's hands lingered on her toes. Reflexology combined with foot erotica. She had underestimated the shoe business.

"At Home Sole Shoes, we measure precisely," Wayne Powell said. "Some rival stores make the customer put on the shoe herself," he said with a shudder.

"I have really big feet," Maxie said.

"I'll be back in a moment with your size," Toby said.

"We never discuss foot dimensions unless the customer brings it up," Wayne said.

Fisher cleared her throat. "Did you know that the average shoe measurement has increased a size in the last thirty years? The National Shoe Retailers Association says that what was formerly a woman's eight and a half is the new seven."

Maxie felt a tweak of affection for the possibly duplicitous Fisher Jacobs. Fisher had done her homework. She really did have a Girl Scout aspect to her soul. Her karmic raincoat was probably a Scout poncho.

Toby returned with a pair of boots that looked like they could withstand Armageddon. The footwear smelled deliciously of tanned leather. He inserted her feet into the boots and tied them. "Walk around. These are still made in the good ole USA, over in Red Feather."

Maxie took a few steps. An almost spiritual sense of comfort and protection sparked up through her soles. "I love them." She reached for her wallet.

"Put it on the family account," Hunter said. "Engagement present."

Maxie was getting tired of her own fiancée gimmick, but she accepted the gift. "Thank you," she said. "Special thanks for the nice customer service."

With the transaction completed, Wayne handed them three tickets. "I'm honored that you came to do this. You could have just sent in a donation."

Maxie studied her ticket. Her pulse quickened. "Rodeo?"

"Just a charity exhibition," Wayne said. "The kids put it on in conjunction with the Harvest Fair."

"Will the Princess Kay of the Milky Way be there?" Maxie asked.

"As a matter of fact, she will. She's leading a Harvest Dance around the bonfire, followed by free buttered crackers."

Maxie almost exploded with anticipation. Maybe she did have a date with karma, revolving around queens.

"Pictures?" Wayne prompted.

"Of course." Maxie took a series of State Fair ribbon photos for marketing and publicity, as promised.

"IT'S THE GRANDDAUGHTER," Hunter said as they drove south on a two-lane highway headed out of town. "She's some kind of high-school rodeo phenomena. Wayne was a pro-rodeo star until he fractured his hip. This is how the Jacobs demonstrate that the Home Sole employees are family. We won't tell animal-rights activist brother Trapper about this adventure, though."

They'd been on the road fifteen minutes when they heard a loud honk. An extended cab Dodge Ram pickup with, if possible, even bigger tires than Grandpa Gunter's Ford, passed them, going nearly ninety miles an hour. Wayne Powell waved and barreled down the road, leaving them in the dust. "I see he hasn't lost all of his rodeo machismo," Maxie said.

"He's a part-time preacher now," Hunter said. "Driving like that, he may become a saint in heaven."

"THIS IS PERFECT," Maxie said, as they pulled into the crowded parking lot outside of a bustling fair grounds dominated by a large indoors arena.

Hunter wagged a finger. "Maxie, please. I saw what you were taking in the mall. Be good. No nasty pictures."

"I'll take nice ones, too." She eyed the crowd pouring through the gates. Little tykes in chaps and plastic guns in holsters. Grown men and women dressed like Roy Rogers and Dale Evans, including sharp spurs on their boots for poking the soft hides of animals.

"*Travels across the Heartland of America with Maxie Wolfe: Exploring Human Sadomasochist Dominance Over God's Creatures,*" she said. "A book of photographs."

Fisher groaned. "You're hopeless. I'm not marrying you."

"You want to live in sin? Fine by me," Maxie said.

"What's with you two?" Hunter asked. "I'm assuming you're joking around."

"It's complicated," Fisher said. "Especially if some people don't believe in true love."

"No kidding," Hunter said. "I'm still looking."

"Best not to look," Maxie said.

WAYNE POWELL WAITED near the ticket booths. "We're in a family box front row, but first to the stalls."

They entered a long, narrow barn. The air smelled of manure, veterinarian ointments and the pungent, sensual odor of horses.

"Hey, Grandpa," a young woman called. She rose from a straw bale in a supply area between a set of stalls, holding a bag of corn chips. She was a pretty, sinewy girl decked out like Annie Oakley. "Thanks for coming." She turned to two miniature cowboys lounging in camp chairs. "Be polite."

The boys shuffled over.

"I'm Katie and these are my brothers, Jimmy and Jason. Jimmy, wipe your nose."

"With a tissue," someone said. An older version of Katie came over.

"This is Rose, my daughter-in-law," Wayne said. "Where's my son?"

"Talking to the vet about Doolittle. He's got a boil on his rear end." Rose smiled. "Not my husband. Doolittle has the boil. He's our best cutting horse, but he'll take a sick day."

"Miss Lacy needs the experience anyway," Katie said. "We have to convince her not to be crowd shy." She watched Maxie pull the camera from her bag. "I hate pictures. I look skinny."

"She's seventeen and she still has no boobs," the youngest cowboy, Jimmy, said.

Katie yelped.

Rose wagged a finger at her son, followed by a shrug. "Grandpa Wayne says these people are a part of our family, so I guess we'll let it all hang out." She clapped her hands. "C'mon, gang. We have work to do."

Maxie backed up to take a shot and stepped on the foot of someone behind her.

"*Wowsa!!!!*" a squeaky voice screamed.

"Sorry," Maxie said, turning. An ancient alarm gripped her. A clown with green hair hopped around, clutching one of his huge feet.

"Hi, Dad." Jimmy hugged the clown.

"Maxie, this is my husband," Rose said.

"Knuckles," the clown said, holding out a hand.

Maxie froze. Clown karma. Everyone stared at her. She forced herself to shake the clown mitt. A mild, painless electric current ran up her arm. She jumped a foot into the air, provoking a round of laughter. She managed a weak smile.

While the family bustled, Maxie took pictures, but the clown had rattled her. After half an hour, the family kneeled on the floor for prayers, except for Grandpa Wayne, whose injuries left him standing. They bowed their heads.

"Lord, we are grateful for all you have provided us," Knuckles said. "And if you should see a continued history of championship trophies in your divine plan, we wouldn't be opposed to that."

"Amen," the Powell family said.

"Fear is our friend," Knuckles said.

"Amen," Maxie said. Not a word she used often.

VINCE GILL BLARED from huge speakers as their entourage took seats in the arena. A few minutes later, Knuckles sprinted out of a chute. He frolicked on the packed dirt, performing cartwheels like a teenager.

"Take Dad's picture," Jimmy said.

Knuckles scaled a wall and propelled into the audience. He dropped into the lap of a young woman wearing a sexy blouse and planted a kiss on her cheek. The audience roared.

"I'm reporting this to his wife," the announcer called over a microphone from his booth.

Knuckles jumped out of the girl's lap, fell over the wall and landed upright on the arena floor. A clown in a fat woman's suit swatted at him with a frying pan.

"Uh oh," the announcer called with glee. "His wife already found out."

While the audience delighted at the misogynistic shenanigans,

Maxie delighted in capturing their reactions. Gospel music brought the antics to an abrupt halt. Everyone, including the clowns, bent their heads. The announcer led the audience in a group prayer.

Maxie continued taking pictures, maybe one of seven people in the arena who wasn't praying. She noticed a few glares, but she was used to that. Next, predictably, "The Star-Spangled Banner" and a rousing salute to active members of the military and their families.

Maxie sank momentarily into the seductive quicksand of traditional family, stars and stripes patriotism and Judeo-Christian values. What was it about this stuff? Judy Oyster would have been ashamed of her. Maybe that's what made it so appealing. Her mental ramblings were interrupted by a poke.

"Katie's event is first. She rocks," Jimmy said.

"We are proud to introduce our first young lady today, the pride of Minnesota high school rodeo, Miss Katie Powell. Go, cowgirl!" the announcer said.

A panicked goat burst from an opened gate, followed by Katie on a palomino. In seconds, Katie caught up with the fleeing animal, captured it with her rope and flew off her horse. She tackled the goat and tied three of its legs together in a complicated-looking knot. She backed off quickly and threw her hands up. The goat twitched on the ground.

The crowd chanted, "Katie! Katie!"

"A fine performance, cowgirl," the announcer said. "Katie will be attending the University of Nevada Las Vegas this fall on a full scholarship. We have no doubt she'll be a top contender in collegiate rodeo."

"Let me see the pictures," Jimmy said.

She showed him the images.

"Awesome," Jimmy said.

HALFWAY THROUGH THE program, Jimmy pulled on her sleeve. "Gotta go."

What followed was either endearing or disturbing or both. A series of tiny cowboys and cowgirls clung on the backs of annoyed sheep as the animals burst from the holding stalls.

"Most of the kids don't last more than a second or two," Rose informed Maxie.

Maxie aimed her camera as Katie helped Jimmy mount a sheep in the closed chute. When the gate opened, the animal burst out with helmeted Jimmy clinging with a death grip. He appeared to be glued to the wooly back. Finally, the mutton gave a great shake and the boy flew through the air. He landed with a thud, head hitting the packed dirt. After a scary moment, he jumped up as the crowd cheered. Katie gave him a high-five.

Nice, really nice, Maxie thought. The road to brain damage.

"Ten seconds," the announcer said. "A phenomenal effort by a little cowboy who will surely be following in his family's footsteps."

Jimmy came back to the box and rushed over to Maxie. "Did you get my picture?"

She showed him the series she'd taken of him. He threw himself into her arms and gripped her in a hug.

"You've got a friend for life," his mother said.

Maxie closed her eyes and held the child, feeling him burrow into her.

PRINCESS KAY OF the Milky Way arrived in a Ford Taurus painted like a Holstein cow. In a field behind the arena, a crude boat shaped from desiccated wood was mounted over a pile of huge dried logs. Tied up in the boat was a dummy in a horned helmet.

"It's a funeral pyre," Wayne Powell said. "In the old days, Vikings cremated their dead. We have a lot of Swedes in this area. We took on this ritual for the Harvest, the death of summer."

The crowd cheered as Princess Kay approached the pyre, carrying a torch. Someone squirted lighter fluid onto kindling surrounding the logs. The princess lit her torch and ignited the pyre.

"Burn, burn," the crowd chanted.

Maxie captured twisted faces as the boat caught fire. She was fine until the dummy burst into flames. Maxie clutched her camera to her breast and ran for her life.

Her new Talerius boots felt like they'd grown wings as she flew away. When she reached an isolated weedy patch behind a dumpster, she threw up on a pile of fast-food wrappers.

"Are you okay?" Fisher asked, coming up behind her.

"I wish you hadn't followed me." Maxie wiped her mouth. "Let's go back. Act like everything's normal. You're good at that."

Fisher flinched.

She'd jabbed Fisher in her weak spot. Well, they were in the same boat, so to speak.

"Maxie, I don't want to fight," Fisher said. "Meet me halfway."

"Two steps forward, one back is the best I can do."

They arrived back at the funeral pyre as the flames died down to a smolder. Maxie hooked her arm around Fisher's waist.

"Just a little romantic stroll," she informed the group. "Fisher, would you get me a buttered cracker?"

ON THE WAY back to the parking lot after the buttered head fest, Maxie noticed the flashing lights, whirling rides and oompah-pah music of the carnival midway. She grabbed Hunter's sleeve.

"I want to go."

"I could use a bratwurst and some cotton candy," Fisher said. "C'mon, bro. I'll buy you a pork chop on a stick. With cheese curds on the side."

"You know my addictions, sis. Okay."

After consuming numerous fried products on a stick, they were nearly at the end of the midway when Maxie spied a basketball booth. Stuffed animals, including an enormous teddy bear, dangled from ropes.

"Do you want that teddy?" Fisher asked.

"No one wins the grand prize," Maxie said. "It's a scam."

"I once dated an actress who worked as a carnie in her youth. I know the secret." Fisher handed several bills to the surly attendant.

The boy glanced down at the money, probably enough for six ratty teddies. He retrieved three basketballs hidden beneath the counter, apparently not members of the general ball population meant for the chumps. "Three out of three wins the grand prize."

"This may make hanging out with messed-up NBA All-Stars worth it." Fisher took a shot and made a basket. "One down, two to go." The second ball hit the rim and dropped in.

A small crowd of onlookers gathered, stuffing cotton candy into their mouths.

Fisher took aim, threw the third ball. It rebounded off the backdrop and plunked in. The crowd cheered.

"We have a grand prize winner," the boy shouted.

The attendant cut the bear from its noose and handed it to Maxie. It smelled moldy. The fur was stiff like pre-shaped taxidermy hide. "Pete the Second," she said.

"I don't want to complain, but my stump is irritated, too much standing around," Hunter said. "Can we go?"

As Maxie, Fisher and Hunter neared the exit gates, a motley group of teenage boys in cowboy hats blocked the path. They inspected the trio with the glazed eyes of kids who'd had a few illegal beers.

"Excuse me, boys," Hunter said.

The boys puffed up. "Go around," said a pimply-faced bow-legged kid with a huge hat perched on his small head.

"Get out of the way, friends," Hunter said.

"Eat horse shit," the kid replied.

"We don't have to feed into this." Maxie took a step toward the boys. "Let us by, fellas."

The boys didn't budge from the path.

Maxie stepped closer.

Their leader, the pimply kid with the big hat, sneered. "Dyke."

Maxie raised her camera and captured the kid's shaky bravado.

"I could break that camera," the boy said. "Who said you can take my picture without my permission?"

"You watch it, punk." Hunter made a fist and advanced. He

probably had fifty pounds over the boy. "Leave the camera alone. It's worth more than you."

Before anyone could move, a rope flew through the air, circled the kid and tightened.

At the other end of the rope Katie tugged, jerking the boy off the path. A posse of sneering girls flanked her, giggling. "Corey Barnes, you are such a turd," she said. "These are my new friends from the city."

Corey Barnes stared at Katie with a look of worship. His deflated gang of bullies scampered off the path. She undid the rope and gave Corey a shove. "Tell your mama I said hello. Beat it."

Corey fled. Katie turned to Maxie, Hunter and Fisher. "Corey has had a crush on me since we were five."

"Thanks," Maxie said.

"I didn't want you leaving with bad impressions. I want you guys to come back and see me next summer." Katie twirled her rope in elaborate circles. "We take our friends and family seriously."

"We'll try our best. Maybe Fisher and I will have our wedding here in Minnesota," Maxie said. She was rewarded with a look of exasperation from the Jacobs siblings.

As Marcello would say, fight fire with fire, *shaine maidela*.

"Cool," Katie said. "Our new minister has a lady friend." She winked at the trio. "Don't make assumptions. Even us rednecks know the world is changing."

"For better or worse?" Maxie said. "That is the question."

Chapter Twenty-one

Mall of America

"YOU'VE NEVER SHOPPED at a Nordstrom?" Artemis asked.

Two days after they'd returned from the rodeo excursion, Maxie and Artemis were in Artemis's Mercedes, pulling into a parking garage the size of a small airport attached to the Mall of America, the Twin Cities shopping destination the size of a metropolis.

"I was raised by people who boycotted elitist establishments," Maxie said. "My mother probably bombed a Saks Fifth Avenue."

Fisher had informed Maxie that the family thought Maxie's usual attire was not appropriate for the up-coming events. Maxie was in the thick of things now. So, what was a little dress-up? She'd live.

"I'm completely dependent on a stylist here," Artemis said. "I have poor fashion instincts and no desire to learn."

"Stylist?"

"A personal shopping assistant. They're called stylists at Nordstrom. It's worth the hassle getting to her in this hellish mall."

They joined a torrent of foreign tourists, local shoppers, teenagers, children on school trips and senior mall-walkers. The hordes poured through the entry with Maxie and Artemis caught up in the near stampede. They were sucked into a domed cacophony of music and psychedelic lighting.

"They say seven Yankee stadiums could fit inside this mall," Artemis said. "Or thirty-two Boeing 747s."

"How about five starving African villages?"

"I try to block that out."

Maxie wasn't exactly Mother Teresa. "Tell me what a hypocrite I am."

Artemis hooked her arm through Maxie's. "If we were all abandoned because of hypocrisies, we wouldn't have anyone, would we?"

"I guess not." Maxie gasped at the sight before them.

Spine tingling rides swelled up towards the glass-enclosed sky. Cars dropped from great heights, circled wildly, while riders screamed. Haunted houses, name-brand trinket stores, junk food stands and game booths lined the twisting linoleum maze. There was something particularly disturbing about the indoor midway. It was Andy Warhol psychedelic. Worse, the bubbled energy had nowhere to escape. Children shrieked, either in frenzied delight or horrific overstimulation.

"Hang in there," Artemis said. "Follow me."

They darted down one of the multiple pathways. Maxie swayed like a drunken sailor.

AS SOON AS they crossed the Nordstrom entry, an aura of elitist calm tempered the populist atmosphere of the mall. Botanical derivatives from organic cosmetics saturated the air. Racks of non-necessities produced by underpaid workers in third-world countries lined the polished pathways.

"All the stylists are experienced sales people," Artemis said on the escalator. "Doreen has a background in theatre design. I'd rather be wearing hunting camouflage or sweat pants. Doreen is my fashion savior. I tell her what I need and she takes care of the rest. I called ahead about you."

Maxie was tempted to ask what the call had entailed, but decided she didn't want to know.

In the women's department on the second floor, Maxie was introduced to the exceptional Doreen, a woman with no obvious physical flaws, make-up imperfections or emotional issues. Doreen appraised Maxie. "You have wonderful bones," she observed, ignoring the attire that Maxie's bones were draped in. In fact, her eyes glowed with the challenge.

"I told you. You have a lot to work with," Artemis said. "She's a diamond in the rough."

Lump of coal. Block of sculptor's stone. Adam's rib. Maxie didn't care. She hoped Artemis appreciated her cooperation in this endeavor.

Doreen led them to a muted gray dressing room. An hour of dress-up followed. The final choice was a gauzy plum-colored pantsuit with a tantalizingly low-cut blouse. The fabric caressed Maxie's skin. She preened before a three-paneled mirror. Not bad. So what if the get-up cost as much as a used car?

When they reached the cash register, Artemis pulled out her Nordstrom's card. "My treat. We coerced you into this."

Maxie decided to use the Midwestern rules to deal with the situation. "Oh no. You mustn't," she said without reaching for her wallet.

Artemis laughed. "I insist."

"Thank you, thank you, thank you," Maxie said.

Back on the mall concourse, Artemis slipped an arm through Maxie's again. "This is fun. I'm going to confide in you. I love my children. But we don't tend to have fun in the same way you and I have managed in such a short time. Stay with us as long as you like."

"Is this a trap?" Maxie blurted out.

Artemis blinked and her gaze slid away from Maxie.

"I was joking," Maxie said. She could hear Dr. Dani's voice in her head. *You weren't joking, were you? You were expressing your misplaced fear and anger.*

Sorry Dr. Dani, Maxie thought. Maxie Wolfe might be messed up, but she knew how to survive. Survivors listened to alarm bells and hers rang loud and clear.

THE EVENING OF Mallory Doyle's opening, Fisher and Maxie took West Seventh Street to the gallery, so Fisher could give Maxie yet another tour. It was sweet that Fisher wanted her to love Minnesota, so she didn't yawn or roll her eyes. Instead she took I ♥ Minnesota pictures as Fisher yammered historical facts and tedious legends involving weather extremes and/or pioneer tenacity.

Before they got out of the car, Fisher cleared her throat. "Purple is perfect for you. The blouse is a tad low-cut." She blushed. "No, it's great." She glanced down at Maxie's feet. "You got a pair of Rachel Zoe flats. Classy alternative for women who don't like high heels."

"They had a pair for big feet." Maxie wiggled a foot. "From the Mall of America Home Sole shoe outlet."

"We appreciate your support of the family," Fisher said.

Maxie noted once more Fisher's growing involvement with shoes and family. Even she was getting mixed up in it all. They'd both come to their senses when they got back to Hollywood.

Honey's XYZ Gallery was located in Lowertown, four blocks west of the Mississippi River in downtown Saint Paul. The building was a brick former warehouse. Honey's place was set prominently on the first floor, with glass doors facing the curb. A neon sign exclaiming *XYZ* flashed boldly, patterning the entry. "This is the place to be these days," Fisher said. "Honey's establishment defines it all. She wants Minnesota gallery owners to think more like New Yorkers. Aggressive acquisitions and marketing."

They pushed through the gallery doors into a crowd of nattily dressed bodies. Honey spotted them immediately. Her high-octane exuberance was on overdrive. Her black sequined silk dress short-circuited in the lights as she rushed over.

"We installed twenty pieces in an impossibly short time," Honey said. "We've gotten amazing pre-opening press. I called in a few favors, including a piece from a former fling, one of the art critics with the *New York Times Arts and Leisure* section, a real dick-head." Honey flinched. "But Mallory Doyle is worth it."

Artemis appeared holding a glass of champagne, in time to hear this last comment. "You're going to great lengths for Mallory," she said. "Her behavior seems ungrateful."

A troubled look crossed Honey's face. "I have to overlook terrible behavior when it comes to genius."

A low whistle interrupted their discussion. "Don't you look hot, Maxie Wolfe?" Trapper came up to stand next to Honey.

Maxie shrugged, but was pleased by the compliment.

"No flirting," Honey said to Trapper.

"It's just Maxie," Trapper said.

Maxie decided to take the comment as a sign of inclusion.

"Is anyone safe from failed vows of fidelity?" Honey asked.

Fisher took Maxie's elbow. "Let's go appreciate the artwork."

As soon as they were out of earshot, she spoke. "I don't know what's going on with Honey and my brother."

"Relationship crap," Maxie said.

"Well, neither you nor I have room to judge," Fisher said.

"I was merely observing."

Maxie was drawn to a mixed media piece that hung prominently on a detached wall in the center of the gallery. Once she was close enough to make out the details, she blanched. Rebecca was stitched onto a canvas. Her severed head writhed in a corner awash in fake blood. Maxie flashed back on Judy Oyster's work. Her pity for the doll transformed into derision for Mallory Doyle. Judy Oyster had always used *real* blood. Maxie raised her camera and photographed Rebecca anyway.

Before Maxie could lower the camera, Mallory Doyle rushed up, draped in red silk, but still looking like an Irish schoolgirl gone cuckoo. She mugged in front of the doll piece. Mallory may have thought she looked wonderfully outrageous, but in Maxie's frame, she looked like an abused child faking bravado. Maxie took three marvelous shots.

"How about that one?" Maxie asked, gesturing to another display.

Mallory ran over to a canvas splattered with fake human entrails. She grabbed a young man with green spiked hair. "Your fifteen minutes of fame," she said. She shoved him up to the canvas. "Lick it." The boy pretended to lick the entrails. Mallory pushed her torso against the boy's behind.

Maxie almost had an artistic orgasm. She took a quick succession of shots.

Mallory pushed the boy away and sneered at Maxie. "Sell the photos to the media, I don't care. Hack journalism."

"You're right, I'm nothing," Maxie said.

Rule 4 of Marcello's Paparazzi Way: Let insults blow right past you.

MAXIE SPENT THE next half hour capturing the reception, weaving through the heavily perfumed crowd, making something interesting out of people looking variously puzzled, mesmerized, bored and pretentious. A few art students appeared to be seriously taking in the work.

Maxie was happy. Still, the rumblings of her inner voices warned of disaster. She was discussing camera technique with a cute fine arts photography major when a distinct rustle ran through the crowd. Maxie turn to see what was up and gasped.

Danny King. The TV Man was coming through the door.

He was impossible to miss. Danny King was an icon. His silver-streaked brown hair fell to his collar in a retro-seventies cut. He wore a black silk turtleneck under a cashmere cardigan. He searched the crowd.

Maxie stepped behind the mutilated Rebecca piece and waited until he was well into the room. As soon as she was sure he couldn't see her, she fled into the evening dusk.

She stepped into a doorway next to the gallery and put in a call with shaking hands. "Marcello, I need a contact in Minneapolis." After he'd scraped up the information, she sent an email with a photo attachment to the address he'd given her. Just as she pushed the send button Fisher appeared on the sidewalk in front of her.

"I'm leaving on the next plane," Maxie said. "I don't know how or why you arranged this, but it was twisted and mean."

Fisher tried to touch her arm, but Maxie pulled away. "Artemis was in on this."

Fisher grimaced.

"Traitors, both of you." Maxie spotted a cab and ran to the curb.

"It's complicated," Fisher called after her.

Maxie spun around. "What did Danny King promise you to throw us together? His lawyer? New clients?"

"Danny contacted me after our sentencing from the Bad Mama incident. He asked me to help get you and him together. In return, yes, his lawyer pulled strings. First, he got us in the same anger-management class. Then he got us out of the anger-management class when it seemed like an even better plan to get you to Minnesota. Of course, I also got referrals for new clients."

"Did he give you the Donna Street tip?"

"He and Street go back a long ways." Fisher looked about to cry. "No one thought Street would go that far. You're not to blame. Danny and I are the villains."

"Go to hell." Maxie jumped into a waiting cab. "Airport." She had her camera. She'd have the backstabbing Jacobs ship the rest of her stuff to California.

Just as the cab was about to pull away, the door flung open.

"Go away," Maxie said.

"I'm coming in."

The cab driver turned around. "Ladies, please."

Looking at Artemis's determined expression, Maxie felt her heart breaking. "Leave me alone."

Artemis slid into the back seat. Maxie's only choice would have been to physically throw Artemis from the car, which was ridiculous. Artemis was five times stronger than Maxie, no matter how many calisthenics Maxie did. "I'm going to the airport and you can't stop me."

Artemis tapped on the bulletproof barrier. "Cabbie, what are you waiting for? The airport."

Maxie groaned. "Cabbie, get going, for Pete's sake."

The cab driver turned and inspected them, apparently trying to decide if he'd picked up two dangerous nut cases or just drunks. Artemis took sixty dollars from her purse and waved it. The driver shrugged and drove. Maxie glanced back. Fisher stood drooping on the sidewalk.

"Give me until the airport," Artemis said. "If you still want to go when we get there, that's fine."

"You and Fisher lied to me."

"There were some things we didn't tell you."

"What's the difference?"

"Sometimes people can't handle the truth at first. We must let it develop gradually."

Maxie's memory bank swung open. "As Lightening to the Children eased/With explanation kind/The Truth must dazzle gradually/Or every man be blind."

All right, now she was officially going psycho.

"That's perfect! Forgive my ignorance, who was that?" Artemis asked.

"Emily Dickinson."

"Maxie, you are truly a delight. Do you have a stack of poems stored in that brain of yours?"

Maxie frowned. "Danny bribed Fisher. What was in it for you?"

"At first, I was just doing Fisher a favor. She was helping a father who wanted a chance to reconnect with his estranged daughter."

"Danny's not my father. He's a jerk who contributed chromosomes related to my existence."

"That isn't my impression," Artemis said.

"What did Fisher tell you?" Maxie asked.

"Everything she knew about you and Danny. Mainly that he was your real father and that you wouldn't speak to him. I'm her mother. She trusts me."

"Fisher got her information from Danny. It's all bullshit." Maxie slammed her fist on the worn vinyl seat. "Danny's stalking me. He'll say anything." She pounded on the barrier. "How long to the airport?"

"Ten minutes," the driver said.

"Danny asked Fisher to convince you to reconnect with him. Fisher tried. Apparently, you were not going to relent. Well, she was coming to Minnesota anyway, and things were not so good for either of you in Hollywood, so she and I hatched the plan to get you here and have Danny show up. Of course, there was the risk that we'd be doing this — streaking off to the airport."

"You're damned right." Maxie swallowed a lump in her throat. "I thought you liked me."

Artemis's expression was mournful. "I didn't expect to like you as much as I did."

"You don't like me, stop lying. Why should I believe anything you tell me?"

"You're talented, funny and you have a big heart. You want to believe me."

"Shut up," Maxie said and reddened. "I shouldn't say that to a mother, even if she's a liar."

"I raised three teenagers. I've heard worse. I'm not a liar, but a time-released truth distributor." Artemis placed a hand over Maxie's fist. "Give your father an hour."

The cab exited on a ramp to the airport. Planes flew low in the sky, coming and going, engines roaring. If she got on a departing plane, she could reclaim the numbness she'd been living with for so many years. Annoyingly, Marcello's voice whispered in her head. *Pandora's box, bella.*

When the cab pulled up to the curb at departures, Artemis gave the driver the address of the Jacobs' residence. "Let's go home. You must be exhausted."

Maxie sat back against the seat without protest.

MAXIE WAS ALREADY asleep when a knock woke her up.

"I'm going to get right to the point." Artemis held out a piece of paper. "It's an email print-out of the tip you sent to the *Star Tribune.*"

When Maxie didn't take the paper, Artemis shook it at her. "It just so happens that P.J. Newton is a friend of mine. She warned me to check where else you'd sent this. Naturally, she isn't going to run it in her column, especially the photo."

Maxie didn't need to look at the evidence. P.J. Newton was Marcello's local contact, the gossip columnist for the *Star Tribune.* The photo in question was of Artemis soaked in blood, gutting Big Daddy.

"Who else did you send it to?"

"Just her."

"How can I believe you?"

"To tell you the truth, you're not important enough to sell this to anyone. It was more a local interest shot, maybe rile up the animal activists."

"My kids would have been livid. Would that have pleased you? Creating a bigger rift between me and my children?"

"Would it make it any better to say I sent the tip before we talked in the cab?"

"It doesn't matter. I'm not going to reject you. It's about time someone did that for you."

Maxie shut her eyes. When she opened them, Artemis was gone.

Maxie went to her suitcase and pulled out her Memory Folder. She climbed into bed and pulled out blank paper. Time to write Journal Entry Number Two. Thank you, Dr. Dani.

Chapter Twenty-two

Journal Entry Number Two the TV Man
by Maxie Wolf

AS SOON AS she could understand deception, Maxie was informed that visits from the TV Man must be kept secret. The TV Man's real name was Danny. He brought her stuffed animals, dolls, candy and a rocking horse. One of her favorite gifts was Sneakers the Clown.

Sneakers was a punching bag with a sand-filled bottom. When you punched him, he fell over and sprung back up. No matter how hard you hit. Maxie kicked and punched him until she was breathless. Then her mother stole him.

"Maxie, I need Sneakers."

"You took Barbie last week."

"Barbie is misogynistic propaganda. Sneakers is ambivalent violence. Danny will bring you another one."

"Mommy..."

"No Mommy. It makes me afraid when you call me that."

"I forgot."

Already, Maxie could read the pain etched on her mother's face that drove her to do crazy things.

"Okay, Judy. Take him."

Later, Maxie found Sneakers stabbed. He was a heap of deflated plastic lying on the wooden floor. Her mother found her seated next to Sneakers, cradling the lump of plastic. She wasn't crying. She never cried.

"The clown is not a materialistic toy anymore. Someday you'll understand, Maxie."

AS MUCH AS her mother's behavior agitated Maxie, she hated when Judy went away. She was gone for hours, days, sometimes longer. At least there was Mrs. Wren.

Mrs. Wren was Amber's mother. Amber was her mother's protégé. Before that, there was Mercedes, Caitlin and Brandy. Maxie was glad when the fights came and her mother fired them. Amber stuck around a long time because of Amber's mother, Mrs. Wren. Mrs. Wren was a reliable babysitter who never went anywhere and always had time to watch Maxie. Judy made fun of Mrs. Wren even while relying on her.

"She's a cliché and doesn't care."

"I like Mrs. Wren."

"I know, I know. Just don't listen to everything she says."

MRS. WREN LIVED three blocks up the hill. The climb was so steep it made Maxie's legs ache to get there. She lived in a real house with a small porch and a chain-link fence. She had a television that she kept tuned to shows that stupid non-artistic people watched. Her favorite was *Life With Marnie*. She never missed an episode.

The stars were Marnie, her son Henry and her husband Danny. The TV Man. Mrs. Wren could tell you every detail of their lives, how each week Danny had to rescue Marnie and Henry from the scrapes they got into.

Imagine Maxie's shock when she first saw Danny on *Life With Marnie* at Mrs. Wren's. The shock was too much for her. She blew the secret her mother had sworn her to keep.

"That's him, Mrs. Wren. He brings me presents and takes me to the zoo."

"Danny King comes to visit you?"

"They made me promise not to tell anyone."

"That's funny. The man comes out of the television to visit you. Now look at this episode. Henry has to face a bully in the schoolyard. He and Marnie are hatching a plan."

"I don't like Henry. Or his mother."

"They're very funny."

"I don't care."

WHEN MAXIE WAS seven, *Life With Marnie* went off the air. The real life Henry got killed in a car accident caused by a paparazzo. His parents quit the show, according to the devastated Mrs. Wren.

Months passed. The TV Man stopped coming.

"Where's Danny, Judy?"

"He isn't coming anymore."

"Why not? Is it about Henry? I'm sorry about Henry, but why does Danny have to stop coming?"

Maxie wasn't sorry about Henry. She was secretly glad about Henry.

"It's about a lot of things. I have someone I want you to meet. I think you'll like him."

A week later, Bobby Shepherd became her stepfather.

"He's a poet, Maxie. You'll like him. And we won't need Mrs. Wren anymore. I've fired Amber anyway. Bobby will take care of you."

"Does he like children?"

"He's practically a child himself. He's sweet."

Maxie was not stupid. She was small and dependent and would

be for a number of years. Bring on Bobby Shepherd.

MAXIE COMPLETED HER second journal entry. She inserted it in her Memory Folder. Who knew what might inspire the final entry?

Chapter Twenty-three

Show, No Show

ARTEMIS AND MAXIE arrived on time at The Sleepy Haven Country Club on Saturday afternoon. Maxie left her camera behind.

"No pictures today?"

"I'm not in the mood," Maxie said.

Stu Phelps, the golf pro, sans his Elvis costume, greeted them. Maxie detected subtle condemning vibes about the ringer episode. A hostess led them to a secluded banquet room at the rear of the building. A large window faced out to the elevated green of the eleventh hole. An hour passed. Danny King did not appear.

"Let's give him another few minutes," Artemis said.

Seagulls fought over a hot dog bun dropped by a careless boob onto the course. Although they couldn't hear the screeches, they watched the furious snapping of the gulls' beaks as they fought over the dregs.

"How can there be seagulls?" Maxie asked. "There is no sea."

"Not all gulls live by the sea." Artemis checked her watch.

"I told you so," Maxie said. "Let's go." She was vindicated. Danny King was officially a jerk.

THE CALL CAME when they were on the Mendota Bridge, nearly back to Highland Park. Maxie let the call roll to voice mail as she'd always done with Danny's intermittent stalking.

"I'm sure he has an explanation," Artemis said.

"He's been leaving what I assume were explanations for years."

"Did you ever listen?"

"No."

"Maxie, teach me the Emily Dickinson poem."

"You're trying to bond. I don't want to bond with you."

"I want to bond with you."

Maxie felt like her head was going to explode.

They exited on the Edgcumbe turnoff. Artemis turned into the Saint Paul JCC parking lot and drove to a remote shaded spot near the railroad tracks. A freight train chugged noisily by. After it passed, Maxie and Artemis recited together. "As Lightening to the Children eased/ With explanation kind/ The Truth must dazzle gradually/ Or every man be blind."

They repeated the poem until Artemis could say it alone.

"Thank you," Artemis said.

"I still won't forgive Danny," Maxie said.

"But you'll stay?"

"Don't force us together."

"Trust me," Artemis said.

"Fighting words," Maxie replied.

WHEN THEY REACHED the driveway of the Jacobs property, Artemis jerked to a halt. "Look!"

Next to the entry fence post, Sneakers the Clown leered at them.

"I'll be damned," Maxie said. She climbed out of the Mercedes, walked over to the clown and belted him right in the kisser. He toppled and sprang back up. Maxie kicked and punched until her arms and legs hurt. When she finished, she noticed Danny King staring at her from ten feet away.

"Do you think this is funny?" She giggled. It was funny. Crazy funny.

"Give me fifteen minutes," Danny said.

She gestured to a bus stop bench across the road on the walk/bike path that bordered the river. "Five minutes."

She crossed the street. Danny trailed her. He wore a jaunty beret, a scarf wrapped around his lower face and bug-eyed Ray-Bans. She got a good look at the bench and smiled. The backrest advertisement featured a shot of Leonard holding a Home Sole shoebox.

Cars and trucks were slowing down to inspect Sneakers, who sat acting as sentry to the Jacobs residence. "You won," she said. "I can't believe I'm talking to you."

"My pursuit isn't about winning," Danny said.

"Four minutes left."

"Your mother and I hooked up for one night in San Francisco after a benefit for Arty Bryce, the political comedian who was fighting criminal charges. I knew him from the old days in the Catskills, before he turned radical. Judy Oyster was smart, strange, wonderful and wounded. Later, I found out from Arty that she was pregnant with you. I was there when you were born. I fell in love with you."

"Time's up."

"What would I have to do to get another five minutes?"

"Cause another suicide? Wasn't Donna Street enough?" Maxie watched her father deflate like Sneakers from the emotional knifing. "Quick."

"My supposed reason for coming to Minnesota is an NPR show. I talked a buddy of mine into dropping out and arranged to replace him. Come see me." Danny stared at the majestic river. "I didn't stop coming to see you because I wanted to stop. Your mother stopped me."

Maxie jumped up. "That's it."

"I still have a minute."

"You forfeited your time. Don't talk about my mother." She walked over to the curb and turned back to face him. "I'll come to your damned show."

She crossed over to the other side of the road, dragged Sneakers up the driveway, up the front stairs and into the entry hall. The Pinschers bounded up to her, but screeched to a halt at the sight of Sneakers. They barked ferociously, but no one came to see what was up.

"Where is everyone?" she asked the dogs. Lady Ruckus scampered towards the dining room, followed by her sons.

INSIDE THE DINING room, Artemis, Trapper and Leonard sat at the table. It was dinnertime, but there was no dinner. Leonard had a vodka cocktail, Artemis a glass of wine, and Fisher a bottled beer.

Fisher waved at Maxie. "Come in. I hope you're not hungry."

"What's up?" Maxie asked.

"Charles quit."

"You're kidding. When?"

"This afternoon. Before making dinner, obviously."

"Why?"

"His popovers failed."

Maxie slumped down into a chair. "Probably put too much flax in them."

"Hunter is on his way over. He's bringing take-out from Lunds," Artemis said.

Leonard burst into tears. There followed an embarrassed silence, which Leonard broke with a quavering voice.

"I was just making conversation while he cooked. I was telling him all about Ned's childhood on the Iron Range. Charles was impatient."

"Egomaniac," Maxie said. "Poor listener."

"If I don't discuss Ned's legacy, who will? I thought Charles would appreciate Ned's contributions to the state of Minnesota and how Ned learned his generosity of spirit in a childhood of hardscrabble misery. My dear Ned represents the spirit of Minnesota. He was not meant to die. He was irreplaceable. Charles was so impatient as I related these facts. I was a little harsh at his disinterest. I yelled terrible things at him."

"Screw Charles. Chefs are a dime a dozen," Fisher said. "We'll get another one." She hesitated. "Maybe a woman this time."

"The eyelashes will be hard to replace," Maxie said.

Everyone turned to her with looks of reproach.

"I was inserting a little humor." Maxie raised her hands in surrender.

"Let's quit this topic," Artemis said. "I don't want to dwell on it when Hunter arrives."

Just as the words were out of her mouth, the dogs raced from the room, yapping. They returned with Hunter, who hugged an armful of brown sacks. "I brought enough for an army," he said. "Why is there an inflatable clown in the hallway?"

"He's mine," Maxie said. "He's a form of therapy."

"Trapper and Honey are out of town," Artemis said. "A date night in Red Feather at the St. Jerome hotel."

From what Maxie had observed of Honey and Trapper, the date night was sorely needed.

"I'll have another cocktail," Leonard said.

"It's a weeknight, Leonard," Artemis said.

"Let him drink," Hunter said. "He's stressed."

When they'd all settled at the table with drinks and mounds of prepared food, Hunter waved a fork. "What happened?"

"He threw a fit and stomped out," Fisher said. "His popovers didn't popover."

Apparently no one was going to elaborate on Leonard's outburst to Hunter, Maxie noted.

"That guy was a piece of work. We'll get a new one."

"I won't miss oat grouts," Fisher said.

"It was the bragging," Artemis said. "I won't miss the bragging."

"Lack of salt," Fisher said.

"How about the tight T-shirts?" Hunter threw in. "We pay them to be chefs, not *GQ* models."

Leonard sipped at his cocktail. The rest ignored his cloud. Maxie joined in the denial. She waved a piece of tarragon chicken. "The take-out is delicious. Better than Charles. It has loads of salt."

She excused herself as soon as possible. She dragged Sneakers up the stairs and settled him in a corner of her room. She'd climbed into bed when a tap sounded at her door. She tried ignoring the intrusion, but a short burst of insistent raps followed.

"Oh my god, come in," Maxie called.

Artemis opened the door. "I want you to watch something with me."

"I know what you're up to."

"Please."

"What do I have to lose at this point?" She hopped from the bed and followed Artemis.

Everything, said an inner demon.

After they settled on the couch in the den, Artemis switched on the television. The theme music from *Life with Marnie* played. Same plot, over and over. Henry and Marnie get into trouble. Danny rescues them. Maxie was back in Mrs. Wren's living room. The episodes were burned into her brain.

Artemis shut off the television. "This isn't a man who would want to hurt you."

"That was his television personality," Maxie said.

"I don't think he has another one." Artemis smiled. "You walk like him, did you know that?"

She did walk like him. She was a compilation of Danny King and Judy Oyster. She shivered. This was definitely too much pondering. "I need to go to bed."

"Yes," Artemis said. "You'll need your sleep. We have some big days ahead."

"I can hardly wait," Maxie said.

Chapter Twenty-four

Go to the Museum

THE VERY NEXT day a chef arrived for a hurried audition. Fiona came recommended by her best friend, Doreen, the personal stylist from Nordstrom. They apparently came from a tribe of enchanted young women who radiated calm professionalism. Her résumé included a meditation practice she'd acquired in California while apprenticing with Alice Waters at Chez Panisse. To temper the trappings of egocentric karma, she had abandoned rising culinary fame in order to serve others in family homes. Rich family homes, Maxie observed. But who expected people to be logically consistent when it came to salvation?

At the try-out dinner that evening, the food was sensible and delicious. Honey and Trapper were back from their date weekend and psyched to be part of the trial. Fiona prepared fresh local ingredients with moderate salt. She explained each course with calm delight and obvious love of nourishment as a form of practice. She looked puzzled at Leonard and Honey's repeated requests for cocktail refills, but took her cue from her employers and brought them with transcendent non-judgment.

By dessert, Leonard was drunk and Honey was growing loose-lipped. She withdrew a newspaper section from a bag that she'd set beside her chair. "Seems like Danny King is doing Sydney Gross's show on Thursday. Artemis, isn't Sydney a friend of yours?"

Artemis shrugged. "We've known each other since college. Leonard, Ned and I hung out with him."

"Was he always such a prick? Excuse my language. That show of his is cult level snobby. If you've made it as an artist, he *might* invite you. Danny King? Good god, if you stick around long enough in show business, you get deified. His wife is the one who should be on the show. Whatever became of her?" She turned to Maxie. "You're the gossip authority. Whatever became of Marnie King?"

"She never recovered from the death of her son Henry. She sells Italian designer shoes in Carmel."

"No way," Honey said.

Fisher glared at her. Maxie had made up the last part about the shoes.

"I mean, Andy Griffith, okay," Honey said. "But what about Don Knotts? Who gets to be an icon?"

Hunter jumped in. "Clint Eastwood, okay. But what about Sylvester Stallone?"

"Danny is good," Maxie said. What did this group know about acting talent?

"I heard Danny tried to get a part in a Shakespeare play on Broadway," Honey said. "I heard he's dating the actress who's playing his daughter."

Maxie stabbed her fork into her carrot cake and left it sticking up through the cream cheese frosting. "Artemis and Fisher know Danny is my father. I'll bet that the rest of you have been informed."

"Not me," Hunter said.

"Don't they tell you anything?" Maxie asked.

"That's enough," Artemis broke in. "We're going with Maxie to the taping of Sydney's show." She held her hand up before Maxie could protest. "We got you into this." She looked around. "Who can make it?"

Without hesitation, everyone raised hands, except Leonard, who sat dozing.

"Then it's a date," Artemis said.

Maxie knew it was useless to protest. Strangely, she didn't want to.

MAXIE SPENT THE next three days exploring the Twin Cities without Fisher. Fisher was haunting the corporate shoe office studying the mesmerizing world of shoes.

Maxie went to downtown Saint Paul and walked along the river's edge. The days were clear and bright. Minnesotans crowded the walkways, basking in the glorious weather, which brought shocked and manic joy for them.

On Tuesday, in a span of three hours, she had almost fifteen shots that were potentially fantastic. A mother and a daughter shared a croissant on a bench, picking crumbs from one another's laps. The pair was obese, the shot could have been mocking. Maxie channeled their obvious affection and caught that in the image.

She shot two lovebirds jogging with their arms entwined, a living tangle of sweaty, oversexed limbs. She followed up with a homeless woman and her pug, identical twins. That one was a little on the sugary side. Maybe she'd go over the top and Photoshop some angel wings onto the pug. Better yet, maybe she'd Photoshop snobby Honey's face on the pug and add some wings.

Maxie sat on a bench in the shade and reviewed every image. She thought about how she'd work with each. Then she erased them, slowly, one by aching one. She was her mother's daughter. She was manifesting creative destruction to demonstrate—what? She didn't know. At least she wasn't cutting herself or running into traffic. Maybe she should. Or she could shoot Mallory Doyle, like Valerie Solanas shot Warhol.

On the last day before the Danny's show, she went to Uptown, where she captured the younger generation expressing themselves like peacocks in their trendy neighborhood. Then to a park outside a nursing home populated with elders doing tai chi, then to the opening of a nail salon, to a toy store and a place that sold imported olive oil and aged balsamic vinegars. She sat on a bench, preparing to erase them all when her cell rang.

"*Bella*? Are you all right?"

"Never been better."

"*Skitsnack*."

"What the hell does that mean?"

"Swedish for bullshit, learned it from a new paramour, a Swedish model." Marcello cleared his throat. "Danny King is in Minnesota taping Sydney Gross's show. Interesting coincidence, no?"

Maxie hadn't told Marcello that Danny was her father. She suspected from his tone that he knew the truth of her origins.

"Marcello, I'm going to Danny's damned show. I feel like I'm being squeezed."

"Then get squeezed. You can't put toothpaste back in the tube, as the saying goes."

"I feel much better."

"My Maxie, I wouldn't know you without the sarcasm."

Maxie hesitated then she told him about the erased pictures. "Please, no clichés. I have some ideas. Like collage, but not exactly. I'm making pictures, but they suck."

"Go to the museum."

"Don't go Zen koan on me."

"Go to the museum. Find images that speak to you. Your ideas will multiply."

"How many museums have you been to?" Maxie demanded.

She felt like an unbearable toddler. Marcello was the one who spouted about unconditional love. See if he could take the challenge of a regressing disciple.

"I've been to more museums than you might think," he said. "Go."

"I'll see."

As she disconnected, a prim, well-dressed senior settled on the bench next to her.

"Isn't it a lovely day?" the lady asked.

"Very much so," Maxie said. "Ma'am, are you familiar with the museums in town?"

Chapter Twenty-five

The Creative View

THE ATMOSPHERE OUTSIDE the Fitzgerald Theatre was frigid, afflicted by an arctic blast from Canada. Somewhere in the sky, stars burned bright, but their radiance was obscured by urban haze. The attending press shivered on the sidewalk, their teeth chattering, their fingers fumbling with frozen equipment.

Maxie recalled that one of Dante's circles of hell involved ice. She could take the cold, however, just like she could the heat. It wouldn't be the ice that broke her. Instead of ex-lovers, she'd be running a gauntlet of comedians seeking forgiveness.

The hall was sold out. Maxie and the Jacobs family took front-row seats. She couldn't see the crowd behind her, but she could hear the polite, highbrow murmur. The show was *National Public Radio*'s little darling, *The Creative View*. As Honey had said, if you wanted to feel like you'd made it as an artist in the entertainment industry, then you got on Sidney Gross's show. If you wanted to be in the cultural elite, you got tickets for the taping of Sydney Gross's self-glorifying tributes for his personally selected chosen ones. Once he had the performer on stage, however, watch out.

A rustle rose from the crowd. Sidney strolled onto the stage. He carried his signature research notebook. According to tradition, no one clapped. Sidney walked over to one of two high-backed leather armchairs with a small table between them. The house lights were up halfway, so that the audience was visible from the stage, bringing everyone into the sophisticated family.

Sidney opened his notebook and made a show of studying his notes. "Tonight, we have the honor of spending time with one of our most enduring comedians. He generously agreed to substitute for Billy Frackett, who could not be here as originally scheduled.

"Danny King has been a favorite of mine for as long as I can remember," Sidney continued. "He and Marnie King are a legendary comedy couple, due to go down in the annals of entertainment history, in the realm of Mike Nichols and Elaine May. Lucille Ball and Ricky Ricardo. Dick Van Dyke and Mary Tyler Moore."

As he spoke, scenes from an episode of *Life With Marnie* played on a screen behind him. Maxie shuddered.

"Without further ado, I invite Danny King to my virtual salon," Sidney said. "A comedic icon."

The audience clapped, then rose for a standing ovation. Maxie remained seated. Still, as Danny shambled onto the stage, she felt a slight tinge of — what? Propriety? Pride?

Danny waved to the crowd and motioned for them to sit. As they started to lower themselves, he motioned for them to rise and gestured for more attention. The people laughed. This went on for two more rounds. He shook hands with Sidney and sprawled into his armchair, body language dialed into cherished familiarity.

Sidney glanced down at his notebook. Before he could ask anything, Danny grabbed the notebook. He flipped through the pages, then lifted his rear, placed the journal under his butt and sat on it. The audience was silent except for a few titters. Sidney looked miffed. Maxie detected a certain rehearsed quality to the whole business.

Danny wiggled on the journal, removed it and held it out to Sidney. Sidney waved it away, face repugnant. Danny sniffed at it, grinned and set it on the table.

The audience squirmed.

Danny wasn't being Mr. Perfect Father. The Fitzgerald was the home of *Prairie Home Companion*, not a sleazy comic joint in lower Manhattan featuring a dude doing fart jokes. Maxie nodded approvingly.

Danny picked up the journal and held it to his nose again. He inhaled deeply and grimaced with revulsion. The atmosphere radiated discomfort. The act reeked of dubious performance art, Maxie realized. How do you like that? Maybe her mother and father had more in common than she thought.

By now, the discomfort level was palpable. Maxie glanced behind her at the pursed lips and furrowed brows. Danny, persistent and devilish, stood and set the notebook on his head and strutted across the stage, mimicking a girl practicing her posture while voicing loud fart sounds.

Maxie laughed loudly and enthusiastically. On each side of her, Artemis and Fisher stared.

After a brief pause, the audience tittered.

Maxie laughed even louder.

Finally, the audience laughed, nervously at first, then with gusto and unleashed abandon.

Danny came to the edge of the stage and peered into the crowd.

Maxie waved to him. "Go, Big Daddy!"

"Thanks, kid," Danny said.

He turned and headed back to the chair. He was almost there when he tripped, thrusting the notebook into the air as he fell. He struggled back into his seat and wiped his brow. The audience howled. He settled into his chair with exaggerated dignity. "Questions?" he asked Sidney with a pompous tone.

"My questions were in my notebook," Sidney said with conspiratorial huffiness.

"Extemporize," Danny said.

"Tell us," Sidney said, "the relationship between comedy and aggression."

"Funny is slipping on a banana peel. Better yet, slipping on a banana peel, sliding into a passerby who falls onto another bystander. A burly cop comes and lands on top of the heap. All comedy has its roots in mishap."

"If you'll pardon a challenge," Sidney said.

Artemis poked her. "Just wait," she whispered.

"I see the slapstick and vulgarity you demonstrated just now. It's easy to get laughs from cheap tricks. What in your mind elevates this crap, if you'll pardon the expression, to art that will last for more than a minute, much less into the pantheon of enduring creativity?"

As Sidney spoke, Danny's head began to droop. By the time the question was finished, he fainted onto the floor. The audience clapped and laughed. He got up, brushed himself off and took his seat. "Good comedy challenges the status quo, bad comedy reinforces it." He raised an eyebrow in a precise imitation of Sidney. "Good comedy opens doors, bad comedy closes them."

Much to his credit, Maxie observed, Sidney smiled appreciatively.

"What, then, separates comedy from tragedy?" Sydney asked.

"Comedy tends to end on a hopeful note."

"All's well that ends well," Sidney said.

"The object of art is to give life a shape," Danny said. "Shakespeare was a genius who understood the darkness in comedy and the comic in tragedy."

"You seem to have a familiarity with the Bard," Sidney said. "Perhaps something, you'll pardon my presumption, not necessarily associated with your populist career path."

"Do you really know me?" Danny asked.

Sidney raised an eyebrow. Maxie glanced around. The audience was on the edge of its collective seat.

"If Shakespeare were alive today, he'd be directing *The Sopranos*. He'd be doing Wells Fargo commercials to fund his projects." Danny frowned. "I had a phenomenally successful television sit-com. My son died. The show ended, my wife and I got divorced. The show was canceled. That's tragedy. I survived. I laugh. I enjoy life. That's comedy."

Sidney took a sip of water. "Tell us something about yourself we don't know."

Danny gazed out into the audience.

No, no, Maxie thought. Simultaneously, she felt a hand from the left and a hand from the right squeezing her arms. Artemis and Fisher gave her protective looks. She shrugged off their hands of betrayal. The last thing she needed was sympathy from Benedict Arnold One and Two.

Danny looked sly. "If I've learned anything in this long career, it's to keep a few secrets."

"Point taken," Sidney said. "Tell us about your next project."

"When I was a little boy, I found a copy of the collected works of Shakespeare at my grandparents' Catskills bungalow colony. I read the entire thing. I did serious drama in college. I was good, but I followed my older brother Perry to Las Vegas and took another path. Now, I'm both returning to my past and becoming someone new. I'm thinking of doing a Broadway production of *The Winter's Tale*, directed by Al Pacino."

"A play with a happy ending, the reunion of a man, his wronged wife and his cast-off daughter."

"A man who is almost destroyed by irrational suffering," Danny said.

"A story of redemption and forgiveness."

"Exactly," Danny said. "A story my life reflects."

"Can you elaborate?" Sidney asked.

"Let's talk about *Winter's Tale*."

"So we speak metaphorically to get at the truth. Leontes fell in love with his jealousy. I was not sold on his redemption." Sidney smiled. "On the other hand, I was never much a fan of Job either. I am leery of divine redemption handed down from a god, be it from the heavens or the writer's pen."

"Meaning divine redemption never happens?" Danny asked.

Sidney shrugged. "We've become jaded."

"More reason to celebrate the glory of the human spirit in a divine universe. Why is the heightened dramatics of tragedy valued over the same in comedy?"

Danny got up and limped across the stage, curled over with rage. "My entire being is crippled with a consuming obsession to be right." He faced the audience. "Who hasn't felt that? Who hasn't hurt those they love in order to prove a point?"

The audience performed a collective mesmerized nod.

"I understand in later years how deep creativity involves an obligation to illuminate suffering. Good comedy goes a long way to that end. Comedy is nothing to be ashamed of. We can not only relieve suffering, but foster growth of the mind, body and spirit through comic creativity."

Danny paused mid-stage. He began Leontes' last act repentant speech. "As she might have done/ So much to my good comfort."

He paused and launched into the rest of the passage with the thick Yiddish accent and broad gestures of a Borscht Belt comedian. The gimmick was weird, funny and poked the passage into the realm of kitschy numinosity.

Maxie loved the whole thing.

THE RECEPTION AFTER the show took place in the ballroom of The Saint Paul Hotel. Maxie had struggled for hours before the evening, but wound up bringing her camera. She felt better with her instrument. If nothing else, she could see the world through her lens. Illuminate suffering through creativity, according to Danny King.

Great. Now she had another voice to add to the inner choir. Danny King sound bites.

"Doing okay?" a voice asked. Artemis came up next to her.

"I'm not sure how to answer that," Maxie said. "I still don't trust you."

"Time heals all wounds," Artemis said.

"Everyone quoting Shakespeare. Like a Woody Allen movie."

"I vote for a remake of Annie Hall," Fisher said, joining them. "You'll be lesbian Woody and I'll be lesbian Diane Keaton. Only we don't break up, we live happily ever after."

"In your dreams," Maxie said.

"A girl has her fantasies." Fisher pointed to the other side of the room. An admiring throng surrounded Danny King. "Your father was engrossing."

"Which leads us to the idea that there may be more to him than we first imagined," Artemis said.

"I don't particularly want to be grouped in some collective 'we' having group epiphanies." Maxie watched her father at work.

"You laughed first," Fisher said. "Guffawed, actually, and you got everyone to join you. Believe me, it's hard to get Minnesotans to laugh loudly at smut. We'll titter, gasp, shiver with embarrassed delight, but we're reluctant to display raucous enjoyment at humor involving body parts."

"It was an impulse." Maxie glanced over to the open bar on the other side of the room.

Leonard and Honey appeared to be arguing with the bartender. Leonard waved an empty glass and Honey slapped the counter. Artemis and Fisher followed Maxie's gaze.

Trapper came up, holding a wine glass. He tracked everyone's gaze. "Someone is going to have to talk to them."

Before anyone could say more, Hunter came up. Everyone dialed into neutral, as if they'd been discussing the weather.

"Interesting show," Hunter said. "A little too deep for me. Still, it's cool about your old man. Mom says it's an amazing coincidence that you both wound up here."

"Amazing." Maxie glanced over at Fisher, who stared at her shoes. In the distance things seemed to be heating up between Honey, Leonard and the bartender. Maxie's radar flashed. "Think I'll mosey on over to the bar."

"I'll go with you," Fisher said.

"I should go," said Trapper.

"I'll go with you, bro," Hunter said.

"We'll all go," Artemis said.

Maxie and the Jacobs marched across the ballroom. The place was stultifying warm and over-bright. The group came to within five feet of the bar.

Leonard and Honey were hanging on one another. The bartender looked on the verge of a breakdown. Honey reached over the counter and grabbed a bottle of vodka. She poured herself and Leonard a refill. Glaring at the bartender, she reached into a plastic bin and plopped three olives in each of their glasses. She clinked glasses with Leonard and took a swallow.

"No lectures," Honey slurred when the family arrived. She punched Leonard's bicep. "You and I, we understand one another."

"Damn right," Leonard slurred back, but he shot a guilty look at Artemis.

The bartender leaned over the bar and addressed Artemis. "I'm sorry, Mrs. Jacobs. It's just, we have a limit, you know. Nothing personal."

"Thank you, Douglas. Nothing personal." She smiled coolly. "We have a lot to celebrate these days. Sometimes people get carried away. You know how it is. I'll put in a good word for you with your boss. You've always been a perfect gentleman."

"Yes, Ma'am," the bartender said, looking relieved.

Artemis made a sweeping gesture, like a goddess on a cliff collecting her disciples.

Leonard and Honey stepped back from the bar. As they did, Honey caught a high heel on a thread of carpet. Leonard tried to catch her. They crashed to the ground in a heap of alcohol-soaked clothing and flailing limbs. Maxie had held back, but now she couldn't help it. She took pictures.

Fisher tried to separate the two. Honey pulled her into the heap.

A growing crowd smirked at the shenanigans.

Hunter tried to pry everyone apart and got kicked in the groin. He yelped and stumbled backwards, clutching his parts. Trapper stood frozen next to his mother. Honey's dress threatened to rise up over her underwear, exposing her crotch. Maxie hid behind her camera, capturing it all.

Out of the crowd, Danny rushed up. He ran towards the pile. Just before he reached the heap, he tripped and landed on top.

The crowd laughed nervously at first, then with abandon.

Danny rolled off the heap and stood, took a bow, then helped Fisher up. She helped her father up. Danny reached for Honey, who shook him off. "Leave me alone."

"It's a stunt," Danny cried out. "Thank you, Jacobs family, for being such good sports. You've illustrated everything I was discussing tonight. Take a bow!"

Everyone in the Jacobs clan was on their feet by now except Honey, who was on her knees.

After a brief pause, the Jacobs family bowed a little uncertainly. Honey, after a moment's hesitation, whispered, "Goddammit," then bowed from her crouching position.

Danny joined them. Maxie snapped a shot.

"Thank you for enjoying the show," Danny said to the crowd. "Now, go and enjoy the rest of the evening."

Leonard weaved over to Danny and punched him in the shoulder in an absurd show of paper-thin machismo. "Thanks, man." He leaned over and vomited on the carpet.

"Let's get Dad out of here." Hunter pulled a tissue from a pocket and wiped Leonard's mouth. The rest of the family formed a barrier around them.

Artemis turned to Maxie. "Are you coming?"

"I'll stay for awhile," Maxie said.

Artemis, Fisher and Hunter led Leonard away. Honey trailed behind them.

"Your new family is on the edge of collapse, from what I can see," Danny said.

"I know." Maxie watched the departing group.

"I'm flying out in the morning. Keep me informed. I can help, whatever the problem."

"Apparently. You seem to go to great lengths."

"What did you think of the show?"

"You're a funny guy."

"Thanks for working the audience. Interested in becoming a father-daughter team?"

"I'm still standing here. Don't push your luck."

"You're right. I'm sorry."

"Don't apologize."

"You're right. I don't apologize."

"I told you," Maxie said. "You're a funny guy. Really funny."

"What about the rest? I'm realizing it's okay to be a smart guy. Screw 'em if they try to stereotype me."

"Okay, okay." Maxie fidgeted. "I'm trying to find a way to show some ideas I have. Like you said about comedy and tragedy. Some other side of human nature or both sides put together. I don't know what I'm talking about."

"I know what you mean," Danny said.

"You can't," Maxie said.

"Why not?"

"How can you know if I don't?"

"All you know is creative struggle, you were born into it. You need my help."

"You have some nerve."

"I can make anything happen for you."

"I won't be bribed."

"When you realize it's not bribery, you'll come around. I'm a patient man these days."

"Go away."

Danny turned to walk away.

"Let me think about it," she called after him.

As she was leaving the party, she spotted Danny surrounded by admirers. She left without saying good-bye.

MAXIE LET HERSELF in to the Jacobs' residence. She bent to stroke the Pinschers and tiptoed down the hallway and up the stairs.

"Maxie."

Fisher stood in the second-floor hall, wearing the kitschy calico kitty nightie, but it was unbuttoned at the chest, exposing the top of her breasts. "Can we talk?"

"There's nothing to talk about," Maxie said.

"How about whatever it is you're doing down in the basement? Show me."

"No."

"Let's go," Fisher said, taking her hand.

Maxie pulled her hand away, but led Fisher down the two flights of stairs to her studio. She opened the door.

"What the heck," Fisher said.

"It sucks," Maxie said.

Fisher stepped into the room and studied the project mounted on the wall.

Maxie had stopped destroying her images after her talk with Marcello. She'd gone to the museums and been inspired. She'd taken pictures and transformed them. She'd ripped them from their contexts, taking pieces of images and combined them into a single huge collage.

"It's unsettling and beautiful," Fisher said.

"It's all wrong," Maxie said. "The whole thing is making me sick."

Fisher was inches from the collage. She laughed and then shivered. "Look at photo of the lady with the costumed monkey on a leash. People can be so strange. I like the shot of you and the security guard."

"I asked a teenager to take that one with her phone."

Fisher approached her. She took Maxie in her arms.

"I love you," she said. "It started when we visited your mother and then Roy and June. Granted, I was colluding with Danny. But I was also falling in love with you."

Maxie tried to push away. "I shouldn't have shown you this."

"I wish I could say I'm sorry that I tricked you into coming here, but I'm not. Maxie, you are unique." She pulled Maxie in closer. "The more I'm around you, the more I appreciate you. You aren't my type, which scares me. We can be frightened together."

"I'm not frightened, just uninterested," Maxie said, but she didn't pull away. Instead she pressed against the open nightie, feeling Fisher's warm breasts against her own. Fisher actually had great breasts. Firm. She felt a current of arousal wash through her. Before things progressed, Maxie's panic alarm rang. She pushed Fisher away.

"Don't push me." Fisher stumbled backwards.

Maxie fled from the studio and charged up the two flights of stairs to her room. She locked the door, heart beating rapidly as though she was fleeing a killer. She went into the bathroom and found a sludgy out-of-date bottle of Nyquil in the cabinet. She rarely self-medicated and this was a pathetic, wimpy version, but she choked down two capfuls and crawled into bed fully clothed.

AT THREE IN the morning, barking dogs woke her up. She ran to the window but all she saw was a trail of lights disappearing at the end of the driveway. She descended the stairs and found Artemis and Fisher in the hallway.

"What happened?" Maxie asked.

"Leonard," Artemis said.

"Is he hurt?"

"Dad was arrested," Fisher said.

Chapter Twenty-six

Troubled Fathers

IN LESS THAN an hour, still before dawn, the entire Jacobs family gathered in the living room. Roger Rutledge arrived in a gray suit and a midnight blue tie. He was a thickly built man with bushy eyebrows. Although he looked calm and dapper, Maxie knew an upset lawyer when she saw one.

Rutledge glanced at Maxie. "Who is this? We have a family matter."

"She's a part of the family," Artemis said. "What happened?"

"I'm not going to beat around the bush," Rutledge said. "Leonard was arrested for soliciting sexual favors from a male undercover cop in Crosby Park." He paused to let the news sink in.

Maxie glanced around. Artemis wore her impenetrable look. Trapper appeared clinical, as though he'd just encountered an interesting glitch in a difficult toe surgery. Fisher held her mother's hand. Honey sat prim and uncharacteristically silent. Hunter appeared on the edge of a silent stroke. A vein bulged ominously on his forehead.

Maxie felt right at home. This was what she expected from life. Absurd tragedy.

Rutledge shook his head. "Periodically, St. Paul citizens get agitated about sex in public places. The cops go on an arrest spree. Don't get me wrong. I don't think people should be having sex everywhere. But the vice guys get overenthusiastic. I'll get this dismissed." He frowned.

"What's the problem?" Hunter asked. "He's innocent."

"There were reporters snooping around at the jail. They love this kind of dirt," Rutledge said.

"No dirt," Hunter said. "He didn't do anything."

"Leonard was minding his own business in a very private area of the Crosby parking lot, when an SUV pulled up alongside him," Rutledge said. "The young man at the wheel of the SUV gestured. Leonard thought the guy was in trouble and he went over to the driver's side. The good-looking young man invited Leonard inside the SUV." Rutledge paused.

"Go on," Artemis said. "We have to know."

"Once inside the vehicle, Leonard told the young man that he was feeling sad, had suffered a great loss recently. The young man suggested he could help relieve the sadness with a little comforting diversion. At this point, Leonard touched the man, who then pulled out his badge and arrested Leonard." Rutledge sighed.

"Roger," Artemis said. "Don't pull punches."

"The area touched was allegedly the crotch." Rutledge slapped his knee. "Leonard is the most devoted family man I know. I hate what the press is going to do to him."

"There's more, isn't there?" Artemis asked.

"In order to protect the undercover status of the operation Leonard was led from the parking lot and taken to the booking station in a van out of sight of the sting. He would have been ticketed at the station for indecent conduct and released, that's the usual procedure."

"He's been in some emotional pain," Artemis said.

"I understand," Rutledge said. "When he was being charged, he unfortunately, due to his heightened emotional state, got into a verbal altercation with one of the officers. The altercation escalated, we hope due to police harassment, but to be honest, probably not. These were good officers, to my knowledge. Leonard got physical. He was charged with resisting arrest and was transported to jail."

The Jacobs family, Maxie observed, seemed to have a genetic predisposition for unfortunate escalations with police.

"I could have gotten him out on bail." Rutledge brushed a dog hair off his expensive jacket.

"But?" Artemis prompted.

"He wouldn't come out." Rutledge shrugged. "We'll get him out after his court appearance. You don't have to come to the courthouse."

"Nonsense," Artemis said. "We'll be in the courtroom. Thank you, Roger."

Rutledge heaved himself from the couch. "If there's a family who can weather this crisis, it would be yours. Expect the press to be hounding you in the coming weeks, paparazzi scum included." He looked over to a corner of the room. "Oh, my god. That's a Kenneth Cole."

Lady Ruckus had dragged Rutledge's unattended briefcase to her doggie bed. All three Pinschers were chewing its soft leather. Maxie thought the sight was pretty funny. She glanced around the room. No one else seemed tickled.

WHEN MAXIE GOT back to her room, she dialed a familiar number.

"Maxie," Danny said.

Maxie felt a lump in her throat. "You said you could fix anything."

She explained the unfortunate and absurd situation, including the interlude provided by the Pinschers. Danny laughed at the doggie misbehavior. "Do we need to get Abe Kraptow involved?"

"All I know is that you've been boasting about how you always take care of things. Fix this, Danny."

"If you call me Dad."

"Screw you. Bribery."

"I don't think you understand how much I love you. This is epic love, Maxie. Like Leontes for his atrociously wronged daughter." He paused for effect. "At least I didn't try to send you to your death in a little basket."

Maxie laughed, despite herself. "Even my mother didn't think of that one." She felt like she was expanding like a balloon blowing up with emotional helium.

"Please help," she said. "Dad."

"No problem, kid."

She ended the call and pushed the conversation from her mind. She decided to go down to her studio and work on her new collage, a set of self-images cut up into pieces and attached to circles of hell. Pathetic, comical little Maxies chased by demons. When she was finished for the night, she stepped back. The work was garbage. She wasn't going in the right direction. She was going to quit. Give up. It was too hard.

She slammed the door and marched up to her room. By the time she'd crawled into her bed, she was thinking about how to start again.

BY THE TIME the Jacobs family arrived outside the Ramsey County Courthouse, a battalion of reporters and media vans crowded the sidewalks and curbs, including crews from the local media, CNN, Fox News, the entertainment stations and MSNBC.

Word had been intentionally leaked that Danny King would be there to support Leonard Jacobs, leading to allegations that he was an ex-lover of Leonard's, which made no sense, not that it mattered.

Danny's arrival created pandemonium. The plot was orchestrated brilliantly to manage a raging fire with controlled burning. Maxie felt a fleeting envy at the antics of the manic photographers, vying to get Danny's attention. In any case, she had to hand it to him. He was a guaranteed distraction, stealing the spotlight from the arriving shame-faced Jacobs family.

"Maxie," someone called. "What are you doing here?" It was Piper Trueblood, of all people. The sleazy journalist she'd taken up with during college.

"Where's your camera?" Piper asked.

Everything Piper said sounded oily. She was the cattiest chick on *TMZ*. Piper was a blandly pretty girl with a permanent insecure sneer etched on her face. But during their affair, she'd been great in bed and put Maxie on a pedestal. Maxie would have let the affair continue unusually long if Marcello hadn't come along and disrupted the whole thing.

"None of your business, Piper." Maxie was almost glad to see her old flame. Piper was easy. "What are you doing here? You're not good enough to be getting paid to travel."

"I was at my sister's wedding in Sleepy Eye. I got word of this so I bailed on the reception. No one likes me anyway. Marcello told us you were hiding after the shit hit the fan with Donna Street. I wouldn't call this hiding. Have anything good for a jilted heart-broken cast-off?"

The throngs pressed in on them. Maxie was in danger of losing the Jacobs family in the swelling crowd. "Nothing," she said and hustled towards the screening area of the courthouse to catch up with her cohorts.

"Maxie, you owe me," Piper called after her. "I still love you."

"Get a life," Maxie called back.

Piper was such a passive-aggressive doormat. If her former fling wasn't careful, she'd wind up in Sleepy Eye permanently, writing obituaries for the local weekly.

THE CROWDED COURTROOM held the usual mix of family, friends and spectators of unknown motivations. The press jammed into the back rows. Maxie knew exactly the kind of high they were on.

A stern-looking Asian judge came out from her chambers and took her place at the bench. Artemis leaned over and whispered to Maxie. "Lucy Chen. She's on the United Way executive board with me. She won't recuse herself. We know most of the judges in town. They'd all have to recuse."

After two defeated-looking defendants appeared in succession from the holding area and were given court dates, a buzz of anticipation ran through the room.

"This is no good," Artemis said.

A court deputy led Leonard into the room. He radiated shame. He drooped with remorse. He did not look out into the rows of hard wooden benches. He stared at his shuffling feet. He appeared stripped completely of self-respect.

The proceedings moved quickly. The charges were read. Rutledge spouted technicalities. The judge responded. A court date was set. Due to his status in the community and lack of prior convictions, Judge Chen released Leonard on his own recognizance. The event was over in less than fifteen minutes.

When the family emerged from the courthouse, Danny repeated his offensive line tactics. He and Rutledge blocked the press, taking questions, while Maxie and the others rushed off.

THAT EVENING, MAXIE and the Pinschers met Danny at the door. The dogs paused a nanosecond before jumping on Danny and licking his hands with joy and instantaneous love.

"Good sign," Maxie said. "They don't always like strangers."

"Animals like me. I once went out with a vet."

Maxie held up a hand. "Stop, that's too weird."

"What?"

"I don't want to hear anything about your sex life."

"Maxie, you're a paparazzo. You probably know more about my sex life than I do."

Maxie couldn't help laughing. "True. I tried, but you were impossible to avoid." She pointed down the hallway. "Speaking of sex lives and paparazzi, the Leonard Jacobs scandal has gone viral. It's a slow news week."

Danny nodded sympathetically. "We'll see what we can do. What a team. Father-daughter paparazzo-celebrity duo."

"Okay, okay," Maxie said. "I've noticed that you have a way of belaboring points."

MAXIE AND DANNY joined the Jacobs clan in the entertainment room.

Artemis and Leonard sat side by side on a loveseat. Honey and Trapper, Fisher and Hunter were squeezed together on the sectional. To a person, they looked drained and defeated. The last available seating was another loveseat, which put Maxie uncomfortably close to Danny and left no choice but to endure it.

For the next two hours, they suffered through commentary on five different stations until the repetition had numbed them. Secret sex lives, hidden closets. Leonard lit up the airwaves with trash talk presented as news. He was an international poster boy for sex-infused disgrace. Lawyers, sex experts, counselors, political candidates and nobodies voiced their opinions. Everyone had one. Not that Maxie was surprised. People loved sex scandals, especially when supposedly up-standing members of the community, priests or politicians were involved.

Finally, Danny spoke up.

"I have a genius fixer named Shelley Silver in Hollywood. I want her help," he said. "Fisher is also a fixer and so am I. Between the three of us, you have a publicity department worthy of MGM under Louis Mayer."

"Fixer? Like in fixing games?" Hunter asked. "My sister is a sports-agent, not a bookie."

"Experts in crisis management," Danny said. "They do miraculous damage control when people get themselves into trouble. Ask your sister. Probably half of what she does is either hide bad situations for her naughty clients or put a positive spin on things."

"Mother hen, motivational speaker, ego builder, story-spinner," Fisher said. "I see under their skin. They know I have their backs."

"I love fixers," Maxie chimed in.

"Does that mean you love me?" Fisher asked.

Maxie flushed. "I can't believe you said that."

Fisher tapped her chest, indicating a swollen heart. "I think my vulnerability index is through the roof. I'm off-balance."

"In front of your family," Maxie added.

"I can't believe you think we can't see something's up with you two," Honey said.

"Leave Maxie and Fisher alone," Artemis said. "They'll work it out. Let's get back to the subject at hand. Danny, tell us what to do."

"You're going to appear on selected talk shows with sympathetic hosts. Shelley Silver and I will take care of that end. If we do this right, you'll come out better than you were before. Look at Martha Stewart."

"I hate phony interviews where people look so obviously coached," Artemis said.

"Those people weren't coached by me." Danny smiled and then grew serious. "You have critical reason to interpret the truth at this moment. I know you love Leonard and respect him."

"Of course," Artemis said.

"You accept him for what he is," Danny said.

Artemis blushed.

Danny glanced around the room. "The same is true for the rest of you."

Everyone nodded except Hunter, who threw his hands up in the air. "Over-thinking things to death. I don't know what you're hinting at."

Could Hunter be that clueless? Maxie wondered. She realized she was flirting in dangerous emotional territory concerning denial, however. Girls in ice houses avoid furnaces.

"You're playing a role," Danny said. "Don't take any of it of personally. Hunter is right. Don't over-think it. Family solidity is your platform. Tomorrow is your entry into the world of celebrity."

With that, he stood. "Get some rest, you'll need it. We begin rehearsals tomorrow." He exited stage door right.

"Your father is something else," Honey said. "Maybe I should beg for help with my gallery."

"Let's just see," Maxie said.

FISHER CAUGHT UP to Maxie outside Maxie's room. She looked like an emotional drunk. "Are you ready for all of this?"

"Game on," Maxie said, attempting to slip into her room.

Fisher reached for the doorknob and held the door shut. "This isn't a game, Maxie."

"It was when I was the dysfunctional one."

"You're right. I think we're soul mates. We thrive on crisis."

"Try to keep the delusional romanticism to yourself." Maxie knew she sounded mean. Fisher ought to know that the worst way to pursue Maxie was to pursue her.

Someone came down the hall.

"Am I interrupting something?" Artemis asked.

"Maxie is refusing my advances. I've been blind-sided by a puzzling and profound love for her and she's pushing me away."

"I can't believe you're saying that," Maxie said. "You keep blabbing."

"I'm as shocked as you are," Fisher said. "Don't you have feelings for me?"

"No. Maybe. No."

"Your ambivalence speaks louder than your words. Love conquers all."

"Your cliché speaks louder than your intelligence."

Artemis wagged a finger at them. "My lost children. Go to bed. We'll find our way to a better life."

Maxie wanted to believe her. Artemis appeared to be a certifiable mother archetype. Their force was supposed to be irresistible, like the waxing and waning of the moon.

LEONARD AND HONEY had each had three martinis by the time Danny arrived the next evening. No one in the Jacobs family had the energy to object to their descent from sobriety. They all gathered in the entertainment room. A casual picnic dinner had been set out on folding trays, but no one touched it. Even the Pinschers seemed unsettled, twitching on their pet pillows and licking their paws. Danny blew in like publicity Moses preparing to part the Red Sea of world perception.

"We have you on *Good Morning America*, a spot with Oprah and a special segment with Diane Sawyer, a personal friend of mine." He pointed to the couch. "Hunter, Fisher, Trapper and Artemis, you'll sit together."

"Where will I sit?" Leonard asked.

Danny knelt beside him. "You won't," he said. "It's best if you keep a low profile. Actually, no profile."

Leonard closed his eyes and leaned back. "Of course. I've caused enough trouble."

"You and I will be on the sidelines, Leonard," Honey said, rising unsteadily and holding out her hand. When Leonard attempted to get up, they both tumbled back onto the cushions.

"Oh, my god," Fisher said. "This is humiliating."

"That's it," Hunter said. "No more for you guys tonight."

Leonard and Honey moved from the couch. The interviewees got settled.

"The dogs," Danny said.

"C'mon, Lady. Come here, kids," Trapper called.

The Pinschers hurled themselves onto the available laps, barking with joy, then settled down with endearing photogenic calm. Maxie grinned. Hooray for dogs. They knew how to put on a heartstrings show.

Danny gave the couch occupants their scripts. Maxie held out a hand. Danny looked puzzled.

"I do a great Diane Sawyer. Let me ask the questions."

Maxie pulled up a chair next to the couch. She took a breath. She glanced down at the script and channeled. She gave the introductions. When she finished, she paused.

A moment of silence ensued followed by an appreciative burst of laughter from everyone in the room.

"Who knew you were such a good mimic?" Artemis asked.

"What do you think I've been doing my whole life?" Maxie replied.

THE NEXT WEEK consisted of brilliantly orchestrated interviews. Leonard was not gay, although the family would fully support him even if he were. Yes, they fully supported gay rights, yet understood that there were public places in which sexual activity was inappropriate. Blah, blah, blah.

The Jacobs family had reality show potential, Maxie observed. They appeared to be sincere, supportive and overall good citizens.

By the end of the week, an avalanche of public sympathy rolled in. Supportive letters to the editor in the *Star Tribune* and *Pioneer Press* overwhelmed the few condemnations from right-wing groups. Social media sites buzzed with positivity. Adoring employees greeted Leonard and Hunter at the Home Sole corporate office. Trapper repaired feet surrounded by sympathetic healthcare co-workers. Artemis organized a cystic fibrosis charity half-marathon with a large force of infatuated volunteers.

Honey, however, disappeared. She claimed to be inescapably distracted by work, but Maxie wondered if she was avoiding the limelight. She was still the daughter of conservative religious parents, not to mention extraordinarily ambitious. Maxie didn't blame her. Not everyone could be a publicity warrior.

On the other hand, Danny King was everywhere. He came to dinner every night. He followed the conversational leads provided by the Jacobs family, including shoe sales, ankle surgeries and the roller coaster antics of the Minnesota Twins. He displayed a surprising knowledge of the Vikings and their latest head coach. He traded recipes with Fiona, the new chef.

Maxie remained quiet about her days. She left in the mornings and didn't return until late afternoon. She disappeared into the basement studio until dinner. She developed a routine.

First, she roamed the streets, the pathways around the lakes, anywhere she could get to on foot or public transportation, taking pictures. Later, she went to the Minneapolis Institute of the Arts and the

Walker. She went from gallery to gallery. When she found a piece that resonated, she sat before it and stared, sometimes for as much as an hour. She studied works that seemed to transcend time. She was especially drawn to the Asian scrolls, the medieval tapestries, and the illuminated books, anything that told a story. She wanted to do work that told a story, but what story?

When she felt like her entire being was awash, she returned to the streets and took more pictures. She didn't think. She was in a spell and she was afraid to break it.

ON THE FIFTH day, Danny called her early in the morning. "Maxie, what are you doing today?"

"I'm busy."

"Want company?"

"No."

"Please?"

"That word is probably the most insidious form of coercion in human communication besides thank you."

"You are probably one of the cleverest daughters around."

"Everything you say sounds like a situation comedy."

"That's how I express my world. Kid, I'm burnt out. I can't take any more publicity crap for at least a day. You more than anyone should understand."

Maxie sighed. "Okay. But no heavy discussions and can it with the love stuff."

AT ELEVEN-FIFTEEN A.M., Danny was exactly where she'd told him to be, in the café section of the MIA museum. There was a package on the table. She glanced at it suspiciously.

"Don't say it," he said.

"Bribery," she said anyway, but reached for the large book. It was a collection of up-and-coming women artists. It smelled nice, like new books did, full of promise.

"Read the inscription," Danny said.

Maxie opened to the first page. "To The Comedian's Daughter, in her artistic journey. With love, Dad."

"Thank you," she said, hoping to avoid further discussion.

"Thank you, Dad?"

"You always push it." Maxie stood. "C'mon."

For the next two hours, Maxie led Danny to a selection of her favorite pieces.

They did the tapestries and the Asian scrolls. As for moderns, they sat together in front of a mural-sized Larry Rivers, *The Studio*, and an equally huge piece by Kehinde Wiley depicting two black men in heroic death poses.

"One is abstract, the other is hyper-real," Maxie said. "I want to use photography in unique ways. I don't know which way to go."

"Try both," Danny said. "Try everything."

"Is there enough time to do everything?"

Danny laughed. "Where's the nearest Picasso?"

They stood for a long time in front of a Picasso painting called *Woman by the Sea*.

"He was moving out of cubism," Maxie said. "Into the classical period. He kept changing his whole artistic life. It's amazing."

"Look at how out of proportion she is, bulky body and small head," Danny said. He was wearing his celebrity-in-disguise outfit—beret, scarf and dark glasses, which he lifted to see the artworks they studied—but a middle-aged couple stared at him looking like they were trying to place him.

"He was one of the greatest geniuses of all time," Maxie said. "But he was not a good man."

"I think about this all the time," Danny said. "How do you separate the work from the artist? I do know one thing, however. What a miracle and joy if a person could bring great art into the world and have their life be as artful?"

"Speaking of genius and the sea," she said, "Judy is spending her damaged hours under the sea with SpongeBob."

"I love—hate SpongeBob," Danny said. "Violent, funny and mythical. Like your mother."

"Profound," Maxie said. "See how you feel after one more piece."

"I have a feeling," Danny said.

Maxie led them back into the hall on the third floor.

"You don't have to do this," Danny said.

"Just come with me."

A semi-transparent black curtain shielded the entrance of a small room. A sign warned of graphic violence and sexual content. "No kidding," Maxie said.

They entered the cramped darkened space. The only light came from a television mounted to a black table. A black bench barely big enough for two faced the screen.

Maxie pressed a black button on the table and the screen lit up.

Judy Oyster appeared dressed in a flowing lacy gown that jarred with her tattoos, hacked bleached hair and stubby toed dirty feet. She banged her head against a wall. Maxie forced herself to watch. Judy whipped herself with a leather belt.

"I was fourteen years old," Maxie said. "I was at that opening. One year before her last performance."

"It wasn't right," Danny said. "I'm so sorry."

"Shut up. You don't deserve to comment."

Danny moaned.

"You know how I got through it? Bobby Shepherd. My stepfather."

"He never should have allowed you to be there. I should have been there for you."

"Bobby was there for me."

"Bobby couldn't handle it."

"Bobby was an addict. What's your excuse?"

"I don't have any excuses."

"Can you give me one good reason to trust you?"

"Listen to this joke," Danny said.

"A woman bought a parrot for a pet. All the bird did was treat her badly. It insulted her and tried to bite her arm. One day she got fed up, opened the freezer door and threw him in. From inside, the parrot screeched for about 5 seconds and then it stopped. The woman thought, 'Oh no, I killed it!' She opened the door and the parrot glared at her. She picked it up and cradled it. Then the parrot said: 'I'm very sorry. From now on, I will be a respectful, obedient parrot.' 'Well, okay,' she said. 'Apology accepted.' The parrot said 'Thank you.' Then he said, 'Can I ask you something?' She said, 'What?' The parrot looked back into the freezer and asked, 'What did the chicken do?'"

Maxie laughed. "Good joke. See you tonight."

DANNY DIDN'T SHOW up for dinner that night. Screw him.

What did the chicken do? Flew the coop.

At the dinner table, the family rhapsodized about their appearance on Katie Couric's show. She'd been brought to tears by their story. Maxie let them do an almost line-by-line reconstruction of their performance. She'd seen it before. They had fallen in love with the reconstructed version of themselves. She refrained from bursting their love bubble with insider knowledge about Katie's darker side or the eventual fate of invented selves.

Something inside her was shifting, but she was smart enough to know that lecturing the family wouldn't help her figure out what was going on—and it wouldn't help them either.

She was leaving the dinner table when Danny called on her cell. She went out the foyer and answered.

"I'm going to New York tomorrow to negotiate a contract for *Winter's Tale*."

"Taking up again with that girl who plays your daughter?"

"Tell me where you got that piece of nonsense."

"Bruce Fein at *People Weekly*."

"Believing reports from Bruce Fein? I'm ashamed of you."

Maxie laughed. "Bulls-eye. Why didn't you come to dinner?"

"I thought you might need a break from me. I didn't want to push for a change."

"I wanted to show you something."

"I'll get a cab."

"Don't bother."

"Be right there."

Maxie imagined him dancing from the room, clicking his heels together, at her admission of need.

DANNY ARRIVED QUICKLY. As soon as he was inside, she led him to the studio. She threw open the door, heart beating rapidly.

He proceeded from one piece to another, stopped and studied each piece of work. He was quiet and absorbed. Maxie fidgeted. After he inspected the last one, Danny hugged her. "I've never seen anything like these. There's something old, medieval almost. Grotesquely humorous, Bosch-like, but the level of abstraction is completely modern and unique. I see the Chinese scroll influence. Not to mention Picasso."

Danny walked over to the last piece he'd studied for the longest period of time. "What do you need?"

"I need a very large-format printer. Everything wants to get bigger. I want to print them myself." She shivered.

Danny strode to the desk and picked up pen and paper. "Write the make and model down." He hesitated. "Do I ship it here or California?"

"California. I can't stay here anymore."

"You created from the heart, Maxie, and you didn't die."

"Just send me the printer."

Chapter Twenty-seven

The Parrot and the Chicken

THE NEXT DAY, Maxie returned to the Jacobs residence after a short and depressing photo outing. The world looked uninteresting to her. The clouds in the sky were postcard clouds, the skaters and strollers and cyclists and old people on benches were stereotypical images. Absolutely nothing made a statement that was original in any way. She felt antsy and vaguely premonitory. She decided to give up and go home.

Fiona was in the kitchen singing the libretto from *Madam Butterfly* to Lady Rowdy, Ruckus and Racket. Unlike Charles, Fiona loved the Pinschers. She baked them organic chicken liver biscuits, which she was feeding them from a dish on the center island. A plate of molasses oatmeal raisin cookies for people also graced the counter.

"Where's everyone?" Maxie asked.

Fiona looked troubled. "They're doing Dr. Steve."

"Whose big idea was that? Not Danny, he knows better."

Dr. Steve was a passive-aggressive loose cannon given to planting booby traps for his guests. Only attention-craving fools went on *Whistle Blow Central With Dr. Steve.* His show was shot in Minneapolis, but it was syndicated nationally so the whole country could feast on human pathos.

"Dr. Steve called Hunter and begged him to come on the show. He promised to plug the shoe business," Fiona said. "They play golf together. I guess Hunter thinks that's a basis for trust. The show is just coming on. I can't watch."

"Where's Leonard?" Maxie asked, stomach tightening.

"Ouch," Fiona cried. She held up her left pinkie. She'd cut it with her paring knife. "I never do that. He went for a drive to Red Feather to visit the shoe museum." Fiona applied a little bandage to her finger. "Said he needed to get away."

"Was he drinking?"

"A little glass of wine. I don't think he was drunk. He said he'd be back by dinner."

"For Pete's sake."

Maxie grabbed some people cookies, proceeded to the entertainment room, and switched on the television. Dr. Steve lit up the screen. As soon as his phony face appeared, Maxie felt sick. Even paparazzi thought Dr. Steve was psycho.

In the first portion of the show, Dr. Steve was gently challenging. The Jacobs held their own with well-rehearsed sincerity. Maxie ate five cookies. A pit had developed in her stomach that she needed to fill. The entire family looked eager and trusting. It broke her heart to look at their deluded faces.

Just before the commercial break, Dr. Steve smiled into the camera with a conspiratorial expression. "In our next segment, I have a surprise for our guests." Maxie lost her appetite. She brushed crumbs from her lap and sank deeper into the cushions.

The show returned with the host standing among the audience. "What do you think?" Dr. Steve asked the audience, grinning with naughty pleasure.

A young man in a white shirt and black tie glared at the family. "Homosexuality is a sin against God. Hidden homosexuality in married people is both a sin and a lie. These people will burn in eternal hell." His cohorts applauded. A tag line on the screen identified them as a youth anti-homosexuality group.

A chorus of boos rang out from a row of infuriated young men and women fifty feet away. A tag line on the screen identified them as a radical gender rights group.

Dr. Steve slithered over to the group, who spoke in turn, condemning homophobia. A butch girl in a white shirt and black tie, who looked remarkably like the bible-banger boy across the aisle, pointed an angry finger at the Jacobs family. "Hidden homosexuality in married people is cowardice. You people are actually helping idiots sell ignorance."

Accusations flew, with Dr. Steve egging on the action.

The worst insults targeted the Jacobs family, who sat on the stage, looking like they were trying to maintain the roles Danny had taught them. To Maxie's practiced eyes, they were wounded deer running from the hunter.

By the end of the segment, when it seemed like it couldn't get any worse, Dr. Steve hinted at yet another angle after the commercial break.

MAXIE HALF-EXPECTED THE Jacobs family to have jumped ship when the show returned, but they sat like fools in their little row sporting dying doe eyes.

The host brought out a trio of stiff-postured, gorgeous law enforcement warriors to explain the necessity of sting operations when scum masking as upstanding members of society threatened public safety.

Next, Dr. Steve showed clips of behavioral experts who nattered on about the pathologies of closeted men who cheat on their wives with ugly public sex. The Jacobs family wilted for the entire world to see.

Maxie was especially disappointed in Fisher. She looked bloodless and weak, like the sharks to which she claimed to be impervious had attacked her.

Dr. Steve closed the show with a pompous rant about closets, and the deep-freeze of sexual secrecy. Maxie would have liked to wring his neck and throw *him* into a deep-freeze.

NO ONE HAD an appetite for dinner. Leonard arrived during the appetizers, looking flushed but not inebriated, although he gulped at a large martini as soon as he sat down.

The group filled him in on the afternoon's fiasco. They made a play at eating the lovely meal that Fiona had prepared. When Maxie initiated a rant against Dr. Steve, Artemis held up a hand. "We came off pretty good, considering we were tricked."

"I hope he goes to hell," Honey said. "Although, technically speaking, Jews don't believe in hell. Hell, I don't believe in hell. Maybe we should just set him on fire ourselves."

A clattering of glass interrupted her tirade. Leonard had knocked over his third drink. He looked around defensively. "I need another one."

"You've had enough, Dad," Fisher said.

"Fiona," Leonard called. "Another round. Honey, will you join me?"

Honey looked stricken. "For once, I think I'll pass."

Artemis gave Fiona a silent look. The chef slipped out of the room without fulfilling any liquor demands.

Leonard stood unsteadily. "I'll get it myself."

"Dad's messed up about all this publicity," Hunter said.

"Don't talk like I'm not in the room," Leonard said.

Honey stood. "On second thought, I think I will get us both a drink."

She ran from the room. Leonard slumped back into his chair.

"Asparagus, anyone?" Artemis asked.

Maxie dumped a few spears on her plate to accompany the rest of her untouched food. Honey returned, sloshing two large martinis. She almost spilled Leonard's refill into his lap. They both giggled. Honey held up her glass. "Let's toast our blessings, anyway. For one, Dr. Asshole didn't dredge up Ned Burdock."

In the silence that followed, Maxie knew she was being watched. Did they think she was stupid? Still, she wasn't going to get into anything Ned Burdock-related, not with the layers of weirdness surrounding the man labeled Leonard's best friend. She turned to Hunter. "Even the paparazzi think Dr. Steve is a moron. This'll blow over."

"He's got a right to grieve his best friend. Screw anyone who reads smut into that," Hunter said. "Dad needs rest. He'll feel better when he's back at work. We'll all feel better as we go back to normal."

Maxie listened to Hunter's laundry list of denial with pity.

IN THE MIDDLE of the night, Maxie woke up to sirens.

By the time she got downstairs, paramedics knelt over Leonard, who was splayed out at the bottom of the stairs. He batted at the medics.

"Leave me alone." He attempted to sit up and moaned.

The paramedics probed at his hip. He started crying, rubbing his eyes with his fists.

"Oh my god, oh my god," he slurred. "I'm so sorry." The paramedics hoisted him on a gurney and wheeled him to the waiting ambulance.

"I'll go with him. Meet me at the hospital." Artemis followed the paramedics to the ambulance and climbed into the back. The van took off down the driveway, sirens wailing.

Maxie and Fisher drove in Artemis's Mercedes. Fisher called Trapper and directed him to Fairview Hospital. She hung up and stared at the road ahead, driving just above the speed limit.

"What about Hunter?" Maxie asked.

Fisher tightened her shoulders. "My brother can't tolerate hospitals. It's okay. Dad isn't dying."

IN THE WAITING area, they sat an hour without any word about Leonard. It was a busy night with two shootings, a large house fire and a three-car accident. Although Maxie didn't ask, Artemis took it upon herself to repeat Fisher's explanation of Hunter's absence.

"Hunter spent so much time recuperating from his amputation, he has an intolerance of hospitals. It's all right. He makes up in other ways."

After what seemed like an eternity, an intern in blue scrubs led them to a room with four beds occupied by patients in varying degrees of distress. Everyone crowded by Leonard's bed, hidden from the rest by drapery.

"His hip is badly bruised, but no broken bones." The intern consulted a chart. "His blood alcohol level should be back to normal by morning."

"I slipped on a snag on that damned carpet," Leonard said. "I want to go home. I'm fine."

Maxie hated hospitals. Emergency rooms were bad, followed by ICU. Brain damage units were the worst. She didn't blame Hunter for weaseling out of the visit.

"The doctor wants you to stay overnight for observation," Artemis said. "We arranged for a private room. You'll be very comfortable."

Leonard looked like he was going to put up a fight, but gave up after studying his wife's face.

On the way down the hall, Artemis said, "Someone needs to call Hunter."

"Not me," Fisher said.

"I'm probably to blame for this," Honey said. "But I'm not calling.

He doesn't like my so-called intrusions."

"We're all to blame for this," Trapper said. "I'll call."

MAXIE'S PHONE RANG while she, Artemis and Fisher were in the car headed home.

"It's my father," she announced.

She was aware of two startling things. First, calling Danny her father. Second, not letting his call roll to voice mail.

"Hello." She nodded, listened and hung up. "Danny is at the airport. He said good-bye."

She expected Fisher or Artemis to probe about her feelings regarding his departure and was disappointed by their silence.

IN THE MORNING, Maxie returned to the hospital with Fisher and Artemis. The first floor had a waiting area that looked like a Hilton hotel lobby, complete with leather couches, a fireplace and an espresso cart. Trapper and Honey waited for them, each clutching a huge coffee.

"Is it all arranged?" Artemis asked.

"Yes. The rest is up to Dad."

Everyone nodded with agreement except Maxie, who didn't have a clue as to what was going on. No point in pursuing it, she'd find out soon enough.

LEONARD'S PRIVATE ROOM was located on the third floor. The unit was decorated in Hilton resort colors. A nurse in a pastel smock directed them to Leonard's room. The supervising nurse handed them a customer satisfaction survey to be filled out before they left.

Leonard's door stood open. A huge basket of chocolate truffles and candied fruits sat on the nightstand next to the bed. "It's from Hunter," Leonard announced. "Can't make it here, he's very busy running the business without me."

When no one spoke, he smiled forlornly. "My hip isn't why you made me stay here."

"You have a problem, Dad," Fisher said.

"I've had a rough patch."

As Leonard spoke, a man entered the room. He wasn't wearing a white coat or carrying a stethoscope, but he emanated doctor vibes.

"This is Dr. Savage," Trapper said. "He's an anesthesiologist. I work with him all the time. He's the best."

"I don't need an anesthesiologist," Leonard said.

How do you like that? Maxie thought. An intervention. She knew all about blind-siding addicts. At least ten celebrities she knew had been emotionally tackled recently.

Dr. Savage stepped up to the bed. He had a weary face, creased in the way of men who'd been around the block a few times. "I'm Martin. I'm an alcoholic. I understand you had a terrible loss just recently."

Leonard shivered. "Someone I loved dearly passed away too soon. No one will listen. I want to be strong, but I can't. However, I don't need you."

"The mourning process is different for everyone," Martin said. He waved around the room. "Your family is mourning, too. They're mourning the loss of their father as a functioning member of the family."

"We miss you, Dad," Trapper said. "You've always been our go-to guy."

"You are the best husband a woman could have," Artemis said.

Leonard sobbed.

A nurse peeked in. Artemis waved her away.

"You're suffering," Martin said. "Your family is suffering. They're terrified they're going to lose you."

Leonard clutched his head in his hands.

"They want the father they remember, the one who cared for them through thick and thin," Martin said. "But you have to go through the anger, the pain, and facing the addiction to become that man again."

Leonard glanced around. "Am I hurting you that badly?"

No one spoke.

He turned to Martin. "What next?"

"I'll make some calls," Martin said.

By the end of the day, Leonard was accepted at the world-renowned Pleasanton Center, fifty miles north of the Twin Cities. Martin suggested that Leonard stay in the hospital until morning to avoid any last minute change of heart.

AT A SUBDUED dinner that night, prepared by a silent Fiona, Artemis handed out copies of the Pleasanton Center brochure. She read the brochure aloud, cover to cover, every word, which didn't do much for anyone's appetite.

Two-thirds of the way through the main course, Hunter barged in, looking officious and impatient. He questioned the choice of Pleasanton Center, which was unbelievably expensive, too far away, and overkill as far as he was concerned.

"There are local places," he said. "Dad just needs a tune-up, not an entire overhaul. What about out-patient?"

"Where were you when this was all discussed?" Honey asked. "If you'd been in on it, you'd know why we chose Pleasanton."

"Honey, I'm going to be frank," Hunter said. "First, your role in Dad's drinking is on the table, or at least it should be. Second, you are not immediate family, let's be honest."

Maxie did not expect Honey to cave in, but she fell with the first punch, dropping her gaze and hunching down in defeat.

It was Fisher's turn. "I suppose you'll be the one who drives him up, then," she said to Hunter. "Since you couldn't make it to anything else."

Hunter blanched.

"Of course he won't drive Leonard," Artemis said. "I'm bringing him. I'm going to stay up there in a motel a couple of nights and make sure he's settled in." She picked up the brochure. "There are meetings for the spouses that I can attend." She reread aloud the entire section on spouse opportunities.

By this time, Fiona had crept back into the room, attempting not to look horrified at her food going to waste. She picked up plates and didn't offer dessert.

"Fiona, where's that apple pie? C'mon, folks, let's eat a piece of pie in Dad's honor," Hunter said.

Greeted with silence, he pumped his fist. "Eat pie, for god's sake. The world isn't falling apart. Even if it was, we'd be the last family standing."

Everyone, including Maxie, ate pie.

AS SHE WAS about to curl into bed, someone knocked. When Maxie opened the door, Artemis flung herself into Maxie's arms. She tentatively stroked Artemis's back. Artemis lifted her head. "Please don't judge us," she said.

"I'm about the last person on the entire planet to judge anyone." A tight knot formed in Maxie's throat.

"I thought he'd pass through his grief for Ned, but his behavior is getting worse." Artemis frowned. "You're leaving us, aren't you?"

"I'll be gone before you return from Pleasanton."

"You'll be back," Artemis said. She tightened her hug.

"Don't count on it," Maxie said. "I'm not reliable."

"Sometimes people who are changing are the last ones to see what's happening."

Artemis released Maxie, but Maxie didn't feel released.

ARTEMIS WAS GONE hardly five minutes when another knock sounded.

"Now what?" Maxie stomped from her bed to the door and flung it open. She gasped.

A female Sneakers the Clown leered at her. The inflatable clown sported a fuzzy green plastic perm, long painted eyelashes and blood-red lips.

Fisher stepped into view. "Mrs. Sneakers is a collector's item. They produced a few hundred, but consumers freaked out over hitting a female, even if it was a punching bag. Can we come in? We wanted to say good-bye."

"You're driving me to the airport in the morning, remember?"

Fisher looked away.

"You're not driving me to the airport?"

"I have something I want to say."

"More declarations of love?"

"You know you're interested. Let me in."

Maxie stood her ground. "Mrs. Sneakers can come in."

"She won't without me."

Maxie stepped back from the threshold.

"Let's sit on the bed," Fisher said.

"Are you kidding me?"

"Humor me. You're leaving anyway."

Maxie grabbed Mrs. Sneakers and dragged her next to Mr. Sneakers.

Fisher went to the bed and sat on the edge.

What the hell? Maxie thought.

She plunked next to Fisher on the mattress. Fisher placed her hand on Maxie's thigh.

Maxie giggled. "The Sneakers are watching."

"You're not being very romantic."

"I only do that when I'm seducing someone."

"Aren't you attracted to me, Maxie?" Fisher stroked the exposed skin on Maxie's thigh. Maxie shivered and let the pleasure spread. Fisher had a nice touch. Well-practiced. Assertive but not aggressive. Teasing, intuitive. Nice. Sexy.

She'd had sex for many reasons in her life, including distraction from a bad day. The last few days more than qualified in that category.

She allowed Fisher to lower her down to a supine position. Fisher ran her hands along Maxie's torso. She slowly unbuttoned Maxie's shirt. She placed her ear on Maxie's bare chest and listened to her heartbeat. Meanwhile, her hands did a slow caressing exploration of Maxie's thighs and belly.

When Fisher licked a nipple, Maxie moaned. She closed her eyes and called up the gyrating pole dancer in the Zorro mask. Fisher's caressing stopped.

She opened her eyes. Fisher watched her. "Look at me."

"I have to keep my eyes closed."

"Look in my eyes. See me."

Maxie's eyelids fluttered, struggling to shut. Damn Fisher. Why couldn't she just let Maxie do it her way?

"Keep them open. Look at me."

"No."

"Maxie, give me a chance. Please. Look at me."

Fisher's face was so close that Maxie could smell her warm, sweet breath. Her eyelids seemed to be taking on a life of their own, struggling to open.

Feeling defiant, she looked in Fisher's eyes.

What she saw was love, although the word didn't begin to encompass this thing that struck her from head to toe, as Fisher stroked her rhythmically, persistently. Every nerve fiber in her body was firing.

"Who am I?" Fisher asked.

"Fisher." The name came out unintelligible.

Fisher's fingers reached into her, gently circling. "C'mon," she urged. "Keep those eyes open. Look at me."

Maxie kept looking into Fisher's eyes. Without warning, Maxie's back arched and she shuddered in a series of convulsions. "*Fisher*," she said. "Fisher, Fisher, Fisher." Before the last wave, she wrapped her arms around Fisher and pressed against her.

"Maxie, I saw you. Deep inside you. You saw me."

"No more talk," Maxie said. "Just shut up and hold me. I can barely handle this."

Chapter Twenty-eight

Another Flight

FISHER WAS NOT in bed with her when Maxie woke in the morning.

Of course not, what did she expect?

Fisher would drive her to the airport, acting distant and polite, like a good girl, ignoring the intensity of what they'd experienced. Worse, she'd find Fisher downstairs in the kitchen helping Fiona make breakfast, bursting with post-coital glow and absurd optimism. Either way was messed up.

Maxie decided she was actually quite angry with Fisher. What right did she have, piercing into Maxie's soul? Mr. and Mrs. Sneakers smirked at her as she dressed. She marched over and socked Mr. Sneakers. By the time she stomped down the hallway, she was ready to punch Fisher.

At the bottom of the stairs the Pinschers yapped with unconditional love. Something Fisher had promised in the night, but couldn't deliver. It wasn't part of the human condition and even if it was—which it wasn't—Fisher was not a good candidate. The Pinschers pranced into the dining room. Honey sat at the table with Fiona, who jumped up when Maxie entered.

"I have to check my buns." Fiona fled the room.

"I wouldn't mind checking her buns," Maxie commented with stupid bravado.

"No kidding," Honey said. "On an intellectual level, of course."

"Where is everyone?" Maxie asked. She meant Fisher.

"Inescapable commitments. I'm driving you to the airport."

What kind of inescapable commitments could Fisher have in Minnesota? A shoe convention? It didn't matter. Good riddance to Fisher and to the Jacobs family. She was one airplane trip away from self-sufficiency.

Maxie had just climbed into Honey's SUV when her phone rang. She glanced down at the number. The phone rang until the call dropped into voice mail.

"Was that Fisher?" Honey asked.

"Yes."

"Why didn't you answer it?"

"I don't want to say good-bye." She tried to sound nonchalant, but her voice quavered. She hoped Honey didn't notice.

Honey looked flustered. "It might be important."

They had merged onto the highway leading to the airport and

escape from Minnesota, land of false promises. Honey looked like she was going to burst.

"You might as well tell me," Maxie said.

Honey slapped the steering wheel. "They don't have a clue what they're getting into. Some artists will do anything to get ahead." She glanced at Maxie. "I think you understand. About doing anything to get ahead, I mean."

"Been there, done that."

"Artists can be fragile. Not Mallory Doyle. She has a sensitive side, but so did Hitler. He was a pretty good painter and loved animals."

Maxie stared out the window, observing a black crow scavenging a bloated porcupine carcass on the side of the road. Guts spilled on the asphalt. The crow pecked at them, a tableau of gory opportunism. Relevant symbols were populating the landscape. "That's pretty offensive, comparing Mallory to Hitler."

"My parents are Orthodox Jews. I like to make offensive remarks about Jewish topics." Honey sighed. "I hate families."

They were almost to the terminal. In a very short time, she'd be on the freedom plane.

Honey steered up the departures ramp and double-parked alongside a mini-van disgorging small, energetic Girl Scouts while a troop leader shouted harried commands. Maxie thought of Girl Scout Fisher and her promise of love, but she pushed the thought back into its memory folder. The driver in the car behind them honked.

"Screw you," Honey shouted to the driver. She stuck her arm out the window and gave the driver the finger. "Trapper, Hunter and Fisher drove up to Ishpeming to confront Mallory."

"What?" Maxie said.

"She's blackmailing us."

"*Blackmailing*? That's why she's living in the cabin?"

An airport security cop tapped on the window. "Move on, ladies."

Honey gunned the engine and swerved into the congested maze of exiting lanes, leaving the startled officer shaking his fist at them. She pulled into the short-term parking garage and took the first vacant spot.

The air smelled of toxic fumes. The dank, shadowy parking garage was horror movie sinister. Although Honey didn't strike Maxie as a serial killer, the environment was suggestive of a knife to the gut.

Honey grinned at her. "I'm not homicidal, although I thought about offing Trapper after this whole incident started." She made a gesture as though shooting a pistol.

"Trapper slept with Mallory. He, my beloved supposedly monogamous partner, fucked Mallory Doyle. He swears Mallory seduced him and that bitch probably did. Not real feminist of me to say that, but Mallory transcends good politics."

"No way," Maxie exclaimed.

"Don't you love it? While I courted Mallory in the business sense,

Mallory seduced my darling foot doctor."

"Yuck," Maxie said. "Mallory in the sack, it makes me queasy."

"Give Mallory some credit. She's brilliant, irreverent, persistent and beautiful. They did it the first time after a PETA rabbit farm protest in Winona."

A menacing figure in a hooded sweatshirt approached the car and pulled something from his pocket. Maxie flinched. The object turned out to be a tissue. The perceived assailant sneezed, blew his nose and moved on, but Maxie's heart still raced. "What about the blackmail?"

"It's the Leonard and Ned thing. They were lovers, as you probably guessed. Ned was a wonderful man. The fact that he and Leonard had to hide their sexuality is a tragedy. Mallory threatened to expose the relationship unless she was patronized."

Maxie knew the plot. It was classic film noir. "She demanded more goodies."

Honey nodded. "After Leonard's arrest Mallory asked for an increase in payments and a new studio in town. She was thrilled to take advantage of the soliciting and arrest. The family refused. Mallory responded with another threat to expose Leonard and Ned's sexual relationship. That would effectively ruin Ned's legacy of honesty, which would absolutely destroy Leonard's already broken heart."

"Why on earth did Trapper tell Mallory about Ned and Leonard?"

"Stupidity. Apparently, he was always drunk during his fun and games sessions with Mallory. In addition to sex, he blurted out family history. You know, I kind of understand the affair. Trapper and I have been so busy and distracted. I don't think we made love more than five or six times last year. What I don't understand is blabbing secrets. Well, in a way I do. Mallory is a manipulator. Trapper was ripe for blurting confessions. We've all been under a lot of pressure lately, since Ned's funeral."

"Which Fisher didn't attend," Maxie said.

"I don't blame her," Honey said. "She left town to get away from all the family dynamics. I think the family was hurt, Leonard most of all." She glanced at Maxie. "The funeral was the day of your little fight with Fisher outside the restaurant. I think she's been a little messed up ever since."

Maxie didn't know whether to laugh or to feel sorry for Fisher. No matter. Even if Fisher did have a good excuse for running out on Maxie, forgiving her wasn't an option. All Maxie needed was to get away from this family and their dramatics.

"The amazing part is that Hunter went along on this ill-fated journey," Honey said. "But he's another story." She started the engine. "You'll miss your flight. That's it for you in this mess. I just wanted you to know what happened."

"What are you going to do?" Maxie asked.

"Wait and suffer," Honey said. "They'll give in to Mallory." She drove back to the departure doors.

INSIDE THE TERMINAL Maxie rolled her bag up to the check-in station and set it on the scale. The Delta attendant held out her hand, waiting for the ticket.

Maxie held the ticket out, but snatched it back from the startled representative. She grabbed her suitcase from the scale and rolled it out of the check-in area. When she reached a place where she could hear, she punched a number on her cell phone.

"Hey, kid? Where are you?" Danny asked.

"I'm at the Minneapolis airport. I have a problem that you can't fix."

"Don't be so sure."

"Then I wish you were here."

"I am here."

Maxie glanced over her shoulder. "Where?"

"A hotel downtown."

"You didn't leave. Why?"

"Intuition."

"Far out. We have to take a trip. We need wheels."

"Give me an hour. I'll get a rental car."

"Get a four-wheel drive with GPS," she said. "I'm not exactly sure how to get where we're going."

"We'll find our way."

"No doubt." Maxie hesitated. "You mean it?"

"That I'll fix this?"

"I can't see how."

"Don't worry."

"I'm not worried."

Maxie found a Dunn Brothers in the baggage claim area. She bought a double espresso and found a discarded *People Weekly*. For the next hour, she busied her mind with caffeine and trash reading.

How many tabloid lies would it take to calm her soul?

Chapter Twenty-nine

Big Foot

DANNY ARRIVED AT the curb outside the baggage area in a gleaming black Audi Q7 SUV with a sophisticated navigation system. "I heard there's a storm brewing." He loaded Maxie's suitcase into the rear. "So here we are, a couple of schnooks with *tsuris* in our paths. Know what that means?"

"Two big fools with even bigger problems," Maxie said. "I learned Yiddish from a friend named Marcello." Maxie thought she detected a slight flicker in Danny's eyes at the mention of Marcello. "Of course there's a big storm brewing. It's so Shakespearean."

"Should we forget this particular Shakespeare play?" Danny asked. "We don't know if we have a tragedy or a comedy."

"Are you kidding? We're both drama queens. I am your daughter, for Pete's sake."

Danny gripped the wheel.

Oh, no, thought Maxie.

He was crying. "I can't tell you how long I've waited to hear that. I love you, Maxie."

"I don't love you. Stop crying. You're all right, though."

"Good enough." Danny wiped his eyes. "Now tell me what's up."

Maxie filled in the details of the Jacobs family dilemma and the siblings' quest to conquer Mallory Doyle. She could practically see Danny's mental wheels spinning as he listened to the tale without interrupting.

The sky darkened ominously as they headed north. Danny tuned to a local radio station. The reporters issued dire warnings in thrilled tones reserved for severe weather situations, storm prediction being a joyous spectator sport in Minnesota. They drove straight toward a horizon of roiling black clouds. Wind stripped trees bare. Lightweight economy cars blew across the lanes.

Twenty miles north of the Twin Cities, an accident-related traffic backup delayed their progress. Police and paramedics roamed amongst shaken victims lashed by the furious gusts. Maxie tried hard not to read any ominous oratory signs in the gruesome scene.

By the time they reached the resort lakes area, the wind had picked up to 50 mph, with gusts over 70 according to the nearly orgasmic radio crew. Lightning tore across the sky, followed by booms of thunder. Meteorologists proclaimed the rarity of thunderstorms in October. A quavering voiced young woman recited school closings and event cancellations as long as a Biblical genealogy.

Maxie glanced down at her Talerius boots and felt profoundly protected.

"What about your feet?" she asked.

He looked down at his Clarks ankle boots. "Not good enough?"

"We need to get you some rugged Minnesota shit-kicking gear."

"My feet are your feet."

They detoured to a coliseum-sized sports emporium a few miles south of Brainward called Universal Outfitters. They crossed the parking lot, fighting the wind. Inside they followed signs to the shoe department. Young employees hovered around the cash register, texting on their smart phones. No one came to help them. Maxie glanced around. Not a Brannock Device in sight. Where were Wayne Powell and Toby White when you needed them?

"So much for customer service," she said. She selected a boxed pair of heavy boots in a size thirteen from beneath a display. "You have pretty big feet. Try these. I don't see any Talerius boots in this joint."

Danny struggled to remove his ankle boots. He seemed to be having trouble getting his foot out of the left shoe. Once he had it out, he tried to put the foot into the new boot and groaned in pain.

"Are you all right?" she asked. "Is it too small?"

"It's nothing." He stood up and hobbled a few yards. "Fits like a glove."

"Then why are you limping?"

"I'm fine," Danny insisted.

They each got hooded Gore Tex parkas and rain pants. Then they fought their way back to the Audi, protected from the ever-increasing gusts by their new gear. Maxie felt very resourceful. Artemis would have been proud. She wondered how much Artemis and Leonard knew about the most recent developments.

THE NAVIGATION SYSTEM guided them to Ishpeming Lodge. As they passed the lodge sign, Maxie thought fondly of Gunter and Ilsa. She told Danny about her trip with Fisher and Artemis. "What a family," she concluded.

"Family is important. You're my family now," he said.

Maxie groaned. "Can you spare me the homilies? I asked you to come with me because I believed you about fixing everything." She swallowed a lump in her throat. "Thank you. I mean it." For a moment she considered telling him about her night with Fisher, but then she came to her senses.

Rain pelted the windshield with increased fury. The navigation system would be useless now. It was a matter of finding the parking lot that led to Mallory's hideout. Miraculously, she recognized the turn-off through the splattered windshield. "That's it."

"I can't see anything," Danny said. "I don't know, Maxie. This isn't good." He turned into the parking lot.

"Look." Maxie pointed to a vehicle in the lot. "That's Hunter's van."

As they stepped from the Audi, hail bombarded them. Gusts of frigid wind turned the pellets into nasty projectiles blitzing them like shots from a BB gun. Maxie forged ahead, comforted by her magnificent boots and weatherized parka. When she glanced back, Danny was bent over, clawing at his boots.

"Are you all right?" she asked.

"I'm okay."

He didn't look okay.

"Maybe this *was* a mistake," Maxie said.

"I told you. I can fix this."

"If we get there," Maxie said.

"We'll get there." He limped over and grabbed her arm for support. "Let's go."

Maxie glanced at the sky. The hail had tapered off slightly and the wind was lighter. Maybe the worst was over. "That way."

They passed the patch of grass where she and Artemis had skinned Big Daddy. The carrion had done their job. Nothing of the buck remained except the memory, a deep freezer full of sausage and steaks and probably an accusatory stuffed head on the dining room wall of the Ishpeming Lodge.

They struggled up the path. Danny moaned. "I do have a little pain."

"A little? You look like death. Are you having a heart attack?"

"I have the heart of a bull."

Despite the statement, he really did look like he was dying. Worse, the storm was starting up again with increased frenzy. Danny staggered, as the hail assaulted them and the wind howled. The sky was pitch black, trees bent sideways with the force of the gusts.

Maxie wrapped an arm around Danny's waist. He leaned on her, gripping her shoulders. He was not a small man. She could barely support his weight. They hobbled together in small steps, inching along the increasingly obscured path.

They were almost to the first cabin where Artemis had shot Big Daddy when the storm became biblical. Lightening illuminated the sky with a weird green cast. Danny gasped and fell to his knees. Maxie fought for balance. Then Danny fell onto his back moaning. She stood over him, heart racing, while he panted.

"It's a gout attack," he choked out.

"Gout! Who has gout these days?"

Despite his pain, he grinned. "The ignorantly maligned malady of excess. A thoroughly embarrassing syndrome. Gout. The word makes you want to snicker."

"I thought only tortured kings got gout," Maxie said, hoping

Danny appreciated her participation in the banter.

"And old actors who play tortured kings."

"Why didn't you tell me? Look at us now."

"I haven't had an attack in a long time. Cold and wet conditions can bring it on. Extreme stress can bring it on."

"Extreme stress, no shit."

"I have medicine. I need water."

Maxie ran to the rickety porch of Cabin One. It was locked. She lowered her shoulder and rammed the door, breaking the flimsy latch. She tumbled into the main room, grabbed a filthy mug from the kitchen counter and turned on the tap. Murky water hiccupped from the faucet. She filled the cup and ran back.

"Probably full of pathogens." She handed the cup to Danny.

"Better than this pain." He swallowed his medicine with a grimace.

Maxie stuck her arms under her father's armpits and pulled him to his feet. She half-dragged him up the steps to the cabin's deck. There were still a few stubborn bloodstains from Big Daddy etched like Rorschach tests onto the weathered slats.

Inside the cabin, she lowered Danny onto a musty couch. From the same counter where she'd found the mug, she snatched a good-sized pitcher. She took it outside and filled it with nontoxic rainwater, something she'd seen in a disaster movie.

She returned to the cabin's main room and pushed the door closed. In a cabinet drawer, she found candles and matches in sealed plastic bags. She arranged and lit the candles, creating a warm yellow glow in the wood-paneled room.

When she was done, she stood over Danny. He looked up at her with his usual unfettered adoration. She shook her head with amazement, unable to rouse any more feelings of hatred towards him. When he shivered, she bent down and tugged at his rain pants and jacket, until she had him out of the wet gear. He had a strangely familiar smell, an aftershave that seeped in from early memories. He made moon-eyes at her. She was touched and she wanted to sock him.

"Sneakers," she blurted out, before her vocal sensors could activate.

"Sneakers the clown fell down. And bounced back up with hardly a frown," he said. His voice was melodious, yet intent. Storytelling from a seasoned actor.

What an act, she thought. Then she did something odd for the second time in recent history. She looked into Danny's eyes without her camera for protection. My god, she thought. He's sincere.

"I love you, Maxie," he said.

Maxie jumped away from the couch. "Stop that." No wonder she'd spent practically her whole life not looking in people's eyes without a shield.

In a closet, she found a couple of musty smelling blankets. She covered Danny in one of them, leaving his feet exposed. She carefully removed his boots and peeled his socks away. "Oh my god," she said. Her stomach roiled.

Danny's inflamed big toe looked like it was about to burst. The angry red bloat crept down his foot. The grotesque horror looked like something out of a medical disease manual, hardly a foot anymore but a mockery of a foot designed to scare little children at Halloween. "How are we ever going to get you out of here?"

"The pills attack the inflammation. I should be able to move around by morning."

Maxie settled into a lumpy cushioned chair and wrapped the second cruddy blanket around her shoulders. "Snug."

"Cozy." Danny looked content. "The drug is already kicking in."

"How long has this gout thing been going on?"

"A long time. It runs in the family."

"At least I'm learning my genetics." She yawned. "I'm exhausted. I didn't sleep much last night." She felt a blush warm her cheeks, which she hoped the flickering candlelight hid.

Danny noted the blush and smiled. "Want me to ask you why?"

"Not at this particular point in time."

"Someday you'll confide in me."

"Why would I do that?"

"We'll be safe harbors. We'll unburden to one another with trust."

"This isn't a sitcom. There's no laugh track and everything doesn't tie up nicely in the end."

"You're my daughter. That's never going to change. I won't assign blame about what happened, but it was more complicated than you know. What's done is done."

"Suit yourself." She stood up. "It's freezing in here."

She found a pile of wood in a basket near the fireplace. She stacked the logs, pyramid style and stuffed crumpled newspaper and kindling around the base. When she lit her handiwork with a match, it burst into flames. Just like a funeral pyre. She shuddered.

"Nice work," Danny said.

"Not bad, if I do say so myself." She watched the inferno. She felt disinclined to flee, not that there was anywhere to flee at the moment.

The blaze purged the cold. Flickering orange flames enhanced the yellow candlelight. The pungent smell of wood smoke drove out the air of neglect.

Maxie was getting hungry. Too bad they hadn't thought to bring food. A bright flash of lightning lit up the room, followed by a boom of thunder.

"At least we made it to shelter," Danny said. "The blackmailer and the vigilantes will still be there in the morning. No one's going anywhere tonight."

He was wrong.

Between the rolls of thunder, Maxie heard the roar of an engine. A minute later, the door flew open. Artemis stood in the entry, clothed in high-tech rain gear and carrying a hefty backpack. She turned and secured the door against the blinding storm. "You're both okay?"

"Snug as two bugs in a rug," Danny said from the couch.

"Honestly," Artemis said, removing the pack from her shoulders and hanging her gear on a hook. "What possessed the two of you to do this?"

"What are *you* doing here?" Maxie asked.

"Answering a question with a question. I discouraged my kids from doing that." Artemis glanced at Danny's elevated left foot. "Gout attack?"

Danny nodded. "You know?"

"Naturally. My son is a foot doctor. Do you have your medicine?"

"All taken care of."

Artemis brought the backpack to the low table in front of the couch. She pulled out an assortment of containers. She had smoked fish, sliced cheese, cut fruit, hummus and wheat crackers. She removed a bottle of red wine and an opener. "An excellent vintage of cabernet sauvignon. Too nice to drink from plastic, but that's the circumstances." She poured three glasses. "Nice fire."

"I made it," Maxie said.

"Good girl." Artemis held up her glass. "To women of fire."

"Couldn't think of a better toast." Danny drank.

Maxie took a large gulp. Red wine gave her headaches, but what the hell. She was trapped with two dubious parent symbols for the night. Let the libations flow.

By the time they'd eaten their dinner, they'd also polished off the bottle of wine. Maxie wasn't drunk, but she was mellow. The ferocious storm was a dramatic prop, now that they were protected.

"How'd you wind up here?" she asked Artemis.

"I was on my way back to the Twin Cities from Pleasanton Center. Honey called me. Told me about my kids, what they were up to. I changed routes and headed here."

"To the rescue," Danny said.

"To add my two cents." Artemis reached in the backpack. "Here's the night cap." She pulled out a bottle of cognac. "Now we'll turn our plastic cups into snifters."

Artemis looked pained. "When Leonard comes home, we'll have to make some adjustments about drinking in front of him. But we'll cross that bridge when we come to it. Right now, we have to get through Mallory Doyle." She handed Maxie a glass of brandy.

Maxie held the glass up to the flames. A kaleidoscope formed, swirling like lava. Light, shadow and color in motion. Beautiful.

Artemis looked over at Danny. "My husband is a wonderful man, but he's had his troubles."

"Haven't we all."

"Marriage and children are absolute commitments."

"When I was younger, I threw myself into commitments without understanding the mechanics." Danny drained his glass. "I shouldn't be drinking with this medication. I usually don't. A different choice for tonight's unusual unfolding."

"Not all choices make sense when viewed from the outside. We do things that make sense to us regardless of how they might strike meddlers," Artemis said.

Maxie jumped up from the couch and walked to the fireplace. She added a log to the fire, sending sparks up the chimney. "People tell themselves the stories they want to hear. Screw the explanations."

"Things happen, Maxie," Danny said. "It's how we interpret those things that can be screwed, as you say. The future is open because it hasn't happened yet. That's why we get to make the smarter choices. There is no new truth until it happens."

"Unbelievable," Maxie said. "If you're so smart, why is your life so messed up?"

"Maxie, don't tell me you believe the tabloids. You of all people know better. Slander like the nonsense about me dating the young actress from my upcoming play is one thing. The lies over the years about my general integrity and intelligence are another."

Maxie smiled. "Taste of my own medicine." She turned to Artemis. "And you. How could you live with Leonard, knowing he loved Ned Burdock? Why didn't you divorce him when you found out about them?"

"I didn't just find out. I always knew."

Maxie gaped at her.

"When Leonard and I met in college, he and Ned were already involved. Neither one of them was willing to come out of the closet. In those days, it wasn't like they'd have a life. I fell in love with Leonard. Despite, maybe because, of his relationship with Ned. With Ned around, I had some level of freedom that married women of my generation were often deprived of. Of course it came with a price, but what doesn't?"

Danny moaned, interrupting the confession.

"Your foot?" Artemis asked.

"No, my past." Danny turned to Maxie. "Even if I'd left my wife, Judy Oyster and I didn't have a chance in hell of a relationship. Even if Bobby hadn't come into the picture, she didn't want me. Maxie, I begged to come see you after Bobby showed up. Then I gave up, until Bobby died. That's when the calls started. The ones you ignored. But I always kept track of you."

"Enough," Maxie said. "If you're serious about reconciliation, I never want to hear your side of things. I don't care. If my mother could explain, I wouldn't listen either. I'm not into competing explanations of the truth, even if there is a truth. Move on, I say. Isn't that your point about the future?"

Danny was silent. Artemis, too, kept her tongue.

Maxie had to give them both credit for knowing when to shut up. She glanced over to the two single beds on the other side of the room. Danny and Artemis could each take one and she'd sleep on the couch.

"*Mispocheh*," Artemis said. "Leonard taught me the Yiddish term. That's us."

"Did Marcello teach you that one?" Danny asked.

"How do you know about Marcello?" Maxie watched a veil form over Danny's face. "*Mispocheh* is like an extended family. Danny, don't avoid the question. You'll ruin every bit of progress you've made."

"I know a lot about you, Maxie." He turned to Artemis. "First, Maxie found out about our plan. Now she knows the truth about you and Leonard. Our *mispocheh* has quite a history."

"Yes," Artemis said. "I hope Maxie will come to forgive us and accept our missteps."

"No promises," Maxie said. "I'm trying to understand, but it's not easy."

"Take your time," Artemis said. "Neither one of us is going anywhere." She glanced at Danny. "Isn't that right?"

"Not anymore," Danny said. "That's a promise."

"We'll see," Maxie said.

Chapter Thirty

Doppelgangers

THE SUN ROSE without remorse. Birds celebrated in song. Rays of light poured into the cabin. Artemis bustled in the kitchen, arranging pastries and brewing coffee in some kind of camping gizmo. A fire crackled spreading comforting warmth. Maxie got up and looked outside. Aside from a scattering of broken branches, peace was restored to the natural world.

Danny was still completely out, breathing through his mouth, lips quivering. She went over, lifted the blanket and checked his foot. The swelling looked less gruesome.

His eyes opened. "Morning, kid."

"You feel any better?"

He sniffed the air. "Glorious."

"Coffee and cinnamon rolls," Artemis called over. "But we shouldn't linger. I don't know how long we have before the party breaks up at Mallory's cabin."

After breakfast, Maxie and Artemis loaded Danny onto the all-terrain vehicle. He was already walking more comfortably, but with a decided limp.

"I got the ATV from the Lodge," Artemis said, "I didn't want to involve my parents, but I had to." She frowned at Danny's awkwardness climbing into the seat. "I made Gunter promise to wait this out until tonight without interference. Are you sure you're up for this, Danny?"

"Can't wait."

They were about to leave when a roar came from the path. Another ATV raced into view. Honey jerked to a stop three inches from their bumper. Her springy hair stood up on her head and she was mud splattered. "You didn't think I was going to be left out of this, did you? By the way, Gunter and Ilsa are going insane. I hope this comes to good."

"We have a trio of furies and a recuperating comedian," Danny said. "Who can withstand us?"

"We'll fly like the wind!" Artemis said.

Honey cackled like a witch. "Hee, hee, hee."

Maxie got into the spirit of things. "Bearing swords of righteousness."

They roared down the path, wind flying through their hair.

"Yippee," Maxie cried.

MALLORY LOOKED PUZZLED when she opened the cabin door. "How do you like that? The more the merrier." She squinted at Danny.

"Danny King. You were at my opening. That was weird, this is weirder." Her eyes lit up. "Is there something I should know?"

"No more ammunition for you," Honey said.

Mallory shrugged. "I have plenty."

IN THE LIVING room Fisher, Trapper and Hunter sat slumped on a couch. A sheet of paper on the coffee table showed a mass of scribbling. They glanced up with dull eyes.

"The negotiations broke off at midnight. No progress at all this morning either," Mallory informed the newcomers.

Trapper watched Danny hobble to a chair near the couch, his foot swathed in thick cloth. "What's going on with your foot?"

"Gout attack," Danny said.

Trapper's eyes lit up. "Did you do anything to treat it?"

"Indomethacin."

"How much?"

"50 milligrams, three times a day."

"Let me see."

Danny removed the cloth.

Trapper inspected the foot. "The anti-inflammatory is the best course of action for now." He turned to the group. "I'm seeing more gout. It's an immunity issue, a form of arthritis caused when uric acid builds up in the blood."

"Can we get back to the matter at hand?" Mallory asked.

"What the hell are the four of you doing here anyway?" Trapper asked.

"Intervention," Maxie said. "We thought you might need emotional blind-siding."

"Not funny," Trapper said.

"This isn't the time for jokes, Maxie," Fisher said.

"I wasn't joking. Besides, you're the one..." She was going to call Fisher on deserting her after their night together. The whole group stared at her. "Forget it."

"I didn't abandon you," Fisher said. "I explained in the voice mail."

"I didn't listen."

"She never listened to mine either," Danny piped in.

"This little escapade isn't about my answering machine habits," Maxie said.

"It's about me," Mallory said. "Trapper, could you do a recap for the newcomers?"

"Screw you," Trapper said. "I can't believe I fell for you."

"Just do what I say."

"Let him be," Hunter snapped.

He looked terrible. His eyes were bloodshot. His hands trembled. He turned to his mother. "I had to find out about this situation at the last minute, when all hell broke loose. What did the rest of you think was going to come of giving in to this woman's demands?"

"Don't refer to me in the third person," Mallory said. "I'm here, I'm real and I mean business."

Maxie almost laughed. She was afraid to look at Danny. Mallory sounded like an imitation Dorothy Malone in a film noir B-movie.

"My point," Hunter said, "is that Mallory wants an increase right now. Fine. We give her more money. We rent her a studio in town. In a year or so, it'll be more. This is not good business. It's a slippery slope with no end in sight. What if we refuse?"

"Then I give all the sordid details of your father and his gay lover to the press," Mallory said. "I'm getting tired of repeating this." She turned to the newcomers. "Danny King. Could you explain to this naïve group about funding art? They need to be educated as to patronage, including deluded bourgeois interpretations of the paycheck. I am trying to accomplish something great. I'm asking for a fair exchange with a reasonable income."

"I can do better than that," Danny said.

Mallory's eyes narrowed. "I doubt it."

"Young lady, I saw your work. You have a vision, one that I don't share, but that's irrelevant. Let me make a proposal."

Mallory sneered, but she didn't interrupt.

"My connections are deep. My connections' connections are deeper. You want to be famous. I can make you famous."

"Don't bullshit me."

"Here's the thing. If I do this, you deal with me. You will never bother the Jacobs family again. You will be expected to follow a simple rule. Stay true to your vision. Your desire to create is keeping you in touch with the rest of humanity."

"You are one devious dude," Mallory said.

"Deal?" Danny asked.

"I would love to disengage from the Jacobs clan. Talk about hypocrisy. This family cracks me up. Mr. Trapper Foot Doctor is one lousy drunk. I got secrets I didn't want to know."

"You just can't let well enough alone, can you?" Hunter broke in. "Our family will survive and you'll probably wind up committing suicide, too lonely and mean to ever have enjoyed any benefits you got from Danny's deal."

"*You*," Mallory said to Hunter. "The rest are boring. You're the fool." She turned to Danny. "I have one point to make then I'll take your deal."

Maxie glanced over at Fisher, who had turned ghostly pale. The entire family had gone rigid.

"Once upon a time," Mallory said, "there was a little boy who had a horrible accident. His mother ran him over in the driveway as he was riding his little bicycle behind her big SUV."

Hunter slammed his fist onto the coffee table. "Shut up."

"Why, sweetie?" Mallory asked. "Don't you want the truth?"

Short of tackling and gagging her, there seemed to be no way to get her to stop.

"The little boy's leg had to be amputated. He grew up to be an accomplished man who never let his infirmity stop him. Why was his mother racing so hysterically out of the house, so upset that she failed to see her son?"

"Is this really necessary?" Artemis asked.

"What did you see?" Mallory persisted.

Hunter jumped up. Trapper stood, too.

Honey remained seated, but she looked like she was going to explode. "You can't do this."

Mallory waved impatiently at them. "I should get bonus points. But why should I tell the story? Why not the actual participants?" She turned to Trapper. "You start."

"Forget it," Trapper said.

"Cough it up," Mallory said. "Otherwise you get my interpretation with details about the pornographic circumstances under which I was told the ugly truth."

Trapper reddened. "Honey and I were playing doctor in my room." He grew redder. "I had my pants off. Honey had her undies around her ankles. Dad walked in. He started explaining that it wasn't such a good idea to be diddling around like that. Mom walked in and saw us. Honey and me undressed. Dad standing there."

Honey wailed. "I've never forgiven myself. I screamed to Artemis that Leonard told us to take our clothes off."

"I panicked," Artemis said. "Ned was one thing. My husband molesting kids was another. I was crazy. I rushed out to the SUV. I backed up without looking." She trembled.

"That's why you ran me over," Hunter said.

"That's why I ran you over." Artemis turned to Honey. "You were a frightened child making panicked accusations. I was the adult. I should have stayed and gotten things straightened out."

"You're being awfully quiet over there, missy," Mallory said to Fisher.

Fisher was crying. "I saw Mom run out. I went to Trapper's room and saw him and Honey pulling on their clothes. I ran down the stairs and went to the window, saw Mom backing the car down the driveway and then she ran over Hunter. It was horrible."

"You ran me over because you thought Dad was molesting children," Hunter said. "Great."

"Later, Honey recanted her story," Artemis said. "Leonard forgave her. We all did."

Mallory laughed. "What if Leonard threatened them? What if this is all another lie?"

Silence fell over the group.

"No," Trapper said.

"No," Honey said. "Screw you, bitch."

"My husband is not a pedophile," Artemis said. She turned to Hunter. "This wasn't information you needed to know after your leg was gone. You were a boy who needed stability. We made the whole incident disappear."

"I caused the accident. I still don't know why you forgave me. Next, I bring the evil artist into the picture," Honey said.

"Evil?" Mallory said. "I think that's a little exaggerated. Evil is for genocides. And pedophiles."

"It's my fault," Trapper said. "Getting even for all the problems in my relationship by fucking Mallory and blabbing secrets."

"My fault," Fisher threw out. "I ran away to California."

"Blah, blah, blah," Mallory said, turning to Maxie. "No camera?"

"This event will have to be preserved in the mind's eye."

"Too bad." Mallory yawned. "Now everyone will kiss and make up, all purged and cleansed."

Artemis looked around the room. "She can't break us."

Maxie had an ah-hah moment worthy of Dr. Dani. The Jacobs clan *would* survive. She laughed out loud.

Everyone focused on her. "Never mind," she said. "I'd explain, but it would just be words."

FISHER DROVE HER to the airport. On the front stoop of the Jacobs' residence, she'd submitted to good-byes from Artemis, Trapper, Honey, Hunter, Fiona and the Pinschers. Leonard sent his best from Pleasanton Center.

They were nearly to Terminal One when Fisher pulled off on a turnout bordering the highway. "I want to see you when I get back to L.A."

"You're coming back?" Maxie asked.

"Definitely, if it means you'll see me."

"Don't let it rest on me."

"Why not? My love for you isn't going to magically go poof after you leave."

A semi hauling a huge grated trailer crammed with chickens rumbled by emitting a fragrance of manure and feathers. "Whew, that stinks," Maxie said.

"Those are the mothers of your deviled eggs," Fisher said.

"Not to mention frozen chicken carcasses. I may have to give up eggs entirely."

"Answer my question," Fisher said.

"If you come back, we'll see."

"Not good enough."

"As good as I can do."

"Maxie, I will not give up. We're made for each other. Like Mr. and Mrs. Sneakers."

"Not the most compelling argument."

At the Departures curb, she hopped out and retrieved her bag. Fisher jumped out of the driver's seat and blocked Maxie's exit. "Hug me, Maxie."

Maxie plunged into Fisher's arms and pressed against her chest, but she could not look into Fisher's eyes.

On the plane, she pulled out her Memory Folder and completed the third and final entry.

Chapter Thirty-one

Journal Entry Number Three Bobby's Funeral
by Maxie Wolfe

MAXIE WAS IN bed with Lucinda Frazier, UCLA assistant women's golf coach when the call came. They were in a seedy motel in the Valley registered under fake names.

In those days, Maxie didn't have a cell phone, so she didn't get the news until she got back to the dorm room she shared with Wendy Underhill, volleyball middle-blocker.

Usually, Wendy was tolerant of Maxie's flings with other students, graduate assistants and an occasional professor. Wendy was a born-again Christian from Orange County, but she'd been taught charity to sinners, which was everybody but the people in her sect anyway.

Maxie knew from Wendy's expression that something was seriously wrong.

"I hope you and that assistant coach of yours were having a good time, because I have news for you."

"Not a real good time. I'm bummed out." Maxie recalled the ugly scene with her assistant coach in the moldy plywood-paneled motel room.

"Lucinda, you're in a relationship, for Pete's sake."

"I'm breaking it off with Caroline."

"I hope not for me. Caroline's a great person. Besides, I have a crush on Dr. Crenshaw."

"Your photography professor? She's married and has five kids."

"Probably won't happen. She blew me off."

"I hate you, Maxie. I'm like really hurt."

Maxie hoped Lucinda could shake it off. The fling had lasted three weeks. The sex was mediocre. They had a meet coming up in five days. How could anyone get that attached in less than a month?

Until she got to college, Maxie had not been much interested in sex. When she got to college, she discovered she had a knack for seduction that was like drinking, only better. No hangover.

As soon as she saw Wendy's face, she knew what happened. It wasn't like a great shock or anything. Since her mother's final accident and the resulting brain damage, Bobby had been going downhill. By the time she headed off to her full-ride UCLA scholarship, he was getting scraped up from under freeway ramps along with the other homeless losers. She wouldn't go to the funeral. What a downer that would be.

In a week, however, Wendy wore her down with torture at the water boarding level.

"He was your anchor. He loved you dearly."

"Some anchor."

She wished she hadn't shared a few secrets with Wendy. Confessions turned people into targets for lectures from moralizers.

SHE FLEW TO San Francisco and rented a rattletrap. She drove to Petaluma experiencing flashbacks and located the crematorium in a strip mall on the east side of town. The service had already started. Maxie thought cremation was against Catholic rules. Maybe there was an exception clause for failed poets. She saw the gratitude in Roy and June's eyes at her late arrival, which tore at her heart.

Things got worse after the crematorium.

A hundred people filed in and out of Roy and June's house, bringing casseroles, salads, beer and whiskey. Every person in Petaluma who knew Bobby attended. A few burnouts from his addict days lurked along back walls. None of the elite who'd survived the early flameout years, the critics and the celebrity artists, attended except one. Maxie didn't know if she was more horrified, amused or touched.

The Lizard Lady, who now resembled a tanned leather purse more than a living creature, ate a plate of assorted casseroles and offered condolences to a puzzled looking Roy and June.

The last straw of the whole miserable event?

Roy and June coming up to Maxie with a plate of deviled eggs and a framed picture of Bobby in a cap and gown.

"Maxie, why aren't you eating? We brought these eggs for you," June said.

"Maxie, we want you to take this picture. You're doing so well in college. Bobby would have been proud of you," Roy said.

"If you're not hungry now, I'll wrap these up for you," June said.

Maxie took the bacteria-laden egg dish and the photograph. As soon as she got five blocks away, she dumped the food.

Not long after that, Maxie failed her journalism class with Dr. Crenshaw. She blew three collegiate matches and was benched from the team.

One night, she was at a trendy club with a girl who sang in a famous band and they were mobbed by paparazzi. The next day, one of the media girls, a fledgling reporter for a tabloid, accosted her on campus. Her name was Piper Trueblood. Maxie dropped the girl singer and took up with Piper, who got her into crappy journalism. And that was how Maxie Wolfe became a paparazzo.

Bye-bye, Bobby. I love you.

MAXIE SLIPPED HER final entry into her Memory Folder. Three memorable incidents. Not one. Not a million. Maxie was a good girl. She'd done all the homework.

Chapter Thirty-two

Redux

MAXIE WASN'T circulating in her usual circles in Hollywood. She didn't know where she was headed, but she couldn't be a paparazzo anymore. She felt as if she'd been released from prison into a murky parole with obscure rules.

Her landlords got her a part-time job at *Celery and Buzz*, a juice and espresso bar in Beverly Center where she made soy lattes and veggie shakes for ten bucks per hour plus tips. She produced sloppy concoctions but landed great tips, because she was cute and projected budding genius vibes. She hadn't seduced anyone as recent events had paralyzed her libido.

One day, an espresso machine repairperson named Serafina showed up, tool belt slung on her narrow hips. One thing led to another. Serafina wound up at Maxie's hideaway repairing Marcello's machine and succumbing to Maxie's advances. One gasket and two arguments later, the fling was over. Before Minnesota, she would have shrugged it off. Before Minnesota, she had no definition for frozen loneliness. Now, she suffered in isolation and she didn't like it.

SHE CALLED HER former college coach Glenn Livvey.

"You still doing that First Tee thing?"

"I thought you hated children. Not to mention hiding your golf chops."

Danny's advice rang in her head. Plunge into what repels you. What better way than to teach little brats? "Forget whatever I've said. Bring on the little monsters."

She drove up to the Valley and faced a bunch of damaged preteens who looked at her like she was an inept crone. She proceeded to hit a few two hundred forty yard tee shots and that shut them up.

After four sessions, she was a mother hen. The kids followed her around like adoring chicks. One particularly creepy delinquent, saddled with the name Gypsy Boner, started out slamming clubs into the turf, but she saw something in him beyond the impenetrable shell. If she knew anything, she knew about shells. She ordered him off the driving range and onto the putting green until he could one-putt sixty balls in a row. He stomped out of the practice area, but was back the next day. He'd made his putts. The brat was a wunderkind, just as she had suspected.

Fisher didn't call, which suited Maxie just fine. She decided that

Fisher was a complication. The entire Jacobs family was a complication. She blocked them out during daylight hours, but they came to her in her dreams.

SHE DIDN'T WATCH much television, but it was impossible to live in the United States of America and ignore media, unless you were part of some isolationist fringe group. She was making a coconut milk cappuccino at the cafe one morning when a customer pointed to a commotion unraveling on a flat screen suspended from a wall.

"Bum," the scowling woman said. "Hypocrite. A conservative family man serving our government demanding horrible acts from a prostitute."

"Amber," Maxie called to a girl with seven piercings on her face. "Take over for me for a minute." She went out to the sitting area for a closer view.

Franny Glass was engulfed in paparazzi as she and her new attorney, Helen Dubois, fought their way through the frantic crowd, up the stairs of a courthouse.

"A call girl is about to give testimony regarding State Representative Marcus and a request for abominable sex acts, despite what she claims were dire threats from him and his staff," a breathless young CNN reporter said from the screen.

"She looks like Jane Fonda in *Klute*," a middle-aged man nursing a mango smoothie said from a nearby table.

"Go, ladies," Maxie said. "Jane Fonda, Franny Glass and whistle-blowers everywhere."

TWO WEEKS AFTER SHE returned she received a call from Piper Trueblood.

"Marcello asked me to give you a message," Piper said.

"You?"

"Amazing, huh? That guy is a kook. Anyway, he said he'd be hard to reach. Went back to Italy on family business."

"Thanks."

"Want to go out with me again?"

"No."

She hung up and went out to her art studio. The Iranian couple had let her install a workshop in an unused garden cottage. Jillian the talented carpenter, one of her old flames, had knocked the studio together in two days. Danny's gift, a large scale Canon printer, occupied a prominent place on a long worktable near the new iMac she'd charged on a credit card, along with a scanner and a large electronic drawing tablet. Each time she entered her new retreat, she thought of Judy Oyster and Mallory Doyle.

Mallory had been deposited in a furnished loft in SoHo. She attended all the right events, invited by the movers and shakers in the art world. Maxie tracked Mallory's progress on the Internet, feeling like she was watching illicit pornography.

Danny was also in New York. He'd started rehearsals for *The Winter's Tale*. He was rumored to be dating the woman playing his wife.

Maxie cut the edges off a photograph to add to her collage. Fragments hung on two walls, vague beginnings that excited her, then sent her into despair. Maxie's cell rang. She checked the caller ID and answered.

"Hi, Dad."

"Any progress, kid?"

"I don't know where I'm going."

"I'm trying to find my Leontes, but he's resisting me. His actions are deplorable, but have a logic of their own. I'm trying to find his complexity and express it."

"What do you do?" she asked.

"I show up and create," Danny said.

"I've never been more excited or afraid."

"Despair drops you into the underworld. The solution is persistence. I love you, my daughter."

Maxie closed her eyes. "Ditto."

She didn't tell Danny that, in addition to the Jacobs, she dreamed of her mother's accident. She stomped around Hollywood in her Talerius boots, taking pictures. She returned to the studio and cut them up or layered them in Photoshop. She pasted images into paintings. She glued them to discarded vodka bottles and added used syringes. She painted eggs. Nothing seemed right.

Now she was doing an underwater montage, including images of her mother and characters from SpongeBob. She thought about adding text. T.S. Eliot? "I should have been a pair of ragged claws/ scuttling across the floors of silent seas," she whispered.

The piece bordered on kitschy. Using poetry frightened her. She thought of Danny's advice. Use the fear.

She was staring in frustration at the jumbled mess on the walls when someone knocked. Zari held out a parcel. "Sorry to bother you. UPS delivered this at our door by mistake."

Zari stared at the walls. Maxie took the package and tried to scoot Zari out as graciously as possible. She wasn't ready for anyone to scrutinize her stuff right now.

The mystery parcel was from Needles, California.

SHE DIDN'T OPEN her delivery until she was back in the pool house. She made an espresso with the Italian machine, now in perfect working order. After the espresso, she washed and dried the cup, then placed it back in the cupboard. Eventually she made it back to the couch and picked up the package. She took a long time cutting the tape with a razor.

Inside were three framed photos and a letter.

The photos were of Big Ears, Private First Class Lloyd Hacker, in some unspecified war zone. In one grainy photo, little boys surrounded him, licking lollipops. In the second blurry photo, he huddled with buddies holding weapons of destruction. Finally, in the last fuzzy shot, Lloyd held a camera and waved. His look was penetrating and Maxie knew he was looking right at her.

The letter from his parents explained that the package had arrived just before Lloyd's death, requesting they forward it to Maxie if anything happened to him. They understood she was important to their son, so they had honored his request and hired a private investigator to track her down.

Maxie took the photos and went into her bedroom. She opened the slatted door of her closet, reached back to the farthest corner and dragged out a plastic storage container from Target. She carried it over to the bed and lifted the lid.

On top of a jumbled stack was the Queen of Hearts card Franny had given her. Just underneath it was Bobby's graduation picture. Maxie was about to dump Lloyd's photos into her plastic Pandora's bin. Then, she stood.

She took out Bobby's lovely picture and brought it, along with the photos from Lloyd and the Queen of Hearts, into the living area, where she set her mementos out for display on the coffee table. With Bobby, the Queen and Lloyd watching her, she picked up her cell and selected a number from her contact list.

"Are you coming back?"

"Actually, no," Fisher said.

"Are you dating that veterinarian chick with the attitude? When I didn't hear from you, I got to thinking. She's dating that old flame that's so perfect for her." She was blabbering and ashamed of it.

"I was going to call. I want you to come to Minnesota. Dad's leaving Pleasanton Center. After he graduated, he insisted on staying to take four peer-counseling seminars. Now that he's finally ready to leave, we're picking him up, then on to Ishpeming Lodge to celebrate his and Mom's delayed fortieth anniversary. Gunter and Ilsa insisted on hosting it. We're not exactly sure why."

"A great final chapter in the anger-management workbook. We can suggest it for the next revision," Maxie said.

Fisher laughed. "You wouldn't be Maxie without the irreverence. I wouldn't want you to be." She cleared her throat. "We all want you to come back. Especially Artemis."

"I'll think about it."

"You do that, Maxie."

FOR TWO DAYS she called in sick from her barista gig. She ate take-out and worked feverishly on her mother/SpongeBob piece. She didn't answer her calls. On the third day of her exile, Marcello called.

"You're back from Italy," she said.

"I missed you, *bella*."

"I missed you, too."

Marcello chuckled. "That doesn't sound like you."

"I'm not sure who I am."

"Beginner's mind. Good not knowing who you are."

Maxie shook the phone. "You're a train wreck courting lung cancer and heart failure. Why can't you practice what you preach?"

The line went dead.

"Oh, no," she whispered. "I didn't mean it."

Her phone rang a few seconds later. "I went through a tunnel. I'm tailing English royalty, one of the naughty sons is in town carousing with the Lakers."

"Pull into a parking lot. I need you alive. I have heard the mermaids singing, each to each."

There was a low whistle on the other end. "Quoting T.S. Eliot. I am exiting on Wilshire Boulevard. Give me *uno momento*."

There was a pause followed by a loud screech and the squeal of brakes.

"No, *nada*," Marcello muttered in a tranquil voice.

The line went dead again.

"Marcello," Maxie said into the phone.

MAXIE LOCATED HER dubious mentor at Good Samaritan Hospital on Wilshire. He looked like a hospitalized fifties Hollywood actress, styled and poised. He had a small bandage on one arm and a bruise on his left cheek, but otherwise seemed intact.

"I told you so," she said, coming up to the bed.

"*Va all'inferno*," he said.

Maxie slumped into a designer chair. "We'll go to hell together." She glanced around. "You can't afford this room."

Marcello shrugged. "I'm not paying."

"Tell me you have an old rich mistress like William Holden in *Sunset Boulevard*. Think where debauchery ends. Floating face down in a swimming pool."

Marcello struggled to a sitting position. "I am fine except for nicotine withdrawal and unrequested tests to justify lectures on my lifestyle choices." He cleared his throat. "Damp, jagged, like an old man's mouth driveling, beyond repair, or the toothed gullet of an aged shark."

"T.S. Eliot, of course," Maxie said.

"I will be an aged shark with teeth, I promise you," Marcello said.

He held out a hand. "Maxie, come here."

Maxie hesitated, provoking a sad smile from Marcello. "The shark won't bite, *bella*."

When Marcello took her hand, she didn't pull away.

"I almost died," Marcello said. "I won't beat around the shrub."

"Bush," Maxie said.

"What?"

"Beat around the bush," Maxie said.

"Forget botany, Maxie."

His accent had become decidedly less affected. "All the clichés hold true about near death. I saw my life playing before my eyes. While I am not inspired to change my lifestyle, I am inspired to come clean about certain things."

She went over to the window facing out on Los Angeles. It was a panoramic view worthy of a jaded Ansel Adams, polluted and beautiful. "Okay," she said.

"I have never, in all of this, meant to hurt you."

"Why do I have the feeling this involves Danny King?"

"Because all roads lead to Danny. He asked me to watch over you after you dropped out of college to become one of us. He was worried about your affair with Piper Trueblood and the other scum sniffing around you like mongrels."

"I have to give Danny credit. He gets things done."

She returned to the chair and slumped back down. "We're going to hunker down right now and get to the truth."

"Is there truth?"

"You bet there is. Danny King and I discussed it and he's wise about these things. We'll start with you telling me who you really are."

Chapter Thirty-three

Old Grudges

MAXIE RETURNED TO Minnesota armed with a few new facts and many questions unanswered.

Fisher waited for her at the curb near the exit doors from baggage claim at Terminal One. She drew Maxie into her arms. Maxie allowed the hug. "It's freezing."

"Twenty below by three in the morning. It'll be sunny and in the forties tomorrow by noon. A span of sixty degrees in nine hours. That's Minnesota. The land of extremes."

"Let's get in the car. My nose hairs are freezing."

When they were buckled in, Maxie put a finger to her lips. "No guided tours, please."

Fisher gave her fifteen minutes of reprieve, enough to get them to Crosby Park. She pulled into a remote parking lot at the public reserve. "This is where Dad was arrested."

"The point of coming here is?" Maxie asked.

"I sit in the car and imagine the arrest. I feel Dad's grief over Ned and their secret love. It's either empathetic or self-indulgent. I don't care."

"How's Leonard?"

"Dad's all about admitting his addiction and asking forgiveness. I don't know if he's going to stay with Mom. He insists he wants to have the anniversary celebration, so maybe he is."

"What does Artemis want?"

"She wants everything to go back to normal."

"There's no normal," Maxie said.

"We keep trying to find it," Fisher said.

Despite the defroster blasting on high, ice coated the windows, except for little moons of transparency where the heat vents blew. Fisher shifted into drive. "You'll have to register as my fiancée at Pleasanton Center when we go to pick up Dad. Then you qualify as family."

"I know. Phoenix Damon went there. She explained the whole program."

"New girlfriend?" Fisher asked.

"For about four days."

"I thought you didn't go in for actresses."

"She's also a fine poet and talented painter."

"One of the mumblers."

"The what?"

"The Method types, squinting and mumbling and making art when they're not riding motorcycles or speeding in Ferraris. James Dean lesbians. I'm surprised at you. Poets and artists crossed with actresses. Very Freudian."

"I've been celibate with only two slip-ups. She was one."

Fisher's voice shook as she spoke. "I thought you were coming back because you loved me."

"I kind of love you."

"I could have slept with the veterinarian. I didn't."

"Wise choice. Too many old associations."

"Maxie, damn you. Why did you come?"

"Please don't yell at me."

"You're right. At least you're here."

"At least that," Maxie said. Half the battle was showing up, according to her father.

THE TRIP TO Pleasanton Center from Saint Paul the next morning was unsettling. They had to leave ridiculously early to pack two major events into one day.

On the one hand, there was Dunn Brothers coffee and warm doughnuts from the Scandinavian place. On the other, there was the phoniness of the light talk that everyone embraced with determination, shouting across the seats. Hunter's van sat twelve in comfort, but Maxie still felt like she was crammed into a Volkswagen Beetle with a bunch of clowns performing a sardines-in-a-can routine.

Artemis threw her beseeching looks, and Fisher exuded love vibes. The glazed bear claw she'd eaten sat like a stone in her stomach. The roads were slippery with melting ice, reminding her of Marcello's accident.

It was a relief to arrive at the campus. Hunter turned onto the private drive lined with stately, bare-limbed winter trees, dark silhouettes against a cool gray sky. Deserted paths bordered with meditation benches led to serene coves along the lake. Finally, Hunter stopped the van at a five-star hotel type facility crossed with Ivy League college laced with Lutheran church.

At the building's entrance a guard-type examined everyone's belongings. "Yum," said the inspector, peeking into the brunch basket. She pointed to the waiting area. "You can sit there." After a short interval, Leonard entered the room, looking a little disengaged, until he spotted his family. His face lit up. A flurry of embraces followed.

"We have a table set up for brunch." Leonard turned to Maxie. "I'm glad you came, Maxie. I've missed you."

As Leonard and the family crossed into the dining room the staff and a crowd of residents followed their progress with adoring gazes. A tattooed young man with a goatee gave a thumb's up sign. Artemis unloaded the brunch basket onto a table bearing the name Jacobs. Another rough-looking customer strolled by, beaming at Leonard.

"Listening to the sob stories of meth addicts?" Hunter asked with false heartiness.

"Son, we're all in the same boat here," Leonard said. "Admitting how little control we have."

Hunter swatted at a fruit fly that must have accompanied the bowl of cut organic fruit. "Are you processing every aspect of your existence all the time now?"

"Let's sit," Leonard said. "I'll tell you about it."

The family no sooner settled at the table when a man rushed up. He pointed at Maxie. "Could we have a word?"

"What's wrong?" Artemis asked. "She's my daughter's fiancée."

The young man flushed. "Sorry."

IN THE PUBLIC relations room, a woman who resembled Tina Turner joined Maxie and the man. She introduced herself as Dr. Jane Powers, Head Administrator. Maxie's heart sank. She knew well the look in the administrator's eyes.

"Ms. Wolfe, I'll get right to the point. One of our patients saw you arrive. He identified you as a paparazzo. We have a strict policy of privacy with regard to our patients. You must leave the premises."

She'd seen Boyd Gruber, the train wreck she'd exposed last summer, in the lobby. He was getting his revenge, probably thrilled at outing her. Wasn't forgiveness one of the first things they were supposed to learn here?

"I'm not here as a journalist, Dr. Jane," she said.

"Dr. Powers."

"I'm here with my family."

"Paparazzi lie to get a scoop. I've been around the block a few times."

Revelation struck Maxie. "You sang with Isaac Mains. Isaac and Janie Mains. Isaac fell apart. You went into rehab."

"I did travel a rocky road to arrive at my present situation." Dr. Powers pointed an accusing finger. "Your kind harassed me to the point of despair."

"Not anymore," Maxie said. "I'm done with all that."

Dr. Powers eyed her suspiciously.

"If there's any way you'd let me stay, I'd appreciate it. But even if you don't, I'm telling the truth." She felt like she'd sliced through a layer of skin and was holding the flaps open for Dr. Powers to see inside.

"Will you sign documentation?" Dr. Powers asked.

"I'll sign it in blood."

Dr. Powers smiled. "I don't think that will be necessary."

ALTHOUGH IT SEEMED like the interrogation took hours, only twenty minutes had passed. Maxie described her absolution. Everyone clapped.

Before more corny moments could transpire, Boyd Gruber walked up to the table. "I see they let you stay, bitch."

"Boyd Gruber," Fisher said. "Please refrain from crude language."

"Fisher Jacobs," Boyd said. "Oh, I see. The bitch paparazzo and the bitch sports agent. A pair of female assholes."

"Boyd, we're all assholes, remember?" Leonard said.

"I know, Leonard. However, Maxie Wolfe is really an asshole. She nearly ruined my life."

Because enlightenment can be as mundane as it is profound, Maxie felt an inner glow. "I think it was the last chapter of the workbook, wasn't it?" she asked Fisher.

Fisher smiled at Maxie. "Yes, it was."

"Thank you for sharing," Maxie said to Boyd. "I'm sorry about what I did to you."

She meant it.

Chapter Thirty-four

The Final Act

A RAINBOW-COLORED balloon anchored to the Ishpeming Lodge sign at the beginning of the resort driveway read, "Happy Fortieth Anniversary Dear Artemis and Leonard."

Hunter, fueled by energy drinks, had insisted on driving the entire way from Pleasanton Center. His passengers, including Maxie, napped.

"Awaken," he cried as they crossed into Hagan territory.

Bundled in a down jacket and wool cap, Bunty Preston rushed to greet them under the portal. "Welcome, welcome, welcome," he choked out.

Five bellhops descended on the piles of luggage.

"How's the puppy?" Artemis asked.

Bunty glowed. "She'll always be a runt, but she's the smartest gal. Can't wait to please Papa. Named her Gretchen. My Greta would have loved her. Comes a time when you have to let go of grief."

"What's so good about letting go of grief?" Leonard burst out. He grinned at everyone's pained looks. "Making a joke."

"Yes," Bunty said. "Ha ha."

"Are the folks up in the office?" Artemis asked.

Bunty clutched his pager. "I suppose you want to surprise them?"

"No," Artemis said. "It might be too much for Dad's heart. Let them know we're on our way."

IN THE RECEPTION area, a crowd of employees broke into applause. Maxie glanced past them to the wall of photographs. "Look," she said.

The entire Jacobs family stood open-mouthed.

The walls were festooned with anniversary paraphernalia, including a wedding picture of Artemis and Leonard and a recent picture of Gunter, Ilsa, Artemis, Fisher and Maxie.

The group trooped in a clump to the office and flung open the doors. Gunter and Ilsa sprang into action. A period of extended hugs ensued, accompanied by grunts and sighs, until finally, Gunter faced them all, looking like he might, indeed, have a heart attack.

"I'm okay," he bellowed. "I'm on six goddamned medications. My heart's been super-humanized. Even if it fails, the pacemaker has a defibrillator." He wiped a tear from his eyes. "I am so glad you agreed to this." He turned to Maxie. "And that you, Maxie, decided to come."

Despite his claims to techno-demigod status, Gunter looked

exhausted. Ilsa took his arm. "He's been up since dawn, finishing the arrangements. I'm going to make him take a nap, even if I have to drug him."

"More drugs," Gunter grumbled, then glanced at Leonard with an apologetic look. "Sorry. I didn't mean anything by that."

"I was having a problem with alcohol, not drugs," Leonard said. "Have a problem. I will always be in recovery."

"I think a little down time before the party sounds perfect," Hunter broke in.

Ilsa consulted a card. "Your room assignments are as follows. Leonard and Artemis will be in the Wild Boar suite. Hunter has the lovely Turkey Trot room. Trapper and Honey will love the renovated Smoked Herring suite. Fisher and Maxie will be?" She paused.

"I'll need my own room." Maxie glanced around. Everyone appeared to be disappointed by her request.

AFTER SHE'D SETTLED into her beautiful suite, Maxie checked out the screened porch facing Tick Lake. Fisher was right. Fickle Minnesota had decided on a seductive day of sunny skies. Still, there was a premonitory harsh edge to the unusual warmth. To top it off, it was only four o'clock and the sun was sinking toward the lake. A knock sounded at the door.

"Come in," she called.

The knob rattled, then another knock.

Of course the door was locked. Maxie smiled to herself about her passive-aggressive moment. She unlatched the dead bolt.

"Is your room okay?" Fisher asked. She held two beers. "I was hoping you'd want to hang out a little."

"Did you bring pretzels?"

Fisher gestured to a pocket. "Locally made trail mix."

"Perfect." She allowed Fisher to enter the room. "Let's go out on the balcony and watch the sunset."

When they'd settled into their wooden Adirondack chairs, protected by a glass enclosure, facing the drowning sun, Fisher pointed to her face. "I've developed an uncontrollable eye twitch. There's plotting going on here."

Maxie sipped her beer. "What's Gunter up to?"

"I don't know."

Maxie studied Fisher's face.

"I'm not lying," Fisher said. "I promised I wouldn't lie to you."

"I don't remember that."

"The night we slept together. I guess you blocked it out."

"When?" Maxie waved her hand. "Never mind. We should get ready." She grinned at Fisher. "What should I wear?"

Fisher grinned back. "We're a casual family. Want me to wait for you?"

"No," she said. "I'll be along in a few minutes. I know what to choose."

MAXIE WAS THE last one to arrive in the dining room. A section of the room was cordoned off, including the area by the fireplace and the wall of stuffed animals.

Maxie twirled around. "Do you like it? I know a designer who specializes in casual chic."

She didn't elaborate on her history with the designer, Tracy G., who had provided Maxie with an outfit used in a biopic about Audrey Hepburn.

Why was she trying to impress a family she was about to disappoint?

Maxie glanced nervously at the wall of trophies. Big Daddy wasn't among them.

Artemis spoke up, apparently reading the look on Maxie's face. "We'll only use one taxidermist. He's an artist and there's a waiting list. Big Daddy won't be ready until after the new year."

"Sometimes you have to wait a long time for the best," Maxie said.

Dinner started in a promising manner. In deference to Leonard, soft drinks, sparkling water and non-alcoholic wine were served with the appetizers. Gunter raised the first glass.

"To my beloved and perfect daughter and her..." Gunter paused. A mild shift, like the slip of tectonic plates, occurred, and then Gunter finished his toast. "...beloved and hard-working husband, Leonard. Happy fortieth and many more."

After everyone had sipped, Gunter raised his glass again. "Ilsa and I are going on our sixty-third. I look forward to toasting anniversaries for my grandchildren as well. Including the gay ones." He grunted.

"I kicked him," Ilsa said.

Gunter sat down and the meal was served.

Everyone launched into safe talk, which suited Maxie just fine. Hunter had just filled a good eight minutes on shoe trends when Gunter stood again. He had a small brown gravy stain on his white dress shirt, just above his waist. "My wife doesn't think I should be announcing this. But I disagree." He danced sideways, out of reach of any potential kicks from his wife.

"As you all know, my homosexual son Roman has a successful career in New York. My daughter is living her own life. I lay awake at night, thinking about the future of Ishpeming Lodge."

"Gunter," Ilsa said.

"No, my darling," Gunter said. "Let me say it." He waved away a waiter who was attempting to clear plates. "I have decided to make a generous offer which is also a bit selfish." He cleared his throat.

"I know Fisher is trying to find herself. I have decided to bestow upon her Ishpeming Lodge. I believe she would be a magnificent resort owner. She can train with me before I kick."

Silence hung in the air.

"I look forward to her eventual marriage to a woman who would also love to make this a lifestyle and passion and raise children in nature." Gunter glanced with intent at Maxie. "I know the gays are having children in all sorts of manners."

Fisher's eye twitch palpated wildly. "This is a shock."

"Think about it, gal," Gunter said. "No pressure." He glanced at Maxie again. "No pressure for anyone."

Despite Gunter's words, Maxie did feel pressure. She took only mild relief in how confused Fisher looked at the offer and all its emotional baggage.

"As you all know," Fisher said, "I have been a little lost concerning my life path. Now this interesting opportunity. It's a possibility."

"Really, Sis, sure you want to get into this environment?" Hunter said. "You might be idealizing. I'm only saying."

"I know."

"Grandpa is right," Trapper said. "You need a partner."

Was it Maxie's imagination, or did the entire clan focus on her?

"What she needs is a good veterinarian with outdoor skills," she said. "A nice Minnesota girl. A former cheerleader. Better yet, a Butter Queen."

She hadn't been sure when to make her announcement, but circumstances made it clear. Now. "I'm going to Italy."

"Vacation?" Leonard asked.

"An extended stay."

Honey spoke up. "We all thought you and Fisher were an item. We thought you came back to be with her."

"Ouch," said Maxie. "Blunt."

Silence filled the room.

Artemis spoke first. "Tell us more, Maxie."

"I have a friend named Marcello. Turns out he's a bad sheep member of the Medici family who has a university degree in philosophy. He got me a place to stay in Florence and access to the *Accademia*. My father is giving me a stipend." She took a deep breath. "I'm becoming an artist."

"That's wonderful," Artemis said.

"Do you mean it?" Maxie asked.

"I wouldn't say it otherwise. I'm also disappointed."

"I think we're all disappointed," Leonard said.

"Not me," Honey said. "The *Medici's*. The *Accademia*."

"Are you jealous?" Trapper asked. "You would leave me and go to Europe for an extended stay?"

"I couldn't afford it," Honey said.

"If you want to get rid of me and do your own thing, I'll give you the money," Trapper said.

"I see nothing's changed with you two," Maxie observed.

"We're fine," Trapper said. "This is who we are."

"I'm not going anywhere," Honey said. "Trapper knows it."

"Where's the cake?" Maxie asked.

A waiter wheeled in a multi-tiered cake ringed in candles and topped with a pair of black licorice shoes. Maxie spent the next hour taking shots of every imaginable celebratory act, including Leonard and Artemis feeding each other the black candy shoes.

THE PARTY WRAPPED up at midnight. Maxie staggered to her room and was about to remove her designer outfit when a knock sounded on her door. She stomped over and flung the door open.

"It's me," Gunter said. "Glad you're still dressed."

He led her down the stairs, across the lobby, to the hallway of photographs. A section, she recalled, was enclosed in a glass case and had contained a shrine to Gunter's days of hockey glory, including trophies, photos and yellowing newspaper articles. It was empty.

"I had a case built in the bar for the athletic stuff," Gunter said. "Better in there, anyway. Good for the sports talk." He rested a hand on her shoulder. "Your place on the walls."

Like a sprinter, Maxie went out of the blocks from standstill to sobbing.

Gunter took her in his arms.

She bawled into Gunter's scratchy woolen sweater. He held her, stroking her hair, until she exhausted her tear ducts. He held her out, so he could look in her eyes. "I dreamed of wedding pictures. Eventually children. But you can put anything you like in here."

"I have some images. But, the new stuff is big."

"How big?"

"Very big."

Maxie accessed her cell phone photo folder and gave him the phone. "This one is six feet high and four feet wide." She took the phone back, then returned it to him. "You were looking at it upside down."

Gunter held the image almost to his nose. "Not wearing my glasses. What the heck are they?"

"They're human images set in mythical landscapes. Landscapes of the soul."

She showed him a few more. She watched his puzzled face. So what? What she was reaching for could not be achieved if a person cared too much about how people reacted.

Gunter handed back the phone. "I don't understand, but I don't need to." He rubbed his chin. "We'll take down some of the stuffed animals in the dining room. In the morning you and I will take a tape measure and prepare."

"Thank you, Gunter. We'll see."

MAXIE WAS STILL verklempt as she climbed up the stairs to her room. At the landing, she paused, then turned down the hall and knocked. The door opened slowly.

"Maxie, you've been crying."

"I don't look any worse than you. Can I come in?"

"Don't break my heart more than it's already broken."

"Don't assume I want to hurt you."

"Why not? You have a good track record in the heartbreak department. You weren't crying about me, we know that."

"Your grandfather. I'll explain."

Fisher stood away from the door.

Maxie stepped over the threshold. "I thought I had a killer suite. Look at this luxury pad."

"I'm the favored granddaughter. Beer?"

"No, thanks." Maxie plopped onto the full-sized couch and patted the place next to her. "Sit. I won't bite."

Fisher sat a foot away. By the time Maxie finished telling Fisher about the Gunter encounter, they were both crying.

Maxie Wolfe was officially off the no-cry list.

"That's it," Fisher said. "Now I'm exhausted."

"Ditto."

Maxie looked over to the king-sized bed covered in a spread of deer amongst pine trees.

"I see that," Fisher said. "I see you."

"I see you, too." Maxie knew she had to choose her next words carefully, because she was basically a bozo in the emotion department.

"I can't think of anyone I'd rather sleep with tonight than you."

Fisher slammed her fist on the couch. "Damn, damn, damn. I don't want to be one of your seduce and reject victims."

"Is that a yes?" Maxie asked.

"It's a maybe."

"What would I have to do to turn it into a 'yes'?"

"No sex," Fisher said. "I'm too vulnerable."

"Agreed."

"That we look deeply into one another's eyes and profess our love."

"Don't push it," Maxie said.

She got to her feet. Fisher remained stubbornly seated.

"Please?" Maxie said.

"The most overused phrase on the planet, as you would say." Fisher stood. "Except thank you."

Maxie took Fisher's hand. "Hansel and Gretel," she said.

BECAUSE HAPPY ENDINGS require uncertainty, Maxie Wolfe and Fisher Jacobs followed a metaphorical path of crumbs leading deeper into the metaphorical forest.

Other Books From Linda Morganstein:

My Life With Stella Kane

In 1948, Nina Weiss, a snobby college girl from Scarsdale, goes to Hollywood to work at her uncle's movie studio. She is assigned to help publicize a young actress named Stella Kane. Nina is immediately thrown into the maelstrom of the declining studio system and repressive fifties Hollywood. Adding to her difficulties is her growing attraction to Stella. When a gay actor at the studio is threatened by tabloid exposure, Nina invents a romance between Stella and the actor. The trio become hopelessly entangled when the invented romance succeeds beyond anyone's dreams. This is the "behind-the scenes" story of the trio's compromises and secrets that still has relevance for today.

eISBN 978-1-61929-036-5

Ordinary Furies

Alexis Pope's life has come undone. Just when she thought she'd found guaranteed security and conventionality, her husband's death casts her into a self-imposed solitary confinement in her suburban mansion. Unsure as to whether she'll ever stop grieving, she's reluctant to accept her gay cousin Jeffrey's offer to come up to the Russian River resort where he works.

Then, a revelation in the form of a nosy fundamentalist neighbor signals enough. Little suspecting she's jumping from the frying pan into the fire, Alex plunges into the refreshingly frantic world of restaurants in the funky chic town of Guerneville, California, a gay and New-Age haven in the redwoods. But peace of mind is elusive. A series of vicious events at the resort forces Alex to revive her abandoned skills as a self-defense instructor.

In this first book of the series, Alex begins to explore her changing sexuality. Like many women, she must face her denials and repressions before coming to terms with her attraction to women. For some women, these are issues not easy to face, and this series explores both the difficulties and rewards of lesbian "late-bloomers."

eISBN: 978-1-935053-47-7

Harpies' Feast

In Dante's circle of hell for suicides, those who take their own lives are transformed into dead trees that can still feel pain. Sitting on their withered branches are the harpies, birds with women's faces, who peck at their limbs. In *Harpies' Feast*, the second in the Alexis Pope mystery series, Alex is once again confronted with a crime that doesn't seem to be what it really is. She is plunged into a mystery exploring suicide and its repercussions.

After solving a crime at the Overlook Lodge in *Ordinary Furies*, Alex no longer feels welcome in the resort town of Guerneville, California. She flees down the road to the village of Sebastopol, home to a melting pot of old hippies, wine estate owners, apple farmers and retired baby boomers. She gets a job teaching "cardio self-defense" at a trendy fitness center, courtesy of her new landlady, Sandy Knight, bisexual personal trainer and part-time philosophy professor.

Through the class, Alex meets two intriguing newcomers to town, a teenage actress and a striking lesbian playwright who've both arrived to work on a local theatre production. Much to her dismay, Alex feels attracted to Nickie, the playwright, and maternally protective of Jaycee, the teenager, who is becoming the victim of a group of jealous local girls.

The bullying and nastiness lead to disaster. In their search for answers to the perplexing events, Alex and her friends, both old and new, explore the glory and sting of relationships and confront the bounds of sexual orientations and attractions.

eISBN: 978-1-61929-019-8

On A Silver Platter

When a film company begins production of a low-budget modern-day horror movie based on the beheading of Saint John the Baptist, Alexis Pope is asked to lend a hand as a stunt double. In no time, she's immersed in the intrigues of the cast and crew, culminating in a terrible calamity that sends her, once again, on the trail of a killer

In this the third installment of the series, Alex continues to explore her attraction to women and her fears of intimacy, as well as the inner demons that drive people to live out fantasy lives that shun the hard reality of regular life-and may lead to deadly acts.

eISBN 978-1-61929-020-4

Other Regal Crest books you may enjoy:

Better Together
by Pat Cronin

Mac Bradenton has never been south of the Mason Dixon Line or across a body of water wider than the Ohio River. But her best friend is sick and on a quest to complete her bucket list. First stop is Paris, France. Mac goes along expecting to enjoy the time with Kristy, never anticipating just how much her life will change.

They meet up with Kristy's friend, Lenie, who has promised to give them a guided tour of Paris and while there, romance blossoms between Mac and Lenie.

Once home, life takes some major turns for Mac. As she struggles to deal with the challenges thrown at her, will everything fall apart? Or will she be able to lean on Lenie knowing that, no matter what happens, they are better together?

ISBN: 978-1-61929-154-6
eISBN 978-1-61929-155-3

Leave of Absence
by S. Renée Bess

Corey Lomax, a writer and English professor at Allerton University in suburban Philadelphia, continues to recover from the rupture of a six year relationship with Jennifer Renfrew, the university's Assistant Dean of Admissions. Jennifer has embarked on a new relationship with Pat Adamson, a Philadelphia police officer.

Kinshasa Jordan, a novelist and teacher on leave from her public high school position in Connecticut, accepts a writer-in-residence post at Allerton. When she relocates, Kinshasa leaves behind a secure job as well as an abusive relationship.

Corey and Kinshasa meet as colleagues, writers, and minority women who must navigate their way through the sometimes unfriendly territory of white male dominated academia. Corey is proudly "out." Kinshasa's sexuality is a matter of conjecture. What is clear is both Corey's and Kinshasa's determination to avoid any romantic entanglements.

As the story unfolds, so do secrets, betrayals, a murder, and the slowly smoldering attraction between Corey Lomax and Kinshasa Jordan.

ISBN: 978-1-61929-106-5
eISBN 978-1-61929-107-2

The Rules
by S. Renée Bess

Blackmail, murder, missing persons, and hidden identities link lives that otherwise, would have remained unconnected.

London Phillips' suburban black middle class background has made her vulnerable to the alienation she feels as she tap dances between the expectations she holds for herself and the expectations other people impose upon her. A full-time realtor and part-time writer, London encounters frustration when she tries to contact Milagros Farrow, a revered lesbian author whose work London would like to include in an anthology she's compiling. Milagros has disappeared from the face of the earth.

Rand Carson is a prominent newspaper journalist who is forced to deal with the sudden loss of her financial security and the dissolution of her long term interracial relationship with Willa. Rand seems compelled to pursue London, although it's possible she's more attracted to London's ethnicity than to London herself.

Candace Dickerson, a corporate event planner, is married to avarice. In order to chase a more lucrative future, Candace has abandoned her lover, Lenah and Lenah's perceived lack of ambition. She's moved into the city where she executes a plot designed to augment her earnings with other people's money.

Lenah Miller is content with her job at a local hospital's Emergency Department. For reasons known only to her, she distrusts women she considers too ambitious or from different social strata. Steeped in cynicism and memories held in secret, Lenah finds it easier to criticize a woman whose gentle nature differs from hers than to accept their differences.

The threads entwined around London's desire to connect with a kindred spirit, Lenah's wary skepticism, Rand's inappropriate ardor, and Candace's greed come undone when three people fall victim to blackmail, one reappears, and another succumbs to murder.

ISBN: 978-1-61929-156-0
eISBN ISBN 978-1-61929-157-7

OTHER REGAL CREST PUBLICATIONS

Be sure to check out our other imprints,
Yellow Rose Books, Quest Books, Mystic Books,
Silver Dragon Books, Troubadour Books, Young Adult Books
and Blue Beacon Books.

About the Author

Linda Morganstein is an award-winning fiction writer who also happens to be the product of a Borscht Belt childhood in the Jewish hotels of the Catskills. In the seventies, she dropped out of Vassar College and drove a VW van to California, where she lived in Sonoma County for many years. She currently resides in the Twin Cities of Minnesota with her understanding spouse Melanie and amazing dog, Courage.

For more information go to: www.lindamorganstein.com

CPSIA information can be obtained
at www.ICGtesting.com
Printed in the USA
FFOW04n1538260115
10525FF